When Ben wakes up from a nap in his Jeep, he is horrified to find two strangers driving it. His car's been stolen, with him in the back seat. Ben overhears just enough to discover they are brothers on the run for murder. Randall is a thug, delighting in showing off his gun and vowing to use it if Ben tries to escape.

Ben just wants to get out of this alive but soon finds himself fighting a dangerous attraction to Randall's younger brother Murphy. His tough exterior hides someone sweet, vulnerable, and completely gorgeous. The sexual tension between Ben and Murphy becomes impossible to ignore as they are kept in forced proximity. Bound together, made to share a room and even a bed night after night in increasingly weird motels, they slowly turn from enemies to secret lovers. When Murphy discovers Randall's true plans for Ben, he must choose between the brother who has always been his everything, and Ben—the man it might be worth losing everything for.

NORTHWEST OF NORMAL

Blue Jones

A NineStar Press Publication

Published by NineStar Press
P.O. Box 91792,
Albuquerque, New Mexico, 87199 USA.
www.ninestarpress.com

Northwest of Normal

Printed in the USA
First Edition
June, 2019

Print ISBN: 978-1-950412-87-7

Also available in eBook, ISBN: 978-1-950412-86-0

Warning: This book contains sexually explicit content, which may only be suitable for mature readers, mention of off-page murder, scenes of physical injury, and some violence.

Chapter One

BEN WOKE UP facedown in the backseat of his car, one cheek pressed hard against the warm leather seat and a hand hanging down to the bristled mat on the floor. He yawned into his sleeve. He'd driven for hours yesterday and was still exhausted. The last thing he remembered was parking up at the roadside late last night and pulling a blanket and coat over himself for warmth. He'd only intended to take a quick nap, but judging from the bright light, he must have slept until late morning. His groggy mind started to clear, and he turned over onto his back, pushed his coat away from his face, and stretched out.

He gazed up lazily at the roof of the car as a shadow passed over it. Then another. He pushed the coat down farther and squinted at the opposite window. Trees rushed by. It was only then that he noticed the steady purr of the engine and the vibration of the car beneath him. The car was moving. Someone had stolen his Jeep. With him in it.

He was suddenly very awake. He smelled cigarette smoke and stale beer and heard someone breathing in the driver's seat by his head. As he edged slightly to his right, he saw a stocky man with short hair and a dirty, green shirt sitting on the passenger's side. Ben slowly lay back down and kept his breathing quiet, even though he felt like his heart was beating out of his chest. For one surreal moment, he wasn't quite sure what to do. They were the ones who had stolen his car, but it felt somehow impolite to interrupt them.

What was he supposed to say? Should he shout at them to get the hell out? Or should he tell them they could keep the car and politely ask them to let him go? He breathed in through his nose and out through his mouth and listened as the man in the passenger seat spoke.

"You chose a decent car, kid. Full tank of gas."

Ben jolted. For a second, Ben thought the man was talking to him. The guy looked about forty and had a southern accent, local to where they were in Georgia. He leaned forward in his seat as he spoke, like he had a surfeit of energy coiled up.

"Thanks."

Ben only had that one word to go on, but the man driving sounded younger and calmer, with a softer voice.

There was a long moment of silence before the younger man driving spoke again. "Why'd you have to do it?"

"I did it for you, and you know it," said the older man sharply.

"Don't give me that," said the driver, sounding defensive.

"I told you one day I'd end up killin' him. Just a matter of time."

"Never thought you meant it."

Jesus Christ. Forget confronting them. Ben would curl back up under the blanket and hide. Perhaps he could slip out unseen next time they stopped for gas or food or to kill their next victim. He was about to duck down under his coat when the passenger looked in the rearview mirror—his shocked gaze meeting Ben's.

"What the hell?"

The driver followed his partner's gaze and whipped around, shouting in surprise. The passenger reached out one meaty hand to grab the blanket off Ben and grip his wrist tight. His ruddy cheeks contrasted sharply with his pale, wrinkled forehead and the puffy bags under his eyes.

"Nice work, little brother," the older one mocked loudly. "The one time I let you drive, you pick an occupied car."

"Shut up, Randall," said the younger guy.

"If this isn't the dumbest shit you've ever pulled." Randall threw his hands up in exasperation.

"I said shut up. You didn't notice him either."

"Weren't my job to look."

The car slowed and pulled to the right.

"What're you doing?" Randall let go of Ben and reached out, jerking the steering wheel back toward his brother so the car stayed on course.

"Pullin' over to get rid of this guy."

"No way, Murphy. I'm not havin' him run off to the cops. He's seen my face. Anyway"—Randall turned in his seat and winked at Ben but continued to talk about him as though he weren't there—"never look a gift horse in the mouth. We can use him."

"What the hell for?" Murphy gave Ben a worried glance in the mirror before turning his attention back to the road.

"I'll think of somethin'."

Shit.

"Why do I always go along with your stupid, dumbass plans?" Murphy muttered.

"Because you love me." Randall stared at Ben. "What's your name, kid?"

Ben licked his lips and sat up, pushing the coat off himself and freeing his legs from the blanket. "Benedict... Ben." He tried hard not to let his voice tremble.

"Why'd you leave your car unlocked, Benedict Ben?" Randall asked.

"I didn't know I had."

Had he really done that? If the man was lying and they'd broken into the car, he surely would have been woken by the noise. Maybe he was just that stupid and had left the car unlocked all night. Ben slid to the middle of the backseat where he could see them both—the driver in profile and Randall, who was still staring at Ben. A male voice with an English accent spoke, and all three men jumped.

"*Make a left turn at your earliest convenience.*"

"Shit, sorry. That's my GPS. It's sort of temperamental. Never makes any sense. I don't even use it," Ben rambled.

"Switch the fucker off, brother."

Murphy scrabbled with the buttons with one hand, and it spoke again.

"*Please make a U-turn.*"

Murphy gave up on the buttons and yanked out a wire. The device bleeped, and its red light went out.

Randall turned sideways in his seat and stared at Ben once more, a smile transforming half his face into deep crow's feet. He scratched at the light gray stubble covering his chin and jaw.

"Gimme your phone."

Ben pulled it from his jeans pocket and handed it over.

"Where's your money at?"

"Uh." Ben couldn't think straight. He patted all his pockets and then remembered. "Oh, my wallet's in the glove compartment."

Randall yanked it open and went through everything. He rifled through Ben's collection of napkins and ketchup packets from fast-food restaurants, his bug spray, and mini bottles of hand sanitizer and finally found Ben's black leather wallet. Ben sighed as he remembered he'd taken out five hundred dollars in cash before he'd set off. More than enough for food, gas, and motel rooms all along his route.

Randall opened the wallet and whistled. "We hit the payload."

Murphy let out an uninterested grunt. He hadn't said a word since they'd found Ben in the back of the car. Randall pulled out the wad of bills, then slipped out Ben's debit card and tucked them into his pocket along with Ben's phone. He threw the wallet carelessly out the open window.

Great. Ben said a silent good-bye to his driver's license, the untouched condom he'd been carrying for three months, and damn it, the free pizza he was due after one more stamp on his Papa Luigi reward card. Ben's gaze flicked back and forth between the two brothers. He'd been right about the driver. Murphy was definitely younger than Randall. His face was clean-shaven, and his dark-blond hair was long, the ends brushing his lips. He wore a black T-shirt, the short sleeves folded up a couple of times, like a redneck James Dean. His arm was slim but sinewy and toned, flexing slightly as he gripped the steering wheel. The muscles chased one another up and down his tanned arm every time he pulled the wheel to round a corner.

"You know what, maybe we should pull over," said Randall.

Ben felt hopeful. Now that Randall had taken the money, maybe he'd let Ben go. But Murphy's nervous glance at Randall prevented Ben from celebrating just yet. Somehow that look didn't suggest his release was imminent. Murphy pulled into a rest stop. The long, curved stretch of road for picnickers was hidden from the main road by leafy trees. The car came to a stop right next to a wooden table with two benches. There was no one else in sight.

"Stay there," Randall ordered as he opened his passenger door.

They listened to a series of soft electronic beeps until Murphy turned off the ignition. For a moment they were alone in the silence, and Murphy turned around in his seat properly for the first time. He pushed dirty-blond hair out of his face to reveal dark, nervous eyes that looked Ben over. But before they could lock gazes, the door opened, and Randall dragged Ben away from Murphy and out of the car. Randall pushed Ben against the wooden table, and Ben's hands scrabbled against its thick layer of leaves until they found purchase on the splintered surface.

Randall hit Ben across the back of the head. "Stop squirmin'."

It was probably only meant as a warning tap. But the bastard was strong, and the blow made Ben's ears ring. Randall patted him down like a cop, his massive hands roughly checking Ben's chest and sides. Ben gasped in surprise when Randall ran his fingers quickly over Ben's ass and down his inner thighs.

Randall rolled his eyes. "Don't get excited, kid. I'm not gonna ask you to prom." He finished his search at Ben's ankles. "You're not armed."

"Of course not."

"Well, we are." Randall reached back to the belt of his jeans and yanked out a big black revolver. Ben's eyes widened, and Randall chuckled. "Seen one of these before?"

"Not in person."

"Didn't think so. I call her Cruella." Randall pulled Ben roughly back to the car and pushed him into the front passenger seat. The leather was still warm. "I'll take the back, since you made it look so comfy. Murphy, pop the hatch." Randall slammed the door in Ben's face, and Murphy flinched at the loud noise. Randall pulled the hatch up and rooted around in the back. "Bingo."

He slammed the hatch shut and returned to Ben's door. He'd found the blue nylon rope Ben had stowed in the back with his camping gear in case he couldn't find a motel. Randall yanked the door open again and pushed Ben back farther against the leather, wrapping the rope several times around both him and the back of the seat. Then Randall bound it firmly around Ben's chest and upper arms, securing him tightly down. Randall leaned over to tie a complicated knot by his waist.

"You got mighty clean hands for a man, Benedict Ben. You a homosexual?"

Ben frowned. That didn't even make sense. He didn't know how to respond, so he kept his mouth shut. He leaned away from Randall as best he could as the man straightened up. Ben couldn't tell from one minute to the next if Randall was going to laugh in his face or punch him in it.

"Relax. But you'd better not be. I don't allow 'em in my car."

His car? Randall patted his handiwork. "There. A pretty neat job, if I say so myself. Now, Murphy, I want you to walk back to that gas station we passed and get me a pack of cigarettes."

"Why don't we just drive there?"

"Me and the Chinese kid are gonna get to know each other a little bit while you're gone." Randall sneered at Ben.

Ben's heart sank, and Murphy hesitated.

"Go on now, boy. Do as I say. We'll be fine."

Ben tried not to look scared as Murphy backed away. Ben stared after him as he set off toward the gas station. As Ben's gaze flickered from Murphy to Randall, he found that Randall was watching him. Ben's cheeks flushed.

"I'm Korean, by the way. Not Chinese." Ben thought he heard Murphy snort as he walked away.

"Whatever," Randall muttered.

Randall sank onto the picnic table by the car and stared wordlessly at Ben, lighting a cigarette. If he had cigarettes, why had he sent Murphy to get more?

"What are we gonna do with you?" Randall said slowly.

His words sent a chill through Ben, and he turned away from the man's pale eyes. He stared at the trees in the distance and concentrated on not shaking. Randall finished his cigarette, and from the corner of his eye, Ben saw him tap the ash off the end. Then in one quick movement he flicked the lit cigarette at him. It bounced off Ben's bare arm twice before falling to the ground. Ben flinched and tried hard not to react further, but it hurt. Randall lit another one and only took a few drags before flicking it again. This time it missed and fell to the floor of the car. Ben shifted his foot and stamped it out.

"Nice shot," Ben muttered under his breath.

It was a mistake. Randall crouched forward into the car and smacked Ben in the face. His head bounced off the headrest.

"You don't know what a good shot I can be, boy. You don't know nothin' about me," Randall snarled.

"I know you killed someone," Ben blurted out and darted his tongue over his lip to check for blood. He regretted saying it before the last word left his mouth.

"Oh yeah?" Randall replied, dangerously quiet.

Ben blinked, his vision a little hazy. While he was in this mess, he might as well continue. "Why'd you do it?"

"They pissed me off."

"Is that all it takes?"

"Randall?" Murphy hovered behind him, holding out a blue-and-white pack of cigarettes.

Randall's huge frame finally moved out of Ben's personal space, and he settled back on the table. He lit up a new cigarette and smoked half of it this time before tossing it at Ben. This one hit more accurately, and the pain in his arm burned brighter. Any hope Ben had of Murphy stopping his brother died as Murphy winced but said nothing, only gazing sadly as the cigarette fell to the ground to join the first. He might have looked like an angel, but he was just as much of a dick as his big brother.

Randall stalked off to relieve himself behind the trees. As soon as he was out of sight, Murphy pulled a blue bandanna from his back pocket and took Ben's jaw gently in one hand. Ben flinched back, but Murphy simply leaned in closer and wiped the blood from the corner of Ben's mouth. Up close, he looked almost as angry as his brother, so Ben avoided eye contact and stared at the faint freckles on Murphy's nose.

He shouldn't have talked back to Randall. He was used to his smart mouth getting him in trouble, but never trouble like this. He resolved to keep his mouth shut from now on.

While Murphy was concentrating on his lip, Ben dared to look a little longer. Murphy's long eyelashes framed dark-blue eyes that were almond-shaped, giving him the look of a cat. This close, Ben could feel the boy's body heat and Murphy's warm breath on his face. Murphy caught him looking and glared back, neither of them saying a word.

Once Randall returned, Murphy pulled the car out of the rest stop, and they continued on down the almost empty highway.

"Put the radio on. Local station," said Randall.

Murphy pressed a few buttons on Ben's radio and tuned it in to something called WCON-FM. Ben tried not to snort at the backwoods country music that immediately filled the car. He could have guessed the redneck would be into this stuff. They listened in silence to three songs, all country, and then the local news. After that, Randall told Murphy to switch it off, and he lay down, echoing Ben's original position. He balled up Ben's blankets and used them as a pillow, pushing Ben's coat away with his dirty boots. It was quiet without the radio and Randall's loud voice. Normally, Ben would have filled the silence with chatter; he liked talking to people. But this was hardly a normal situation, and he'd vowed to keep his mouth shut.

After ten minutes of silence had passed, Ben couldn't take it anymore. He bit at his lip and then cleared his throat, speaking hesitantly. "You kidnap people a lot?"

Murphy didn't answer, but a frown passed over the man's forehead. A snore came from the backseat, and Ben twisted his head around awkwardly, unable to move anything below his neck. He watched for a second as Randall drooled on his blanket.

Great. Which detergent was recommended for getting redneck drool out of cotton-polyester blend?

He glanced over at Murphy's profile as he drove. The man appeared a year or two older than Ben but definitely way younger than Randall. He had sharply defined cheekbones that tapered down diagonally to his mouth. His body was all lean, hard muscle. Murphy lifted his thumb to his mouth, and his narrow, pink lips parted to let him chew on the edge of his nail. Ben turned resolutely back to the road just as Murphy glanced around at Randall in the backseat. Maybe to check that he was still asleep.

"Sorry 'bout my brother."

"What about him?"

Murphy took a deep breath. "Everything. Talking to you like that. I'm really sorry. He don't mean it."

"Oh." It seemed like being an ignorant homophobe didn't run in the family.

"It don't hurt, does it? The rope?"

"No, no. It's fine." *I get tied to the passenger seat all the time. No problem.* He didn't know why he was compelled to be so polite to this guy. But on reflection, it was probably his best move. Maybe if Ben kept Murphy happy, he wouldn't end up dead.

"How's your face?"

"Okay."

Murphy reached out to the middle of the dashboard, and Ben flinched away.

"Relax. I'm just..." Murphy gestured at the cigarette lighter and pressed it in to heat up.

Relieved, Ben let out a breath and fidgeted in his seat, trying to get more comfortable. The truth was, Randall had tied him way too tight. The nylon rope was digging painfully into his arms. Murphy lit a cigarette and then returned the lighter to its holder. Ben hoped only one brother was into flicking cigarettes.

"Where were you headed before?" Murphy asked.

"Before you...borrowed my car?"

Murphy nodded.

"Florida." Ben paused. "You ever been?"

"Never been out of Georgia in my life," Murphy drawled.

His voice was so deep and gravelly Ben felt the vibrations of it rumble through his bones. The discomforting thing was, the rumble seemed to connect right to Ben's groin. He rambled to distract himself from what he was feeling.

"I drove for six hours straight last night. I was starving. I planned to stop and eat, then rent a room somewhere. But I nearly fell asleep at the wheel, so I stopped at the side of the road and crashed in the backseat. And that's where you found me."

"You didn't eat?"

Ben shook his head and cursed his decision not to grab something out of the cooler in his trunk when he'd had the chance.

"You hungry?"

"Yeah, I guess I am."

"Here." Murphy checked behind him and then, after digging into the pocket of his jacket, brought out a slightly melted chocolate bar. He threw it onto Ben's lap, where it hit his thigh and came to a stop over his crotch. Ben smiled weakly and glanced at his tied arms. "Oh yeah, right."

Murphy steered with his left hand and grabbed the chocolate bar with his right. His warm hand crept over Ben's thigh as he watched the road, and then his long fingers skimmed accidentally over Ben's cock as he reached the chocolate bar. Ben inhaled sharply and tensed his whole body. His stomach flipped as Murphy brought the chocolate bar up to his pink lips, ripped open the packaging with his teeth, and squeezed the bar halfway out of the wrapper. He held it up to Ben's mouth, completely unaware of the effect he'd just had. Ben hesitantly took a bite, his eyes on Murphy's face.

Murphy continued to drive with one hand, the other resolutely holding up the chocolate bar for Ben, until it was all gone. Murphy shoved the empty wrapper in the ashtray. "Better?"

"Yeah." Ben swallowed. "Thanks, man."

Murphy shrugged and checked the rearview mirror. He angled it more toward the backseat, presumably so he could keep an easier eye on his brother.

Ben licked the chocolate off his lips and wondered if Murphy could tell he'd been lying about Florida.

"He still asleep?" Ben whispered.

"Yeah."

"He's your older brother?"

Murphy nodded.

"He's kind of scary."

"Randall's all right."

"Your name's Murphy, right?" *Didn't they always say you should connect with your kidnapper? Make them see you as human?*

"Yeah."

"My cousin's called Murphy." Another lie. But Murphy didn't look all that impressed. "Where are we going?"

Murphy hesitated. "Not Florida. Sorry."

Ben wondered how sorry he was. "You could let me go while he's asleep."

Murphy shook his head. "No, I couldn't."

Ben nodded. He hadn't expected him to say any different. "Murphy..." He didn't really want to hear the answer to his next question. "What are you going to do to me?" Ben's self-control wavered, and he let himself look as scared as he felt.

Chapter Two

THE KID SURE knew how to look like a baby rabbit. Soft black hair and big, pleading eyes the color of Coca-Cola. His face shone with a weird mixture of fear and curiosity. *Come to think of it, do baby rabbits look like that?* Maybe cartoon ones. Unfortunately for the kid, Murphy and his brother shot rabbits—baby or otherwise—and ate them for dinner. They had to. Wild animals were free, and they didn't always have enough money for food.

He wished the kid would shut up. He'd barely stopped talking since they'd found him in the back. But to be fair, the poor bastard probably wasn't used to this shit. He was just some guy trying to take a nap in his car, and they'd come along and messed up his plans. He'd probably never even met people like Murphy and his brother before. He definitely wasn't from around here. Murphy couldn't identify his accent, but he looked like some rich kid from the city.

Murphy knew Ben was scared shitless. He'd seen the kid's eyes when Randall had felt the need to show off his gun. He had wanted to get that frightened look off the kid's face, but the fact was, Randall was unpredictable. He loved his brother, but the guy was an asshole. Randall could be cold, cruel, and violent when he thought he needed to be.

"Listen, just do what Randall says. Don't piss him off, and everything will be fine." He hoped he was telling the truth.

AS THEY APPROACHED the edge of Georgia, Murphy couldn't help but start shifting in his seat and breathing a little quicker. This would be his first time leaving the state he'd been born in. Pretty pathetic for a grown man, but he'd never needed to leave before. Not that he hadn't fantasized about it. He almost wanted to wake his brother to mark the occasion, but Randall wouldn't care. And anyway, what did he want him to do? Sing him a fucking song? It was no big deal. He still smiled, though, as they approached a sign declaring TENNESSEE WELCOMES YOU.

"Congrats," said Ben.

"What?"

"First time out of Georgia, right?"

Murphy nodded and scratched the back of his head. He frowned and turned away from the kid's sweet, nervous smile. It was too hard to look at. But there was a warm feeling in Murphy's stomach as he drove into Tennessee.

Randall had been set on getting out of the state. As if crossing state lines could have stopped them from getting arrested for a crime as serious as his. Even now that they'd reached another state, Murphy wouldn't be surprised if Randall wanted to keep going and get as much distance between them and Georgia as possible. Maybe continue all the way to Canada. He just didn't know how long Randall was going to keep this kid with them. Or what the hell he was planning to do with him. Murphy switched the radio back on but lowered the volume so as not to wake Randall. A bunch of swearing and shouting about being woken up was the last thing he needed. But the radio might keep the kid from talking his ear off. Murphy needed quiet. Of all the people to kidnap accidentally, it had to be this chatty pain in the ass.

Chapter Three

THEY DROVE FOR three hours, Randall sleeping for most of them. Ben took Murphy's obvious hint and surrendered to silence. Despite the chocolate bar, Ben's stomach started growling around hour number three.

"That you?"

Ben had no reason to be embarrassed, but his cheeks burned a little more every time his belly gurgled. He shifted in his seat, but Randall's rope-tying skills meant he could hardly move a millimeter.

Randall stirred and grunted from the backseat. "Where are we?"

"We're out of Georgia."

"Good work, baby brother." He stretched and rolled down the window to spit. "Time to eat."

Murphy took the next exit to a roadside diner and parked the Jeep in the far corner of the lot. Once out of the car, Randall kneeled beside Ben and untied the knots. He unraveled the rope completely, then pointed his gun low and rammed it into Ben's side.

"Now listen, kid. I need to make something very fucking crystal clear to you. I'll have this gun on me at all times. I have no qualms ending your life. I'll do it in front of people if I have to. I've done it before."

Ben nodded down at his lap, unable to look away from the barrel of the gun.

"You do what I say, I let you eat. You act normal, I don't shoot you in the face. Sound reasonable?"

Ben nodded again, feeling slightly manic. Finally, Randall pulled the gun away and tucked it back into the waistband of his jeans.

"I'm in the mood for grits! Who's with me?" Randall said.

Ben rubbed his bruised stomach as Randall set off across the parking lot. Murphy raised his eyebrows and shrugged an apology at Ben with one shoulder.

THE DINER WAS small and decorated in faded red leather and grimy chrome. A dozen square tables sat along the glass wall, and a counter ran beside them. The smell of bacon and coffee made Ben's stomach ache with hunger. As they crossed the room, the sticky floor and sugary tables were at once both disgusting and reassuringly familiar.

Randall chose a table by the window and slipped onto the red-cushioned bench. Murphy directed Ben gently onto the bench opposite Randall and flopped down next to him, hemming him in against the window. Ben's shoes stuck to the tacky floor under the table as he moved over to make room for him. For one second, Murphy's thigh and shoulder pressed warmly against Ben's, but Murphy quickly maneuvered away, making sure to leave a few inches of space between them.

A young waitress brought three glasses of ice water to the table and left them some menus to look at. Ben rubbed his upper arms. The rope had pushed deep red marks into them, and he ran his fingertips over the channels still left in his skin. He stopped when Murphy laid one laminated menu out between them so they could both read it and winced as the menu brushed his arm. The two spots Randall's lit cigarettes had hit were tiny but still red and sore.

Randall snatched up a menu and searched through it for what he wanted. After a minute, he threw it at Murphy. "I'm gonna take a piss. Watch him."

As soon as Randall left, Murphy grabbed Ben's hand and stretched out his arm, taking his drink with the other hand and pressing the cold, wet glass against the cigarette burns on his forearm. Ben gasped at the cold but let him continue. Murphy turned the glass to press the cooler side against his burns one at a time. A minute later the waitress dropped a tray, sending dirty plates crashing to the floor and broken china scattering under the tables. They both jumped, and Murphy let go of Ben's arm like he'd been the one burned. And it was lucky he did. Randall returned, clapping and cheering as he sauntered past the waitress on her knees.

WHEN THE WAITRESS finally made it back to their table, chewing on her pencil, Randall and Murphy ordered and then both turned to Ben. He blinked at Randall's ice-blue stare and couldn't speak. He didn't know whether he should make do with a drink or if Randall really was offering to pay for his food. It didn't seem like him.

"Aw, look at him. He don't know his ass from his elbow."

"Leave it, Randall. I'm surprised he has an appetite at all with you around."

Randall smiled at the menu. "Get what you want, kid." His voice was soft for once.

Ben still wasn't sure if it was a trick but ordered pancakes and bacon, like Murphy had. He was grateful they were letting him eat, although Randall was probably going to be paying with the money he'd taken from Ben's wallet.

"You all want coffee?" the waitress asked.

Murphy and Randall nodded.

"No, I'll just have water. Thank you." Ben liked the smell of coffee but couldn't stand the bitter taste.

The food came a few minutes later. The pancakes were fluffy and sticky and delicious. Murphy licked the butter and maple syrup off his fingers, and Ben tried not to look. He thought twice before speaking, but there was no way he could hold it in for another long drive.

"I need to use the bathroom," Ben said.

Randall rolled his eyes and stuffed another bite of sausage in his mouth.

"Me too," said Murphy. "I'll watch him."

"Gay," said Randall, through his mouthful of food.

"I don't mean I'll watch... Oh, forget it." Murphy stood and let Ben out. Murphy followed Ben closely through the diner, and they both entered the men's room.

Ben was very conscious of what he was doing with his hands. He tried to walk normally to a urinal. He couldn't think of anything to say. Did Murphy feel awkward too? Probably not. Murphy reached into his pocket and pulled a cigarette out of a pack. He flicked it easily into his mouth and held it comfortably but made no move toward lighting it. He rolled it around between his lips, sniffed, and scratched the back of his head.

"I don't know what the hell I'm supposed to do with you."

"Wait for me to use the bathroom?"

"Don't mean that," Murphy murmured.

Ben had no idea what he did mean but didn't want to ask. They both used the urinals, Ben staring carefully at the white tiles in front of his face. Murphy washed his hands and left the tap running for Ben while he dried off his hands, making dark marks on his black jeans. Murphy held the door open for Ben, and as Ben brushed past him, their hips touched for a brief moment. Ben was shocked when Murphy flinched away.

"Don't touch me," Murphy snapped.

"Sorry," said Ben.

Randall paid the bill, and they walked back to the car. This time Randall didn't tie Ben to the passenger seat. Instead, he tied the rope around Ben's wrists, lashing them tightly together, keeping the other end of the rope in his grip, and holding Ben on a makeshift leash from the backseat. Ben raised both his hands to scratch his nose with one finger. This was certainly preferable to being tied to the chair.

THEY SPENT THE next few hours driving through Tennessee in near silence. The only interruption was the occasional cruel comment from Randall about people they passed who had the temerity to be overweight or less attractive than he deemed acceptable, and grunted requests from Murphy asking him to shut the hell up.

As it got darker, Ben's mood changed. He'd been distracted by pancakes, adventure, and Murphy's blue eyes. But it was quickly starting to dawn on him that this situation wasn't a joke. These were two dangerous men, and he was alone with them. Anything could happen. As soon as the sky darkened, everything seemed a little more real and a lot more terrifying.

Bad things happened at night. He guessed that was something primal he'd learned as a child. Ben was just starting to wonder if they'd be driving all through the night or sleeping in the car when Randall nudged Murphy's shoulder and told him to pull into a motel.

They slowly passed a neon sign for the Loveless Motel and drove down a curved stretch of road. The long row of motel rooms was painted white, each with a sloping green roof and a parking space outside. They stopped under a broken streetlight, and Randall sauntered off to reception to book a room.

Murphy leaned against the car, leaving Ben in the passenger seat. His firm, jean-clad ass pressed up against Ben's door, and Ben couldn't help but reluctantly stare at Murphy's arms and broad shoulders. His gaze idly traced the shape of Murphy's biceps while he waited for Randall to return. Randall came back with a key attached to a small square of plastic and the number fifteen printed on it. Murphy pushed off the car and let Ben out. He got to stare at Murphy's face instead. The tip of his nose and his ears were red from the cold night air.

Murphy grabbed Ben's overnight bag from the trunk and a small backpack Ben didn't recognize and tugged him into room number fifteen. The walls, carpet, and bedspreads were all varying shades of beige. There were two twin beds, a battered old TV set, and a door leading to a small bathroom. Murphy dumped the bags on one of the beds, and Randall threw himself down next to them, bouncing slightly. Ben kept quiet as Randall went through Ben's overnight bag, taking out anything he fancied keeping, and checking through the rest. He grabbed the tablet and headphones first and put them aside.

"We got a reader," Randall said, holding up Ben's battered old copy of Kafka's *Metamorphosis*. "I read this once. Didn't like the ending." Randall paused and looked closer at the graduation photo being used as a bookmark. "Who's this pretty little piece? Your fuck buddy?" He smiled widely, showing all his teeth.

Ben wished he could slap the photo and all his other belongings out of Randall's grimy hands.

"I asked you a question, boy." Randall turned his cold blue gaze on Ben. His mouth was a straight, hard line. God, he could turn terrifying in the space of a second.

"It's my sister." As soon as Ben told him, he realized it was a mistake. He should have pretended she was his girlfriend. Might have stopped Randall from making any more comments about his sexuality.

"Ah, shame. Still, maybe you Chinese are into that."

"He's Korean," Murphy muttered.

"Shut the fuck up, brother."

It was a good reminder that even if Randall stopped making gay gibes, he'd continue with the race crap ad nauseam anyway. Ben would just have to tune him out.

AFTER CHECKING THE bathroom for windows, escape routes, or anything that could be used as a weapon, Randall untied Ben and allowed him to use the bathroom for five minutes. As soon as Ben closed the door, they started talking in hushed, urgent voices. So he stepped back to the door and jammed his ear against the edge. He caught the end of Randall's sentence.

"...might have to dump him."

"What? You mean kill him?"

Ben's heart stopped.

"Nah. I'm not gonna kill the kid. Probably not. Just beat the shit out of him. Tell him we'll hunt down his sister if he goes to the cops. Then dump him somewhere it'll take him a while to get out of. We'll be long gone, and he'll be having nightmares about my face for the rest of his life."

"Like half the women in Georgia."

"Watch it."

When Ben returned from the bathroom, Randall tied Ben's ankles together and secured the end of the rope to the headboard.

"You're sleeping on the floor, kid."

With the presence of only two beds, Ben hadn't expected any different. He sat down on the narrow beige rug between the beds and lay back, using his bag as a pillow. The floor was hard and uncomfortable, but he was grateful to still be breathing and able to feel anything at all. After a minute, Randall switched off the lamp, and Ben blinked into the darkness. He was so close to Murphy's bed that the sheets hung down and brushed Ben's knee. He heard Murphy moving around above him, the mattress creaking as he got comfortable. All three were sleeping in their clothes. Randall and Murphy had taken their boots off, but Ben had kept his red Converse on, not knowing when he might be ordered out of the room. And it might be useful if he had the chance to escape. Although he didn't see that happening—he was constantly tethered down like a badly behaved dog.

A few minutes later, something large and soft landed on Ben. He grabbed at his stomach in surprise and found a pillow. Murphy's hand loomed out of the darkness and dropped a blanket on top.

"Thanks," Ben whispered.

"Shut up. Tryin' to sleep," Murphy rasped back.

Ben smiled and replaced his lumpy bag with the pillow and then spread the blanket out.

This was the first time Ben had really had a moment to think, and his brain was well and truly racing now that it had the chance. No one would be missing him yet. The weeklong road trip he'd planned had morphed into a very different one, but it had similarities. He'd still be out of reach on the road. He couldn't use his phone now that Randall had stolen it. But when people didn't hear from him, they'd probably assume he had no reception. He was glad his mother wouldn't worry, but it also meant no one would have a clue he was in danger. No one would be calling the police or getting him any help. He was all on his own. Which, ironically, was all he'd wanted in the world when he'd set off.

He'd made a huge deal out of being able to drive across the country alone and had offended his whole family by refusing to accept the plane ticket his parents had offered him. The flight would have delivered him safely to them in a few short hours, but he hadn't wanted to be safe. He'd wanted an adventure. Instead of flying, he had chosen to drive. His mother had kept saying she wanted him home safe. She'd made some joke about how this was an extreme way to get some alone time with his precious car. And he did love his Jeep. He'd never even let anyone else wash it, let alone drive it. But he wasn't some obsessed weirdo, and today proved it. He'd allowed a random stranger with a gun to drive it all day, and he hadn't said a word.

Anyway, she'd laughed at him and said he would hate every minute alone, which rubbed him up the wrong way. He had insisted she didn't know what the hell she was talking about, accused her of not knowing him as well as she thought she did, and told her in no uncertain terms to keep out of his business. He'd upset her and pissed the rest of his family off in the process. Of course, by the second day of driving, he'd been bored to tears. That night he'd slept in the Jeep, a bit depressed and wishing he had some company. And the very next morning, he'd been blessed with the company of these two assholes. He'd be due the mother of all I-told-you-so's when his parents found out about this. If he'd accepted the damned plane ticket, he'd be home in bed right now instead of in a motel room that smelled like mold, sandwiched between a sociopath and his brother.

As if on cue, Randall snored loudly. Ben should probably be hatching some kind of escape plan. What would Jason Bourne do? Maybe that was aiming a little high. Bourne had epic fighting skills and could take down a man with nothing more than a pen. What on earth could Ben do? He should use all those years in college studying science and try to be methodical about this. He looked at the situation logically. Fighting was out of the question. He'd never even gotten into a fistfight at school—nothing beyond a push and a shove. Both these men were badass, especially Randall. Besides, it was two against one. The only possibility was to outsmart them somehow. But attempting to run off when they were otherwise engaged would risk angering a man with a gun, a man who already hated him, a man who could easily recapture him and then beat the shit out of him, or worse, as revenge.

All things considered, it really might have been more sensible to wait. If he learned how they thought and saw how they worked, maybe he could figure out what Randall had planned for him, if anything. Then he could formulate a plan of escape that would really have a chance of working. Of course, that was assuming Randall didn't kill him in the meantime.

Ben made a decision. He would play the long game. And if he got the idea that the situation was quickly heading south, he would shout for help and try to run. But that was only if things got desperate. He didn't want to risk getting some poor stranger shot and killed in the cross fire.

He hadn't forgotten the first words he'd heard them say. Randall had killed someone. It wasn't a dream or the product of Ben's half-asleep brain. Randall had murdered a man. Murphy might well have helped, and now they were on the run. And just like Randall had said, Ben had seen their faces in great detail. He knew their names. Knew they were from Georgia.

He also remembered something else Randall had said. It was seared pretty thoroughly into his memory. *"We can use him." Use me for what?* Oh God, that wasn't why Randall was so interested in discovering his sexual orientation, was it? No, no. Ben tried to calm down. He got absolutely no gay vibe whatsoever from Randall. He was a dyed-in-the-wool right-wing, neo-Nazi-leaning redneck Southerner. He wouldn't want to use Ben for sex. Maybe he'd meant they could continue to use him for his car and his money—what he had left of it. Ben locked that hope in his heart and hung on to it.

Ben heard a quiet sigh from Murphy's bed. Murphy was a little different. Ben had to admit he found it almost cute when Murphy frowned or drawled at him to shut up. Somehow there was no real malice in it. It was obviously just his way. Maybe learned from his older brother. Murphy always came across as more confused than angry. Confused when Ben smiled at him or talked to him.

Except when he'd snapped at Ben not to touch him. Then he'd nearly seemed scared. Even though it had only lasted a second, Ben was sure he'd seen fear in Murphy's blue eyes. But there was no way someone like Ben could ever scare Murphy. He had a few inches on Ben, and his shoulders seemed twice as wide. He'd probably taken on Randall in dozens of fights over the years. He was still living, so he must be pretty tough. It couldn't be Ben who had scared him. It was the mere act of being touched.

Still, he shouldn't get too hung up on the guy, no matter how intriguing he was. It was nice of him to give Ben a pillow, and yeah, he was gorgeous. But he was still a criminal. And brother to a neo-Nazi. Ben would do well to remember that.

Ben felt a little better after the impromptu mental pep talk. His brain had calmed enough to stop thinking at a hundred miles a minute, and he even felt ready to sleep. He snuggled down into the blanket that smelled a tiny bit like Murphy and drifted off.

SOMETHING JOLTED BEN awake. He panicked for a moment in the pitch black, bracing for Randall and flinching at the potential of a verbal or physical attack. But he was met with silence. He lifted his head from the pillow and listened more carefully. He heard a strange noise like the whimpering of a hurt puppy. And it came from just above his head. Murphy.

Ben sat up and waited for his eyes to adjust to the darkness. Murphy lay on his side fast asleep, but the soft noises continued to spill from his lips. He must have been having a bad dream. Ben glanced over at Randall, but his hulking shape was unmoving. He probably couldn't hear from his bed. Murphy's quiet whimpers made Ben's heart ache a little bit. Maybe he was dreaming about what had happened before they stole Ben's car. Maybe he felt guilty about what he'd been made to do.

Ben shook his head. He had to stop projecting onto this guy. Murphy wasn't a vulnerable, sweet bad boy with a heart. He was a kidnapper and—at the very least—an accomplice to murder. Murphy was more likely dreaming that the next diner had run out of grits. Or the radio station had banned country music, or whatever else it was that scared rednecks. Maybe a giant homosexual was chasing him down the street like Godzilla. The whimpers slowly grew less frequent and eventually stopped altogether. Murphy had probably tired himself out, and the noises faded away to nothing.

Chapter Four

BEN WAS WOKEN up by Murphy grabbing the pillow from under his head and whisking it away.

"Hey," Ben grunted.

"Shh." Murphy pointed at a sleeping Randall, and Ben understood. Randall shouldn't know that Murphy had given him the pillow and blanket. Ben blinked himself awake and remembered the previous night.

Murphy didn't give off any impression of having experienced bad dreams or even a bad night's sleep. His eyes were bright and clear, and all things considered, he was pretty damned chirpy. Ben, on the other hand, felt like he hadn't slept at all.

Randall woke a few minutes later and staggered, bleary-eyed, to the bathroom. When Randall was done, Ben brushed his teeth with Murphy guarding him from the bathroom door at Randall's command. Ben realized Murphy was watching him in the tiny mirror, so he stopped brushing his teeth, white foam all around his mouth.

"What?"

Murphy shook his head as if waking from a trance. "Nothin'. I just need to buy a toothbrush."

Ben paused. "You wanna borrow mine?" He waved his toothbrush at Murphy.

"No way, man. Get outta here."

Ben shrugged and spat out toothpaste in the sink, then ran the cold water and rinsed his mouth out.

RANDALL HAD MURPHY stop at a big roadside supermarket. Murphy untied Ben's hands, but Randall flashed him the gun and a smile. Ben was under no illusion as to what would happen if he didn't stick by Murphy's side as Randall instructed. Luckily, it wasn't something he minded doing. At all.

Randall grabbed a basket and headed off toward the alcohol. The aisles were empty of customers—it was too early yet—but the shelves were freshly stocked, and bland music echoed out from speakers in the cavernous ceiling. Ben felt Murphy's body heat every time they bumped arms, which was quite often if Ben had anything to do with it. They slowly made their way up each aisle in turn, Murphy swinging a basket in one large hand. He grabbed razors, shaving foam, one green toothbrush, and a tube of toothpaste, then headed to the clothes section, where he picked up two plain black T-shirts and a multipack of underwear.

"You didn't get time to pack anything, huh?" Ben asked.

Murphy shook his head.

"You can borrow anything of mine." Ben eyed Murphy's sinfully wide shoulders. "Not that my shirts would probably fit you."

Murphy gave Ben an uncertain look. "Thanks."

"You going to get your brother anything?"

"He can take care of his own damn underwear."

Ben couldn't imagine Randall wearing any of this stuff anyway. Or shopping for clothes at all. He couldn't picture him in anything but the dirty white wife-beater, khaki shirt, and dirty, aged jeans of indecipherable color he had on now.

Murphy stopped at the fruit section and pulled a purple grape from a bunch on a shelf. He put it in his mouth and chewed slowly, staring at the grapes and seeming to think about something. He pulled another one off and offered it to Ben, who shook his head. He didn't want to get caught stealing and glanced around, checking for any nearby staff. When Murphy popped the second one in his mouth, Ben saw a flash of pink tongue, and he wished he'd said yes. He remembered being fed the chocolate bar, and the thought of Murphy pushing the cold, sweet grape into Ben's mouth with his fingers made him flush and turn away. Not that Murphy would have put it in his mouth anyway. Ben wasn't tied up now. At most, they would have touched hands briefly as Murphy passed it over. When Ben finally got himself under control, he turned to find Murphy had already left. Ben trotted to catch up.

"Where are we going?"

"The checkout."

"Murphy." That wasn't what he meant.

"I know," said Murphy, as though he'd heard the unspoken words. He stopped walking and pushed one last grape into his mouth. "We're going to Canada."

They must have decided that when Ben was in the bathroom. He was pleased for one surreal moment. It'd be nice to see snow. He shook his head. That was hardly important right now.

"Why?"

"Because...we need to get away."

"Why?"

"We just do."

"But why?"

"What are you, five?" Murphy started walking again, and Ben followed.

"No."

"Then ask a different question."

Ben thought for a second. "What did you do?"

"I didn't do anything."

Ben tried to change tack. "The people you need to get away from. Is it the police or bad guys?"

Murphy smiled at Ben's use of the term "bad guys." But Ben didn't care. Maybe he was five after all.

"Police," Murphy whispered, stopping to look at a bag of peanuts.

"But you say you didn't do anything."

Murphy shook his head, looking at the floor. "I didn't."

"So this is all Randall?" Ben knew it. "What did he do?"

"You don't want to know."

But Ben already did. Apparently, Murphy didn't remember that he and his brother had talked about it in the car before they noticed Ben was lying in the backseat. Ben knew Randall had killed someone. He just didn't know who. Or how it had happened. Maybe it had been in self-defense, or maybe it had been in cold blood.

Ben picked up a pack of his favorite potato chips. Hoop-shaped and barbecue-flavored. He stared at it for a long moment and then put it back. It would have been useful to know just how scared of Randall he needed to be. But it was a relief to know Murphy hadn't done anything.

"If it was Randall, why are you here?"

"Because I always go along with Randall's dumb plans. I can't say no to my brother." Murphy sighed. "Don't you want anything?"

Ben shrugged. "I don't have any money."

"We're using yours. You can get whatever you want."

It was stupid, but Ben found it strangely endearing that Murphy remembered and even admitted they were using the money Randall had stolen from his wallet to buy everything. But he had all he needed in the car, and he was too nervous all the time to be particularly hungry. So he shook his head.

"I'm fine."

Murphy rolled his eyes and picked up the chips, then threw them in the basket with his stuff. Ben followed automatically as he strode ahead, noticing that Murphy's arms even looked good from behind. He'd never seen someone so finely muscled but still so slim. Murphy's hips and waist were narrow, but his shoulders were so wide. He didn't look out of proportion, just kind of breathtaking. Like a Greek statue. The unholy span of his shoulders made Ben lose time. Or a couple of heartbeats. Or his mind.

Ben sighed quietly and tried to tear his eyes away before Randall found them and caught him staring. But before he did, he noticed a scar on Murphy's upper arm. Narrow and pink, the end of it peeked out from the sleeve of his shirt and seemed to turn thicker underneath. It was faded and clearly years old. Perhaps it was the result of a fall from a tree house when he was a kid. Or some kind of sexy knife fight. Or a misjudged scuffle with Randall that went bad. Ben preferred the tree-house idea.

RANDALL MADE MURPHY drive again; it was apparently very important that he slump in the backseat with his feet up and nonchalantly try to polish off two bottles of whiskey. Ben kept his mouth shut for most of the drive. Randall had forgotten to tie him up. The rope was pooled on the floor behind Ben's seat, and he didn't want to draw attention to it. But three hours in, he couldn't keep quiet any longer.

"If you want a break, I could drive." Ben thought after three straight hours of driving Murphy deserved a rest. But Randall disagreed.

"Shut up, kid. He's fine."

So Murphy drove for another couple of hours. Until Randall got so drunk he took pity on him and told him to stop at the next motel. Or maybe he'd simply sobered up enough to get hungry. Ben couldn't identify much difference between drunk Randall and sober Randall. He was similarly sullen, angry, and rude. Ben had started to wonder whether Murphy followed Randall's orders so readily because he wanted to, because he was scared of him, or just because he'd learned over time it was less hassle not to argue.

RANDALL RENTED A room at the next motel. This one boasted an outdoor pool, but as they drove by, Ben saw it was empty of water. It was off-season and too cold to swim. They ate at the motel's tiny café, then checked into the room.

It was small, clad in orange-stained wood, and featured a deer's head mounted above a double bed, antlers slightly askew, pointing at ten and three o'clock. Ben peeked farther into the room. The double bed was the *only* bed.

"A double?" Murphy asked.

"Doubles is all they had left," growled Randall, challenging anyone to have a problem with that.

Ben scouted out where he'd be sleeping that night. There was a wide, low armchair by the window that seemed a little comfier than the floor, but it all depended on what Randall would let him do. He might insist on the floor just to spite him.

Ben used the toilet, which was a lovely shade of avocado, matching the sink and shower unit, and came out to find Randall missing. Murphy sat on the edge of the double bed, hands folded neatly in his lap.

"Where is he?"

Murphy smirked, looking almost mischievous. He jumped up and crossed the room to the window, kneeling on the edge of the low armchair.

"Look outside." Murphy pulled the curtain back.

"What?"

Murphy chuckled. "C'mere."

Ben jumped up next to him on the armchair, and Murphy flinched away. Ben wasn't sure what he'd done until he remembered Murphy didn't like to be touched.

"Sorry."

"Forget it."

Their room was at the back of the motel and faced out over a wide, dark parking lot. Trees lined the far end, and giant trucks were parked in neat lines behind them. Ben recognized the man walking away as Randall, and together, Ben and Murphy watched him march across the lot toward a small group of women standing in the shadows under the trees. Murphy glanced over at Ben and waited for him to figure it out.

"What are those women doing out...? Oh." Ben's and Murphy's gazes met. "No way."

Murphy laughed.

"Which one do you think he'll go for?" asked Ben.

"He loves blondes."

"I bet he goes for the tall one in the red boots."

They watched, both holding their breath as Randall reached the small gaggle of women. He finally stopped by the blonde.

"Ha! Told you." Murphy slapped the back of his hand against Ben's shoulder. "Shoulda bet money on it."

They giggled like schoolboys as Randall walked her back to their room, one hand on her back. She hurriedly sucked her way through a cigarette before they reached the door.

"He's not gonna make us watch, is he?" Ben asked, stricken.

Murphy laughed. "Course not. He'll just chuck us out. We'll smoke a cigarette outside."

Ben didn't smoke. But he didn't think it was quite the time for a lecture on healthy living. And besides, he liked the idea of hanging out in the dark alone with Murphy.

"One cigarette? He doesn't last long, then," he managed to mumble before the door opened.

Murphy smothered a laugh and led Ben toward the door.

"Where you goin'?" Randall planted a large hand firmly on Murphy's chest and stopped him in his tracks.

"Leaving you to it."

"She's for you, brother."

Murphy's face fell. "I don't want her."

Randall plastered a fake smile on his face. "Don't offend the woman."

Murphy slapped Randall's arm away. "I'm not interested. You gotta stop doing this."

Randall grabbed Murphy by his neck and slammed him up against the wall, wedging his huge forearm across Murphy's throat and pinning him there. "You'll have her and be grateful for it. What's wrong with her?"

"Nothin'," Murphy choked out.

"Shit. Anyone would think there was something wrong with you. You gonna do as you're told?"

Ben's eyes widened. Murphy's face was turning red from lack of air, and Ben fought the instinct to pull Randall off, knowing he would have about as much success as a squirrel trying to move an elephant. They were brothers. Surely, Randall would let Murphy go before he stopped breathing. Murphy nodded imperceptibly, and Randall stepped back, dropping Murphy to the floor. Murphy breathed in deep lungfuls of air. Randall grabbed Ben's arm and yanked him out of the motel room, leaving Murphy and the woman behind. Ben felt weightless as he was catapulted out by his arm. He wanted to reach out to Murphy and check if he was okay, but Murphy wouldn't even meet his eyes.

"Have fun, kids," Randall shouted.

The woman had remained silent and unmoved throughout the altercation. Ben guessed she was used to this sort of thing and a whole lot worse. He stumbled after Randall and stood hesitantly behind him in the shadows, watching as Randall sat down on a step about ten feet from their door. Someone had strung twinkle lights around the eaves of the motel. The colors were pretty, but it was way too early for Christmas decorations. The lights had probably gone up one December, and no one had ever bothered to take them down again.

"Sit down," Randall growled. And Ben obeyed immediately. "You know if you run, I'll catch you. And I'll kill you."

Ben believed him. Randall pulled out a cigarette and started to smoke. The silence gave Ben time to think.

How was Murphy going to have sex if he didn't like to be touched? Maybe he was different with women. He had slapped Ben on the shoulder just now. Maybe he didn't mind touching people but didn't like being touched by others. What was that woman doing to Murphy? Were they having sex right now? Or had Murphy refused? Was she about to storm out in anger and make Randall flip out even worse at his brother? Ben was torn between wanting Murphy to do what was necessary to keep Randall happy and wanting that woman nowhere near him.

He sat a few feet from Randall and rubbed his hands over his aching eyes. Why the hell did he care whether one of his captors was screwing a prostitute? It was none of his business if the idiot caught some venereal disease.

TEN MINUTES LATER, Ben wished they'd walked a lot farther away from the motel room. At first he could just hear a distant squeak, and then a soft and steady creaking noise, followed by female-sounding moans. Ben's gaze met Randall's, but he couldn't keep the disgusted expression off his face.

Randall seemed surprised. "Well, what do you know? The little dumbass managed it. Nice to know his dick works. Even if the rest of him don't."

Ben turned away, repulsed by Randall and by the noises coming from inside. He fought the impulse to cover his ears.

The woman came out soon after and left without a word or a glance. Her heels clicked loudly in the dark until she disappeared into the shadows on the other side of the parking lot. After another ten minutes, Murphy emerged. He had wet hair and smelled like soap.

Randall smirked at him. "You did good, boy. I know she ain't exactly...your type."

"Shut up, Randall. And don't do that again."

"A little gratitude wouldn't go amiss, brother." Randall whacked him hard in the back of the head. "I found and paid for her, ya ungrateful son of a bitch."

Murphy lit a cigarette, and Ben stared at the orange burning tip. He realized with a sick feeling that the woman's services were yet another thing Randall had paid for with Ben's money. Randall finished his cigarette, threw it into a bush, and followed the woman's path.

"I can't look at your ugly, ungrateful mug anymore tonight. I'll get my own room and my own whore. Think you can do something right and keep an eye on him for one night?"

"Yes," Murphy said, as though the fight had gone out of him.

"See you bright and early, fuckwads." Randall stopped and turned around. "Don't you two get too friendly, y'hear?" he said sternly, then went on his way, shouting good-bye over his shoulder. "Love ya."

"Love you too," Murphy replied quietly, his brother already out of earshot.

What did he mean by "friendly"? Ben stared at Murphy, eyes wide, feeling a seed of panic bloom deep in his belly. Could Randall tell what he was? Murphy stared at Ben hard for a moment, his eyes glowing in the twinkle lights. A soft breeze ruffled his hair, throwing strands across his eyes, and Ben's hands itched to tuck them back into place. The pink glow of the lights accentuated the sharp line of Murphy's cheekbones as he sucked hard on the cigarette, making his cheeks hollow out deliciously.

"He wants you scared. He knows I gave you that pillow. I'm not supposed to be nice to you. He don't want you to like me."

Too late.

BACK IN THEIR motel room, Ben smelled the sweet, flowery scent of the woman's perfume. He grabbed one of the pillows from the bed and headed toward the armchair. It creaked loudly as he sat down.

"What are you doing?" Murphy asked.

"Going to sleep."

"Over there? Randall's gone. He won't be back till tomorrow. We can share the bed."

Ben stared at the neat white sheets and couldn't help picturing what had just happened on them. "I don't really...I...That woman."

Murphy followed his gaze. "Oh. Then you won't want to sit on that chair, 'cause that's where it happened."

Ben jumped up and looked behind him as the chair creaked again. He brushed off his jeans and backed away from it as Murphy chuckled.

"I wasn't gonna mess up the bed, man. I gotta use it tonight. And so do you, if you want."

The smell of perfume diminished as Ben approached the bed.

Murphy disappeared into the bathroom to brush his teeth with his new toothbrush and get changed for bed. He emerged still wearing the T-shirt he'd worn all day and one of his new pairs of boxer shorts. They still had the creases on them from being folded inside the packaging.

They both sat up in bed, leaning against the pillows and the headboard. Murphy sat as far away from Ben as it was possible to get. So far that Ben was worried he'd fall off the edge.

After a short, awkward silence, Ben ventured a question. "You got any other family?"

Murphy paused. "Are we seriously having a get-to-know-you conversation?"

"Yes."

"Then I need a drink."

Ben laughed as Murphy jumped out of bed and grabbed the half bottle of whiskey that Randall hadn't finished. Maybe a drink was a good idea. Maybe it was a great one. If Murphy got drunk and fell asleep, this would be the perfect time to escape. Especially as he'd said Randall wouldn't be back until tomorrow. Murphy slipped back into bed and took a big gulp, made a face, and passed it over. Ben's eyes flickered down to Murphy's arm and the scar on his shoulder, and Murphy pulled his sleeve down. Ben surreptitiously wiped the neck of the bottle with the sheet of the bed; the thought of putting something in his mouth that Randall had been sucking on all day made him sick. Murphy saw him do it, and Ben knew from the look on his face that he thought it was because of him. Ben's heart dropped. He couldn't bear Murphy to think that when it was just the opposite. He took a swallow and smiled, trying to distract Murphy.

"We can play truth or dare."

Murphy sneered. "We ain't kids."

"Well, forget the dare part. We'll just do truth. You can take a drink but only if you answer a question."

Murphy snorted and shrugged. "Whatever."

"So," Ben tried again. "Do you have any other family besides Randall?"

Murphy paused. "Nope. No one." He took a sip and handed the bottle back.

He obviously didn't want to elaborate.

"Okay. Your turn," said Ben.

"I don't know what to ask."

"Anything. Whatever you want to know about me."

"I don't want to know anything about you."

Ouch. "So ask something embarrassing. Amuse yourself." Ben had played truth or dare and all the other variations on drinking games a million times. He was practically unembarrassable.

"Nah. What's your family like? I bet your parents are still together, right?"

"Yeah." Ben always felt faintly guilty that his parents were still happily married when most of his friends' weren't.

"That's cool."

"I have three brothers and a sister. All younger than me. They all live at home." Ben took a sip and passed the bottle back to Murphy.

"Sounds nice," Murphy murmured.

Ben thought for a second. What question did he really want to know the answer to? He took a deep breath. "Do you have a girlfriend?"

Murphy glanced at him and pushed his hair out of his eyes, only for it to fall right back. Blue eyes behind dark blond. He shook his head. He sipped from the bottle and held it out to Ben, inches from his face.

"Do you?"

Ben shook his head. He took the bottle in one hand, his fingers brushing Murphy's, and then wrapped his lips around the neck of the bottle and tilted it up, swallowing. His ex-boyfriend's face flashed into his mind for a brief second. Light-blond hair, right on the cusp of being red, pale skin covered in freckles. He had dumped Ben months ago. And apparently Ben was very easy to fall out of love with. He was already engaged to someone else. Ben felt that familiar kick in the guts as he remembered how disposable he was. But he didn't miss him, not exactly. Maybe just missed having someone to hold at night.

"What's your job?" Ben asked.

"Don't really have one. Used to fix cars. What's yours?"

Ben smiled. "Stop asking me the same questions I ask you."

"If you don't answer, you can't drink." Murphy grabbed the bottle back.

Ben snorted. Fine by him. He hated the taste anyway, and it meant he got to ask another question. He tapped his fingers on his stomach and thought.

"That wasn't your first time with a prostitute, was it?" Murphy's eyes widened, and Ben immediately regretted asking. "Forget it. Don't answer that. It doesn't matter."

"Wasn't the first time Randall got me one."

It seemed Ben had underestimated how badly Murphy wanted to get drunk. Murphy took a long swallow from the bottle. Ben couldn't even imagine any of his brothers buying him condoms or porn, let alone a prostitute. Besides, books and video games were easier to wrap.

"That's weird, huh?"

"No," Ben automatically denied. "Well, maybe a bit."

"Randall's pretty weird."

"Why does he do it?"

"Thinks it's normal. And I guess maybe he thinks I should sleep with more women or something."

Part of Ben noticed they weren't playing the game anymore. Just talking. And Murphy was the only one drinking.

"Wants me to be more like him."

"But you're not."

"Hope not."

"You're nothing like him," Ben said, unable to keep the disgust from his voice.

Murphy sharply raised his head. "He ain't that bad."

Ben must have sounded more disgusted than he'd meant to. "I don't even know him. Or you. I'm only going on first impressions. Don't listen to what I say. I don't know anything."

Murphy laughed once. "No, you're right. He's an asshole. But deep down, y'know? Deep down, he's all right."

"Really, really, really deep down."

Murphy smiled. "So what's your real name? We can't keep calling you Benedict Ben."

"Oh, were we not formally introduced?" Ben asked. "I guess that's one of the drawbacks of kidnapping people." Ben considered giving him a fake surname. But he'd only forget which name he'd given later on and mess it up. Might as well keep things simple. Ben held out his hand, and Murphy shook it. "Hi. I'm just Ben."

"Just Murphy. Nice to meet ya." Murphy passed the bottle over and winced as he stretched out his shoulder. "Must be your turn by now."

"What's up?"

"Nothin'. My arm hurts from driving so long, I guess."

"You want…" How could Ben make this sound like a normal, everyday activity between two men? "You want a back rub?"

"No way, man. It's fine."

"I'm good at it. I do it for my mother all the time." *That should reiterate that it's nonsexual.* It was true. He was good at it. And it was in no way whatsoever just an excuse to get to touch Murphy. But Murphy did look in pain. Randall shouldn't have made his brother drive for so long, the selfish prick. Maybe if Murphy drank a bit more, he'd agree to a back rub.

"My turn," Ben declared, not really sure whose turn it was. "What's your worst fear?"

"Snakes. Hate 'em." Murphy reached for the bottle, but Ben held it away.

People always said snakes or some kind of insect. That wasn't a real answer. "Really? That's your biggest fear in the whole world?"

"Guess not."

"So what is?" Ben nudged.

Murphy sighed. "You really wanna know?" he asked, an edge of defiance in his voice.

Ben nodded, and Murphy shrugged.

"Turning into my dad. Doing what he did. Leaving." He bit on the edge of his thumb. "That's why we're a team, me and Randall. We're all we got." He paused. "That better than snakes?"

Ben pushed the bottle gently into Murphy's hand.

Chapter Five

MURPHY HAD SCRUBBED himself in the shower, but he still didn't feel clean. The drink wasn't doing its normal job of blocking everything out, and Ben's stupid, endless questions weren't helping. The hot humiliation of what Randall had done hit him again. The whiskey might be loosening his tongue a little, but he wasn't going to share all the gory details with Ben. The first time his brother had made him sleep with a hooker, he'd been sixteen.

It was his birthday, and predictably, his father had forgotten. If someone had held a gun to the old bastard's head, he wouldn't have been able to remember the month of either of his sons' birthdays, let alone the date.

But Randall had remembered. He'd given Murphy a brand-new hunting knife in the morning. Wasn't wrapped, but Murphy had loved it. Then later that night, Randall had insisted he get drunk with Randall and his friends. He didn't like his brother's friends at the best of times, but he hated them when they'd been drinking. It magnified their bad qualities by about 600 percent. Made them loud and obnoxious, even dangerous. But Randall wouldn't take no for an answer. And Murphy was only sixteen, still skinny and shy and unable to refuse his brother anything once the man had his mind set on it.

So they'd gone to Mick's house. There were about a dozen guys there, spread over the small house, half-drunk already. Murphy didn't really drink back then, but he'd willingly taken a few beers to make the evening less unpleasant and end the day sooner. He couldn't wait for the morning to come and his birthday to be over with.

All of them kept laughing at Murphy behind their hands, but no one would explain why. It was like they had a secret that no one was letting him in on. Then there was a knock on the door. A blonde woman with bright-red lips and a leather skirt stepped in, and Murphy knew what the secret was.

He'd always wondered what it would feel like to be Randall. To want someone like her so badly. To want sex so much that you thought about it all the time and pursued it every day. He never had. Not with someone like her, anyway. His cheeks reddened with shame at the fact that Ben had seen it all. He must think they were so fucking hick. Ben was a nice guy—an educated guy from a good family. Murphy could tell from his clothes, his car, and the way he spoke. He was amazed Ben even wanted to talk to him, let alone grace him with that amazing smile. Every time Ben laughed at something he said, Murphy was shocked. No one had ever really found him funny before. Or been generous toward him. Or asked him questions. Or made him feel like he had anything to say worth listening to.

Well, the prostitute fiasco should have thoroughly put Ben off ever talking to him again. Plus Murphy had seen Ben staring at his scars. Ben's skin was flawless, of course. And now the kid wanted to give him a massage or some shit. He'd be able to see his scars real close up. Get the full effect. Murphy sighed. They'd reach Canada soon enough. Then the kid would be free of him. Never have to look at him again.

"The lights are hurting my eyes. Must be the drink. I'm gonna turn them off, okay?" Ben said.

"Okay," Murphy grunted. That figured.

Ben flicked his bedside lamp off and made to reach over to Murphy's.

"I'll get it." Murphy pressed the switch under the bulb and gasped as his shoulder twinged painfully.

"Murphy, let me help you," Ben said in the dark. "Don't worry. I'm the king of back rubs."

"Forget it." Murphy blinked and kept his face neutral. *Damn it.* It wasn't that he couldn't do with a massage. His shoulder was killing him. Every time he moved, it sent a white-hot pain through his neck and arm. He'd probably managed to pinch a nerve. But he'd seen people receiving massages. The groans and noises made him uncomfortable. Touching like that, having your hands all over someone for such a long period of time, it seemed almost sexual. Massages were the kind of thing best kept between a man and a woman. Or whoever. Not something he was interested in. *Not something Ben should be doing to me.* Still, the kid clearly wasn't going to let him get out of it. Maybe he should get it over with.

"I promise it won't be torture, Murphy." He didn't realize he'd been so obvious. "It'll feel nice," Ben continued. Murphy didn't want to feel nice. "I know you don't want to feel nice." The kid was reading his fucking mind. "And I know you don't want me to touch you. But after I'm finished, your shoulder will feel better, and you'll be glad I did this. Okay?"

Murphy grumbled something incoherent. He guessed Ben was making some kind of sense.

"Shift over in front of me."

"If it'll shut you the hell up," Murphy answered quietly. He crawled in front of Ben and sat cross-legged just in front of him. Ben settled behind him and placed his hands gently on Murphy's shoulders. Murphy automatically flinched away, but both of them seemed to be expecting that. Ben simply moved with him, keeping his hands firmly in place. "You don't have to, but it'd be better if you took your shirt off."

"No way."

"You don't have to," he said again. "It'd just be easier to get at your shoulder." Ben paused. "It's not like I can see anything."

"I don't care what you see."

"So take it off, then."

"Jesus." Murphy pushed Ben away and yanked his shirt off over his head, then threw it farther than he meant to in his annoyance. "Happy?" he snapped.

"I'm not trying to piss you off, Murphy," Ben said. "I want to help you."

"So get on with it," Murphy growled. The way Ben said his name so much and so softly made him feel weird. Plus, he was getting goose bumps from the cool night air on his skin. People never just "wanted to help." There was always something in it for them.

So what did Ben want? If he had any sense, he was probably trying to find a good moment to knock Murphy out and escape. And Murphy had half a mind to let him. Randall would probably beat the crap out of Murphy for being dumb enough to let Ben go. But it was no more than he deserved, getting this poor kid mixed up in his brother's stupid plans. Ben brushed his fingers softly from Murphy's nape out to his shoulders and then down over his upper arms.

"So was it your mother or father who gave you your giant shoulders?"

Murphy froze. He thought he had already made it clear he didn't want to talk about his family. But he was pretty sure Ben didn't mean anything by it. Murphy answered honestly. "Neither."

"Ah. Don't suppose you had a mailman with suspiciously broad shoulders?" The kid was on a fucking roll. "Sorry. Sorry. I don't know what I'm saying. It's the whiskey."

"Try not talking."

"Good idea."

The room fell silent again. The only sound was a cricket chirping busily in the corner. Ben's stupid comments had distracted him. He'd forgotten to worry about whether Ben could feel the thick, ropy scar across his back. The kid hadn't jumped away in disgust yet, at least. Murphy held his breath as Ben reached both hands around his throat, almost meeting at the front, and then slid them softly over his shoulders to his back. He pushed the heel of his hand deep into Murphy's shoulder blades and made him groan. Murphy wanted to slam a hand over his mouth. Fuck. His cheeks flushed in the darkness. Now he regretted telling Ben to keep quiet. At least if he were talking, that noise might not have been so obvious.

"That feel good?"

Murphy couldn't leave him hanging. "Mm-hm."

Ben did it again. This time, Murphy let out an involuntary whimper.

"That's it. Just relax," Ben murmured.

Murphy felt Ben's breath on his bare shoulders. He soon forgot all about his desperate need to keep quiet. He deliberately switched off his thoughts and got lost in Ben's firm touch. His chin sank down to his chest as Ben's warm hands worked confidently across his shoulders. He really was good at this. Murphy heard Ben breathing hard as he put all his effort into fixing Murphy's shoulder. Each time Ben pressed into him, Murphy rocked forward slightly and then fell back, melting into his touch. His thumbs pushed hard into the muscles on Murphy's back over and over again, knocking the breath out of him in a series of small sighs.

"You really needed this, didn't you?" Ben whispered. "Your muscles are knotted up so tight."

Ben grabbed Murphy's shoulder with one hand while he worked into his back muscle with the other. Ben's fingers curled down over Murphy's chest and touched the sensitive skin there. Goose bumps flared under the tips of his fingers, and Murphy shivered. He felt Ben shift to his side, moving his hands to Murphy's arm, pressing his palms hard into the muscles there, and rubbing his strong fingers in rhythmic, firm patterns. He worked from Murphy's shoulder down over his upper arm and down to his wrist. He moved again and slowly gave his other arm the same treatment and then returned to his lower back. When he reached the top of Murphy's boxers, Ben pulled his hands away, and one hand slid all the way up Murphy's spine to his neck and into his hair. Ben's long fingers spanned the back of his neck, reaching around to grip it and firmly stroke up and down. His fingers pushed into Murphy's hair on each upward stroke.

Ben gently repositioned Murphy's head, lifting his chin from his chest until he faced the ceiling. Murphy's first instinct would normally have been to pull away, but he let Ben move him without a word. He felt like Mowgli being hypnotized by the snake. Murphy sank back into Ben's chest as Ben leaned against the headboard. Ben buried both hands in Murphy's hair and moved his fingers in soft circles over Murphy's forehead and scalp.

Murphy didn't know how long the massage lasted. It could have been two minutes or twenty. But when Ben finally stopped, Murphy felt like he was waking up from a deep sleep. He scooted forward, self-conscious, and twisted his fingers together in his lap. He cleared his throat, not sure how to say thank-you.

"How's the shoulder feel now?"

It felt amazing. But glad he had the chance to skip the thank-you's, Murphy gave his shoulder an exploratory roll.

"It feels good, man." He turned around, and Ben grinned at him in the dark. He shifted across to the other side of the bed and pushed softly on Murphy's chest with one hand until he was lying back on soft pillows.

"Get some sleep," Ben said.

Murphy realized two things. One, he hadn't flinched when Ben had put a hand on him to push him back into the pillows, and two, he was shirtless and a little cold. But it seemed like way too much work to go and retrieve his shirt from the floor. His body felt heavy, and every movement was an effort. He slowly tucked his legs under the covers and pulled the blanket up to his chest. How had this kid—this kid he didn't even know—made him feel so relaxed? So safe? He was used to Randall's version of protection. He always felt physically safe with him—safe from other people, at least. Murphy knew his brother had his back, knew he would try to keep him out of danger, and now the fresh knowledge that he would kill for him. But this was different. Murphy let his head grow heavy and sink into the soft pillows. Conscious of Ben's comforting, steady presence beside him, Murphy relaxed his whole body into the mattress, feeling utterly content, and fell asleep.

Chapter Six

BEN'S HANDS STILL tingled from giving Murphy the massage. The scar he'd seen a hint of in the supermarket—the scar Murphy was so ashamed of—was so much bigger than he'd thought. Murphy's reticence to let him see it made more sense now, although it broke Ben's heart that Murphy was ashamed of it.

Ben didn't find it ugly at all. He'd wanted to run his fingers across its raised surface, follow its curve right across Murphy's body. But Ben knew it would have made him uncomfortable, and so soon after he'd finally convinced Murphy to relax. The scar spanned Murphy's whole back from the top of his left arm, over his shoulder blades, and then disappeared under his right arm. If it had been anyone else, Ben would have simply asked what happened. Was it a car crash, an accident, or was he attacked? But Murphy didn't want to talk about it, so Ben was happy not to know. If and when Murphy wanted to tell him, he would. Ben would never ask.

He listened until Murphy's breathing grew regular and soft. Ben lay back, careful not to knock into the other man. His eyes grew used to the dark, and he soon saw the room around him in charcoal grays, a square for the window, and bright lines surrounding the door. If he was going to escape, now was the moment. He was about to swing his legs off the bed when Murphy made a noise.

Ben looked over to find Murphy lying on his side facing Ben, eyes closed, fast asleep, and his hands flexing, clutching softly at thin air in his sleep. There were quiet whimpers coming from his throat. More bad dreams. The massage had relaxed him enough to fall dead to the world but not enough to sleep without nightmares.

Ben turned on his side to face him. He reached out to stroke Murphy's hair away from his face but stopped in midair. Every sinew in Ben's body wanted to comfort Murphy, but he knew he should take this opportunity to leave. Murphy wouldn't stop whimpering. He was talking now too, in a small voice, saying words Ben couldn't decipher. Until he said something unmistakable.

"No. No. No."

Murphy's head whipped from side to side. Even in the darkness, Ben could see sweat forming at his temples, and he couldn't let him go through it alone any longer. Ben moved closer to Murphy and hesitantly took one of his hands. He used his free hand to push Murphy's sweat-soaked hair out of his face. Murphy gripped his hand tight, and Ben thought he'd woken up. But the indecipherable whispering started again. Murphy was still locked in his dream. Ben stayed there, holding Murphy's hand and stroking through his hair until the noises stopped. Ben whispered words of his own, vague words of comfort. He didn't really know what he was saying, and Murphy couldn't hear him. He just hoped his voice might be some kind of help.

Eventually Murphy's breathing returned to normal, and his once-damp forehead was dry and cool. Ben tried to let go of Murphy's hand and slide back to make his escape. But even in his sleep, Murphy wouldn't let go. Maybe Ben could stay a little while longer. After all, if he moved now, Murphy might wake up.

BEN WOKE UP on his side hours later, with something against his back. One of his pillows must have moved during the night. He tried to roll over but found a solid mass behind him. He glanced down to discover one of Murphy's strong arms wrapped tightly around his waist. Ben had fallen asleep and missed what might be his only chance to get out of there. Murphy's chest was against his back, thighs pressing into the backs of Ben's legs. He could feel Murphy's warm breath on his neck. Delighted chills ran through Ben's body, and his stomach flipped. He squirmed, and Murphy's grip tightened.

"Murphy?" he whispered. But there was no answer. Ben stared down at the tiny blond hairs on Murphy's tanned arm and followed the slightly raised route of a vein wrapping around his forearm up to his biceps. There was a small black faded star tattoo on his hand where his thumb and forefinger met. Ben wondered if it meant anything. He smelled Murphy all around him, a delicious mix of pine trees and wood smoke and spearmint. How long would he be allowed to stay there? This might be the closest Murphy would ever let him get; Ben wanted to make the most of it. He moved again, trying to shift his leg into a more comfortable position, and realized there was something hard and unmistakable digging into his hip.

Ben's eyes widened. But his initial rush of excitement was soon replaced by awkwardness. As much as Ben loved lying there in the early dawn light with Murphy wrapped tightly around him, he knew it had to stop. It broke his heart to move away, but Murphy would be mortified if he woke up. And more importantly, Randall could burst through the door at any moment. With a sad sigh, Ben untangled himself as carefully as he could. But Murphy's breathing changed. When he went silent and still and his entire body tensed, Ben knew he was awake. Murphy moved the lower half of his body away convulsively, obviously trying not to touch him with his erection.

"It's okay," whispered Ben. There was no way Murphy hadn't noticed that he'd been pressed into Ben's hip. "I won't take it as a compliment."

Murphy didn't answer.

"I know it doesn't mean anything. I just..." Ben stumbled over his words. "It's just one of those things. It's not personal. I get it."

"Shut up."

"It's okay."

"Shut up," Murphy snapped. "You don't know what you're talking about."

"Sorry," said Ben. He took a breath, pulled himself from Murphy's grip, and got out of bed entirely. Murphy seemed frozen in place. It was a classic case of morning wood, nothing to get embarrassed about. Maybe he'd been thinking about that prostitute, wishing she was still here instead of Ben. She hadn't been so bad looking, if you were into that sort of thing. Not too old, pretty face underneath the makeup, and long legs. Whatever else it was straight men were into.

Murphy wouldn't look at him, so Ben went into the bathroom. He exhaled loudly as he stared into the black-flecked mirror. It was well and truly too late for escape now. And a stupid small part of him was almost relieved he wouldn't have to say good-bye just yet.

Trust Ben to be attracted to a guy like Murphy. He and his redneck brother were the most heterosexual men he'd ever met. Whores and beer and country music. Randall was clearly the type to use homophobic slurs as the go-to insult for everyone, but if he knew how accurate it was in Ben's case, he'd probably beat him to death and leave him at the side of the road. Or worse. And Murphy was related to that asshole. He was nicer, sure, gentler, and warmer, but he probably thought the same way. He didn't have a choice, growing up surrounded by guys like Randall, wherever it was they were from. The backwoods of a hick town. He'd slept with that prostitute. He might not have been too enthusiastic about it, but he'd done it.

Ben would just have to forget how it felt when Murphy's bright denim-blue gaze squinted through the sunlight into Ben's. And how warm his body had been crammed tight against Ben's. And how he ran his tongue over his lips when he was nervous. How his cheeks had hollowed out around that cigarette. And how he constantly pushed his soft blond hair uselessly out of his face and how it fell right back in front of his eyes every time.

AN HOUR LATER, they sat on the hood of the Jeep, Murphy's leg pressed against Ben's. The awkwardness from earlier seemed completely forgotten. Or maybe Murphy was pretending it had never happened. As soon as Ben left the bathroom, Murphy had been relaxed and cheerful. Ben couldn't work him out but decided to go with it. Murphy was even feeding Ben potato chips off his fingers, for Christ's sake. Ben was almost giddy.

Murphy stuck his fingers into the packet of chips again and speared one hoop-shaped chip on each of his fingertips like ill-fitting rings. He ate the first one, sucking his finger into his mouth and biting into the crispy hoop. Then he offered the second and third to Ben, letting him bite them off his fingers. Like it was nothing. Like all guys did that.

Ben caught sight of Murphy's hand and the tiny black star again. "I meant to ask, why did you get that?"

Murphy shrugged. "Got it when my dog died. She was called Nebula."

Ben gazed at him. He was so heart-achingly smart. Did all rednecks name their dogs after astronomical terms? Did they all know what words like "nebula" meant? Did they all feel so sad after a pet died that they got a tattoo in its memory? Ben crunched on a chip, swallowed, and then let out a little sigh. He really had to rethink his prejudices against rednecks. And buy more chips.

The door of the motel room farthest from them opened, and Randall strode out, followed by a familiar woman with blonde hair.

Ben's mouth fell open. "Oh God. He used the same woman?"

Murphy shrugged and smiled patiently.

"That's disgusting."

"That's Randall."

Randall didn't spare her a backward glance but seemed a lot more cheerful today. Apparently, all he'd needed was to get laid.

"Remember that fucked-up taxidermy museum we saw on TV a few months back? Run by that albino guy?" he shouted to Murphy. "You remember. All the animals were white with red eyes. Just like him."

Murphy shrugged.

"Where was that place?"

Ben must have watched the same TV show. He knew exactly where it was. "Evansville."

Randall continued as though Ben hadn't spoken. "I'm sure it's somewhere around here. You remember, Murphy?"

"Evansville," Ben repeated.

Randall continued to look expectantly at his brother. Murphy glanced at Ben and back at his brother. "I dunno, Randall. I think it might be in Evansville."

"That's it!" Randall exclaimed. "We should go check it out today."

Ben couldn't tell if Randall was ignoring him on purpose or had genuinely just tuned him out.

"Gimme the map," said Randall.

Despite having GPS, Ben's dad always made him keep a big spiral-bound map book in the car in case the GPS malfunctioned or got stolen. Randall seemed to prefer it old-school, and Ben had noticed him poring over it in the backseat several times already. Murphy opened the car, scooped the map off the floor where it was half-hidden under the front seat and passed it to Randall.

TWO HOURS LATER, they pulled into the gravel-covered parking lot outside Mel's Taxidermy Place. The museum was housed in a huge, sprawling two-story building that looked like a private home. There were trees and woodland all around it, overgrown and unkempt with no other buildings in sight. The bright, painted sign also boasted ownership of the world's largest ape.

"Is it open?" Murphy asked.

"Sure, stupid. Just not busy yet," said Randall.

That was an understatement. There was only one other vehicle there—a midnight-blue Mercedes. From what Ben could remember about the TV show, this place was run by a wealthy eccentric with a huge taxidermy collection. He'd gathered them all together here in one of his many properties and charged hardly anything to let people come in and look at them.

The entrance hall was large but dark and cluttered, the walls covered floor to ceiling in tourist postcards and posters of animals. Randall paid a woman at the desk, and somewhere in the back of his mind, Ben recalled that the woman might be the owner's sister. Her irises were pale gray with a hint of violet. As Randall paid and picked up a guide leaflet, Ben felt nostalgic for all the boring trips he'd been forced to take as a kid with his dad, walking for hours around endless historical monuments and museums.

"Right, fuckwads. Let's take a look around this shit hole."

Okay, that was a little less like his dad.

"That woman is the owner's mom," Murphy whispered into Ben's ear. Murphy looked thrilled, like they were in the presence of some huge celebrity. He was right—mother, not sister.

"I remember now. They had some kind of weird, uncomfortably close relationship," Ben whispered back.

Murphy nodded, grinning. It was the happiest he'd seemed since they met.

"It's kind of funny that we all saw the same show," Ben said. He liked the idea that he and Murphy had a connection, however small.

"I remember the night it was on. Randall was so drunk he lost the remote, and we were stuck on that channel for hours." Murphy scratched behind his ear. "Days, actually."

They wandered through the exhibits, every animal in sight an albino. Randall was uncharacteristically silent as they passed through numerous rooms, inspecting a white badger, a yellowing fox, pale, skinny cream-colored rabbits, countless white dogs, and an insanely long yellow-and-white python wrapped around a white ferret.

All with bright-red glowing eyes. Murphy stared at each animal longer than either Ben or Randall. Randall grew impatient and pushed on ahead, but Ben stayed glued to Murphy's side.

The house still looked like a house. Each creature was set up within in its own surreal homely setting. In some kind of drawing room, there was a big white hedgehog fighting a porcupine on an otherwise empty dinner table, their spines a bright, dazzling white. In a large room with tall windows and a grand piano were birds suspended from the ceiling on wires. A white eagle flew, frozen in place, wings outstretched, toward a dozen smaller birds, all in shades of white and yellow, all with orange eyes. On the gray stone floor of a glass conservatory filled with flowers and herbs was a huge crocodile, its scales buttery and pale.

In the final room, surrounded by a deep-red carpet and four walls lined with antique books, was an enormous albino gorilla, fists beating against its chest like a snowy King Kong. Ben laughed in shock. That was the last thing he'd expected to find in a library.

"I guess we've found the world's largest ape."

"Guess so."

"It doesn't look all that big. I mean, it's pretty big for the room, but if you imagined it in a jungle setting, I'm pretty sure it's an average-sized ape."

"Yeah," Murphy said and stood close to it, staring up into its glowing orange eyes.

"Do you think it's real?" Ben asked.

Murphy reached out to touch its fur, more yellow than pure white. On its stomach, at human-hand level, the fur was almost worn away. Instead, Murphy reached up as high as he could and touched its face softly. "It's real."

They stood in silence for a second or two.

"Randall must be in the gift shop."

"Yeah, I guess," mumbled Murphy.

Murphy crossed the room and sat on the window seat. Leaning toward the glass panes, he tore his gaze away from the gorilla and peered out into the unruly garden. Ben perched next to him, hardly pausing to take a breath.

"Are gorillas technically even apes?"

"Ben. What do I have to do to stop you from talking?"

"I dunno, put your tongue in my mouth?" It came out without Ben thinking. He held his breath, but Murphy's reaction was so adorable Ben was glad he'd said it.

"God, shut up." Murphy's cheeks flushed dark red. "You can't say things like that," he whispered furiously, checking toward the exit.

"Why not?"

Murphy shook his head and opened the window. He stuck his head out of it as if he needed to cool down. Ben could get to like embarrassing Murphy.

A little while later, Ben followed Murphy out through the exit door. They found Randall in the gift shop, stuffing a handful of Mel's Taxidermy Place pens in his pocket. Murphy quickly crossed the shop to stand by his brother, smiling casually across the room at the person behind the counter.

"What's wrong with you?" Murphy whispered.

"Ain't nothin' wrong with me, little brother."

"You have Ben's money."

"Won't last forever."

"We don't even need pens."

Randall shrugged. "They don't have any liquor to steal."

Murphy rolled his eyes and grabbed three Mel's Taxidermy Place apple danish pastries from the refrigerator. He slammed them on the counter and paid. "Keep the change."

All three of them ate sitting on a picnic bench under the trees out back, staring at a fifty-foot ape made from steel and painted white. Its arms reached up to the sky and held an actual 1950s convertible above his head, creaking in the wind.

Chapter Seven

THEY PULLED INTO the parking lot of the next motel sometime that afternoon. They'd clocked another four hours of driving, and Randall said he was tired. Evidently, sitting on the backseat with your feet up was backbreaking work.

Randall paid at reception and led them to room number twenty-seven. He was the first to walk in and stepped right onto a plastic DVD case, snapping it under his boots.

"What the fuck?"

There was a handful of open DVD cases scattered over the floor and the rumpled bed. Ben walked into the room behind Murphy and noticed a magazine lying open by one pillow. He stepped closer and saw several photographs of men in various sexual positions on the glossy pages. Randall snatched up one of the discs and read out the title.

"*Captain Americock?*"

Murphy snorted. "They must not have cleaned in here yet."

Randall picked up another. "*Daddy Bear*? I do not even want to think about what's gone on in this room."

"Looks like they had a good time," said Murphy.

"You *would* say that," Randall said under his breath. Ben wasn't sure Murphy heard him. Randall threw the DVDs back on the bed and wiped his hands on his jeans. "We ain't staying here. This is disgusting."

"You're not gonna catch gay from breathing in the air."

"Might catch somethin'."

Murphy rolled his eyes. "Whatever. Although I gotta admit, I'd appreciate clean sheets."

The bathroom door was ajar, and curiosity made Ben take two steps closer and push it open. His brain could barely process what he found inside.

A body lay on the floor, plastic bath mat rumpled up beneath it. Its feet lay by the toilet, and its head was in the shower. What was left of the head, anyway. The face was intact, but the back of the head wasn't there anymore. The bathroom's white tiled wall was entirely covered in red, all the way to the ceiling. It was like someone had taken a spray gun and painted the room scarlet. Blood pooled in the shower, dark and black. Some of the blood in the tub had already slid down the drain, and a bar of white soap was ruined with tiny neat red circles. The mirror was covered too, small patches of red with congealed lumps splattered here and there. Ben realized what the lumps were and staggered back. The last thing he noticed was a silver gun lying by the body's curled fingers.

"Jesus fucking Christ," Ben sputtered. He jumped back and fell over Randall's feet onto the bed.

Murphy darted into the bathroom, pursued by his brother.

"Randall?" Murphy's voice sounded young and scared for a second. He grabbed at Randall's arm, and his brother stepped back, pulling Murphy gently with him. He swung an arm around Murphy's shoulder and walked him out of the room. Ben followed close behind, wanting desperately not to be alone in there with the body.

Randall pushed Murphy softly back into the wall outside the room. He leaned him fully against it and then let go, his hands hovering over Murphy's shoulders until it was clear he was steady and safe.

"I'm gonna go tell reception. Don't go back in there, okay? You"—Randall pointed at Ben—"stay with him. Do not move."

Randall stalked off to the front office, and Ben heard him shouting in the distance within a minute.

"Murphy, you okay?" Ben asked.

"I'm fine." Murphy ran a hand over his face and pushed away from the wall. "Just...wasn't expecting to see that."

"Me neither."

Randall came back with a young teenage girl trotting after him. She seemed terrified. "There's three things you need to do, girlie. First, you need to get us another room. Second, you need to call the cops. And last, you need to give me your phone number," said Randall.

She stared into the room and through the open bathroom door at the tiled wall spattered in great globs of scarlet blood. Her eyes were huge, and she didn't seem to hear Randall.

"Shut up, man," Murphy said.

"What?" Randall grinned and raised both hands, palms facing out. "Just tryin' to lighten the mood."

Murphy seemed to take over at that point, obviously realizing the girl was young and scared, and Randall was going to continue being an ass.

"Ain't there anyone else you can get, miss?" Murphy asked.

"I'm on my own until six."

"Right. Then go back to your office, and call 911. Tell them you've found a body in one of your rooms. We'll make sure no one else goes in there till you come back, okay?"

"Okay," she said breathlessly and ran back to reception.

Murphy went back inside and collected up the DVDs from the bed and floor and shoved them into his bag.

"What the fuck, brother? I don't want you looking at that crap."

Murphy rolled his eyes and said nothing, grabbing up the magazine too.

Randall shook his head. "Ah, now this is worth taking." Randall, of course, had found the drinks cabinet. He held up a bottle of gleaming green absinthe.

"Put it down, Randall," said Murphy.

"No way. We deserve some compensation for all this here emotional trauma."

Ben snorted. As if Randall was capable of being traumatized. But he was silenced by one hard glance from Randall.

THE GIRL FROM reception led them across the paved courtyard in the center of the motel to their replacement room, opposite the first one. She apologized profusely despite Murphy's insistence that everything was fine. As soon as she left, Murphy pulled the DVDs and magazine out of his bag and shoved them deep inside the refuse bin at the edge of the courtyard.

Randall went across the road to get takeout and make a private phone call. Murphy and Ben watched from their motel room window as an ambulance came and left.

"The guy had half a head. That ambulance was a little redundant," Ben said.

"Guess they have to come and officially declare him," Murphy replied.

They watched for a while as a coroner's van came to take away the body in a black body bag, and someone put up yellow police tape across the door.

"I've never seen so much blood in my life," said Ben, clearing his throat, having not spoken for several minutes—a long time for him. "Didn't even know there was that much in the human body."

"There's the equivalent of three six-packs of blood in each of us."

"How the hell do you know this stuff?"

"Not all rednecks are dumb."

"I didn't mean that."

"I know. I just read stuff and remember it. Can't help it."

"You have an eidetic memory?"

"I'm not Good Will fucking Hunting."

A black van parked up outside. The yellow writing on the side read CRIME SCENE CLEANERS. Two men stepped out and opened the back doors of the van. They both climbed into white bodysuits, pulled the hoods up over their heads, and positioned breathing masks over their faces.

"Holy shit," Ben said.

"We really shouldn't have touched anything in there."

"You think there were chemicals or poison or something?"

"Nah, I seen them before. They always dress like that. Even to clean up blood from a car crash. They gotta be careful now with blood-borne hepatitis C and whatever," Murphy said.

"So basically you know everything?"

"Shut up, college boy. I just mean we shouldn't have messed with it. Legally and stuff."

"Why did you?"

Murphy shrugged. "No one's mom needs to see that sort of thing."

Of course. Ben hadn't even thought of that. It would be bad enough to learn your child was dead and be handed a bag of their belongings. But to open it and find that what your child chose to do with his last moments on earth was watch porn alone in a motel room seemed unimaginably sad. Elvis dying on the toilet was nothing compared to that. Ben didn't know if the police were allowed or had the time to worry about which belongings to give to the grieving family and which they were allowed to "misplace." Murphy's quick thinking might have given that guy a last little bit of dignity.

The men came back out and dumped two huge blue plastic bags in a box in the back of the van.

"Human waste," Murphy said.

"Nice," said Ben.

"Well, cleaning cloths saturated in blood anyway. And maybe some brains."

"TMI, Murphy. TMI."

"And skull fragments."

"Murphy! Shut up."

The crime-scene cleaners pulled off their face masks, and the taller one yanked down his hood and climbed out of the white bodysuit. He even pulled off the T-shirt underneath to reveal a deeply muscled chest and six-pack hewn from rock. His body was obscene. Ben instinctively glanced at Murphy, and it seemed as though he saw Murphy's eyes travel down over the man's body and up again. Ben stared hard at Murphy and then turned to find the man had disappeared behind the van.

"Seems pretty sad to kill yourself in a motel," Ben said.

"Maybe it's better that way. Then your family don't have to find you."

"I guess." Ben paused. "That's the first dead body I've ever seen."

"Hopefully the last."

Ben didn't like how ominous that sounded. It reminded him that Randall had a gun. If Ben pissed him off, it wasn't exactly a great impossibility for him to end up just like that. He didn't really think Randall was planning to kill him. He was still fairly certain that Randall was using him for the car and as a cash machine. But even as he thought that, something in the back of his mind nudged at him, reminding him that Randall could easily have the car without him in it, and if he wanted Ben's money, he could keep his card. Ben was obviously no hero. Threaten him with a couple of punches and he'd hand over the PIN, his savings, and his social security number in a heartbeat. So why was Randall keeping him around?

The van left, and there was nothing to look at but an empty courtyard and flapping ends of police tape. Ben turned away.

"So. Two single beds again. Guess I'm back on the floor." They shared an awkward look. Ben wasn't sure if he was relieved or sad that they wouldn't wake up cuddling again.

Randall slammed in with two bags of food and threw them at Murphy. "I already ate. I got someone to meet. You two are staying here. Don't leave the room."

"Weren't planning to." Murphy seemed surprised and confused by Randall's declaration, but he didn't ask any questions.

"Bye, love ya," Randall shouted over his shoulder and slammed the door behind him.

Murphy flinched at the noise before throwing himself on one of the beds and staring at his hands. "Love you too," he muttered darkly.

Ben swallowed. "You want to watch TV?"

Murphy shook his head. In silence, they ate the burgers and fries Randall had brought back, and Ben wondered what he could do to cheer Murphy up.

"You want to try the absinthe?"

"No."

Ben rummaged through his bag. He pulled out a pack of cards and waggled them at Murphy. "You want to play poker?"

"No."

"We have to do something. Don't you know how to play?"

"I know how. I just don't like to."

"'Cause you always lose?"

"No."

Ben shrugged. "Then play."

"I don't bet for money."

"That's good. I don't have any left," said Ben.

That made Murphy smile.

"We could play for favors instead."

"How do you mean?" asked Murphy.

"Like, if you lose, you can offer to fix the other person's car or make them dinner. Or if you were playing with girls, you could bet them a kiss or whatever."

Murphy pulled out Randall's stolen bottle of absinthe and set it between them.

"Oh, Murphy?"

"Yeah?"

"I'm gonna kick your ass at this."

Murphy snorted quietly.

They played a round, and then it was time to ante up. Ben knocked back a mouthful of absinthe and grimaced, leaning forward on his elbows.

"God, that's disgusting." He stared at Murphy across the bed and bit his lip as he thought about what to bet. "If I lose," Ben said and then paused. There wasn't a single thing he could give Murphy. He hardly had anything with him, and most of what he did have, Randall had already taken. And what sort of favor could he do for him? He was basically trapped doing whatever Randall told him to. "I'm at a loss."

Murphy smiled. "You could let me watch the old movies on your tablet," he said shyly. "Randall was messing with it yesterday. He don't really know how to use it, but I saw him scrolling through them. You have a lot of Marlon Brando movies."

"Okay. We can watch them."

"If I lose," Murphy said, "I'll make sure I'm the one tying you up tomorrow, and I'll do it loose, so it don't hurt." Murphy eyed Ben's wrists, still covered in red marks from the last time Randall had tied him.

Ben automatically rubbed his bruises. "It's a deal." He laid down his cards. Three tens. Murphy smirked and threw down his cards. Three kings.

"Jesus."

"Sorry," Murphy murmured. "I'll still do it, though." He gestured at Ben's wrists.

"No, no. A bet's a bet. Rules are rules." But God, it was sweet of him to offer.

SOMEWHERE ALONG THE line, they started betting forfeits instead of favors. Ben drank a lot more absinthe, lost a few more hands, and then laid down his pair of twos.

Murphy sighed. "How can you be so useless at poker? You even lose when all I have is two fours."

Ben leaned closer to squint at Murphy's cards. "Are you ever gonna let me win?"

"I'm trying."

"Is anyone even keeping track of who won what?"

"So far, you've won exactly nothing. I've won access to your entire movie collection, your titanium watch that tells the time in six different countries, another massage I don't even want, and you giving me half your food tomorrow." Murphy unsuccessfully tried to hide his smile at the dismay on Ben's face.

Ben gathered up the cards and dealt again. He looked up from his cards to find Murphy watching him. "I swear I'd be better at this if I wasn't drinking," Ben said.

"Sure."

Murphy took a small sip from the green bottle. Ben had downed a few inches of the stuff already, but Murphy was taking it much slower. Ben reached across the bed for the bottle. He snatched it up, took a sip, and missed his mouth, spilling it down his chin and shirt. Murphy surprised him by laughing out loud. Ben grinned back.

"You're a clumsy fucking drunk," said Murphy.

Ben swiped at his white T-shirt with one hand, the wet patch spreading. He pulled the shirt away from his skin, and when it fell back against his body, the dark shadow of his nipple showed through the wet fabric. Murphy pulled the dark blue bandanna from his back pocket and threw it into Ben's lap. Ben used it to dab at the stain but made no progress.

"Damn it." Ben pulled his shirt off over his head.

"What the hell are you doing? This ain't strip poker."

Ben balled up his shirt and wiped at the damp patch on his chest. "Can't sit in wet clothes. I'll get a cold."

"Whatever." Murphy grabbed an extra shirt from the back of the chair and threw it at Ben. "Cover yourself up, man."

Ben pulled it on over his head and adjusted it, rubbing his hand over the soft, worn fabric. "It smells good."

"It can't smell good," said Murphy. "It just smells like me."

"We should play strip poker, y'know. It'd be hilarious," mumbled Ben.

"Not a chance."

"You're so boring."

"You're so drunk."

"Not drunk enough."

Ben reached for the bottle again, only managing to spill it all over the bed. Murphy reached over and gently removed the bottle from Ben's hand. He wiped the blanket, the bottle, and Ben's wet hand with his bandanna and then carefully handed him the deck of cards. Ben started to deal again and promptly dropped the deck on the bed and floor. Cards scattered all around him, and he exclaimed despondently, staring at the carpet now covered in hearts and diamonds.

"Don't move. I'll get 'em." Murphy kneeled to collect the cards. Despite his orders, Ben slithered off the bed to try to help, only succeeding in banging his forehead hard on the edge of the bedside table. The collision made a loud bonk, and Murphy laughed.

"Was that a giggle? Tough rednecks giggle?"

"Fuck you. That was a manly expression of mild amusement, if anything." Murphy pulled Ben up by one arm, then dropped him and the pack of cards back on the bed. "Let's make this the last hand."

Ben grumbled an agreement.

"And Ben?"

"Yeah?"

"I'm still waiting for that ass kicking you promised me."

Ben's cheeks reddened. Even through his comfortable drunken haze, he had the grace to feel embarrassed. He hadn't won one hand yet.

They played the round, and Murphy stared at his cards. It was his turn to think up a forfeit.

"I've got one." Murphy's eyes flashed.

Ben felt a burst of nerves. Murphy had obviously thought up something good. Or bad.

"Whoever loses this hand has to say yes to every question they get asked by anyone for the next twenty-four hours. Starting right away."

Ben glanced down at the best hand he'd had all night, possibly his whole life—a straight flush. "Go ahead."

Murphy smiled at him and proudly laid down three jacks.

Ben whooped and threw his cards at Murphy. "In your fucking face!"

Murphy caught the cards and checked them. "Damn it. Swearing does not suit you, Ben. Sit the fuck down."

"Ah, this is what it feels like to win. I almost forgot." He knew he'd beat Murphy eventually. "Murphy, consider your ass kissed. Kicked! I mean kicked. Fuck." He really needed to stop talking. The room was spinning.

Murphy rolled his eyes. "Lie down. And shut up." Murphy pushed him hard into the pillows.

"Wow, I'm flattered, Murphy, but I don't know if we're ready for this yet," Ben slurred.

"Very funny. Shut up and sleep it off. I got movies to watch."

Through half-closed eyes, Ben watched him cross the room to find his tablet in Randall's stuff. Most people would have taken Ben's shoes off and thrown a blanket over him. Maybe even found him a bottle of water for when he woke up hungover. But Murphy wasn't most people.

BEN WOKE LATER to find Murphy lying next to him on his side, staring down at Ben's torso. Shifting lights played over Murphy's face as he stared—transfixed—at Ben's chest. Ben was being used as a screen rest. Murphy's gaze flicked up to meet his.

"Welcome back," Murphy said.

"You enjoying yourself?"

Murphy scratched the side of his nose, his gaze back on the screen. "Yep."

"Can you get me some water?"

"Nope."

"Wrong answer."

"Huh?" That got his attention.

"You have to say yes to every question for the next twenty-four hours. Well, probably only twenty-two or something now."

"You're not actually gonna hold me to that, are ya?"

"You bet I fucking am."

"I told you swearing don't suit you." Murphy paused the movie and jumped off the bed. He filled a coffee cup with cold water from the bathroom sink and brought it back to Ben.

"Thank you." The room was silent. "Is Randall ever coming back?"

"No clue. He might have found another woman crazy enough to sleep with him. Or maybe he's passed out drunk somewhere."

"He does that a lot?"

Murphy shrugged. "Anytime I've ever needed him, you can bet he'll be passed out from drink or drugs somewhere."

Ben smiled. "Like you can talk?"

"Hey, I'm a little buzzed. I'm not drunk. Unlike some people." Murphy reached out to grab the tablet and moved sideways closer to Ben. He pulled his knees up, feet flat on the bed, and leaned the screen against his thighs so they could both watch it.

"She's beautiful, huh?" Murphy muttered, staring intently at the screen.

"Eva Marie Saint?"

"Yeah."

Ben's heart sank as they watched Marlon Brando play with one of her white gloves on screen.

"Yes. She's beautiful."

Ben's leg was falling asleep, and he shifted position. His shoulder was now touching Murphy's, and he watched from the corner of his eye to see if Murphy flinched. He didn't, and for some reason, that made a warm glow spread through Ben's chest.

"My sister's watched this movie about a thousand times. She loves old movies even more than I do." Ben smiled fondly at the screen, and Murphy glanced over at him.

"You really like your family, huh?"

"We're all pretty close. It's a bit sickening, really. I miss them more than I thought I would. I haven't seen them for months."

"Why not?"

"I haven't been able to get home."

"Why?"

"Well, I had to finish college."

"Yeah? Thought as much. What did you study?"

"Marine biology," Ben said. Murphy raised his eyebrows. "Yeah. Really useful, huh?"

"You're smart. That's always useful. I ain't even been to college."

"What would you have done?"

Murphy shrugged. "Never thought about it. No money."

Ben felt like a dick for asking. "Well, anyway, I had to stay for graduation. Then I had to find someone to take over the apartment I was leaving. And I helped a friend move house. Then I assisted in some summer classes."

"Sounds like someone didn't want to go home."

Ben shifted uncomfortably. Sometimes Murphy was a little too intuitive. "You know, it's really late. You'd better get a couple of hours' sleep. Got a busy day tomorrow."

"Doing what?"

"Saying yes to everything."

Murphy snorted. "Lemme just watch the rest of the movie."

What am I? His mother? "Sure, watch to the end."

He'd seen the film a dozen times, and all the absinthe he'd consumed was making him sleepy again. He drifted off to the sound of Marlon Brando's voice.

BEN WOKE AGAIN later, completely sober and very thirsty. Another film was playing, but Murphy was silent. Ben gazed down at Murphy's face and held his breath.

Murphy was fast asleep, snoring like a puppy, his head a hot, heavy weight on Ben's chest. Murphy's hair looked soft, but Ben didn't dare touch it. He stayed motionless and watched Murphy's chest move up and down with each slow breath. Ben's ankle started to itch, but he decided he would let his leg fall off rather than wake Murphy up from a peaceful sleep. A small voice in the back of his head reminded him he was running out of chances to make a break for it. *But screw that.* All he wanted to do in the whole world right now was cup Murphy's face in his hand and run his thumb gently over Murphy's cheekbone. His skin looked so soft, so pink, and so perfect. Ben almost wanted to cry.

Ben couldn't bear to imagine kissing Murphy, because the thought of merely touching his lips made him die a tiny death. Ben squirmed a little. The thought of fucking Murphy practically made him black out. Murphy would be mortified if he knew Ben felt anything like this. Or he'd laugh. He'd think Ben was ridiculous. And he'd be right. Ben was ridiculous. Wanting to cry over cheekbones, for Christ's sake. He almost wished, for the first time in his life, that he'd been born a girl. But even then he probably wouldn't be Murphy's type. Murphy would like beautiful, strong women who could cook stews, skin a deer, and hunt squirrel. Not pathetic biology nerds who were so inept they allowed themselves to get kidnapped in their sleep.

Besides, in a few days, this would all be over. Whether he escaped, whether they left him bruised and beaten in a forest somewhere, and whether they returned his car or took it with them, soon Murphy would be gone from his life forever. They were never going to cross paths again; they lived in different worlds. There was no kidnappers reunion site where they could catch up in ten years' time. This was it. They'd never even kissed and never would, but the thought of not seeing Murphy again made Ben more distraught than he'd felt when his ex had dumped him.

A couple of minutes later, the movie finished, and music played over the credits loudly. Murphy's eyes fluttered open at the noise. He seemed confused as to where he was, his dark-blue eyes glazed and sleepy. He finally saw Ben and sat up.

"Oh, man. I fell asleep on you. Sorry." He swung his legs off the bed, put his feet on the floor, and rubbed a hand swiftly over his face. Ben's chest felt cold and bereft without Murphy's warm weight.

"Is it over?"

Ben nodded and switched off the tablet. Murphy bounced up onto his feet. He ran the water in the bathroom and filled the absinthe bottle back up, then shook it to mix the two liquids together and disguise the fact they'd drunk some.

"I'll take the bed by the door. Then if Randall does come back, it's me he'll punch in the head and push out, not you."

Ben felt a wave of gratitude. That was one brother he did not want to wake up sharing a bed with. "Would he really punch you in the head?"

"What do you think?"

Ben remembered Randall holding Murphy against the wall by his neck.

"I've been woken up by a fist in the face more often than I can remember." Murphy smiled.

"That's horrible."

He shrugged. "Compared to my dad, that was affectionate."

"What did your dad do?"

"Nothing. Forget it. Go to sleep."

Ben stood to switch the light off. There was something he wanted to say, but he knew he had to broach it carefully. Unfortunately his brain didn't get the message.

"Murphy, you know we could just call the police and hand Randall over."

Murphy glared at him.

"And then we—I mean you—could be free of him and stop running away. You wouldn't have to go to Canada. You could go home."

"Are you crazy? Shut the fuck up, man." He grabbed the tablet and took it to Randall's bag.

"I know he's your brother, but you don't have to stay with him forever. If it's only him who's done something wrong, you don't even need to be here. You don't need to be on the run."

Murphy turned to face him. "Don't think you know us, kid. Don't think you know me."

It was back to "kid" again.

"Maybe I know you better than you think."

Murphy threw the tablet back on Ben's bed. "You don't know the first fucking thing about me, and if you think I'm gonna hand my brother over to the police, you ain't as smart as I thought." Murphy grabbed Ben and pushed him onto his bed, hard. Ben bounced and gripped the edge of the mattress to keep from falling to the floor. Murphy hesitated, as if realizing how hard he'd pushed. "Just stop fucking talking," he muttered. "Randall was right. Shoulda gagged you from the start." Murphy reached over to grab the tablet from behind his head, and Ben flinched, squeezing his eyes shut. His whole body tensed, anticipating the strike.

"I'm not gonna hit you. Jesus." Murphy's voice was strained. He sounded offended.

Murphy tucked the tablet back in Randall's bag, making sure it was exactly where he'd found it. Ben caught his breath and then jumped up and crossed the room to stand by Murphy. He was careful not to touch him.

"All right, forget the police. We could just leave, before Randall gets back," Ben said. Murphy didn't answer. "Do you want to get away from him?" Ben asked carefully.

Murphy still didn't answer.

"You have to say yes," Ben continued hesitantly.

Murphy exhaled and gave Ben a sidelong look. "Knock it off." He paused. "I owe him, all right? I owe Randall everything."

At least he didn't sound angry anymore. What was the hold that Randall had over Murphy? He treated him like dirt, and yet Murphy would barely hear a word said against him. Ben understood the whole blood's-thicker-than-water thing. He felt the same way about his family, but blind loyalty made no sense when it all went one way. Murphy seemed to spend his whole life doing everything Randall demanded, but Randall never gave anything back. Ben was sure about only one thing. He no longer wanted to leave. Not until Murphy came with him.

LIKE CLOCKWORK, MURPHY started having nightmares soon after he fell asleep. This time the talking came before the whimpers. It was still hard to discern the words he was mumbling, but Ben made out one word.

"Stop."

Murphy was sleeping on his stomach, facing Ben's bed, and his head shook from side to side—as much as it could against the pillow—in a repeat of the night before. Ben crept over to Murphy's bed and crouched beside him, stroking his damp hair off his sweaty face. He tugged the sheet up, intending to cover more of Murphy's back, and caught sight of his scar again before pulling the sheet up to his neck and smoothing the fabric out.

"It's okay, Murph. You're okay. Just breathe. Relax."

Murphy's whimpers calmed down immediately, and Ben rubbed a soothing thumb back and forth over the soft hair at Murphy's nape.

When Ben was in high school, a tornado had hit their town. It was strong enough to flatten a few small buildings in their neighborhood—the tennis hut at the park, the old bathroom block at school, and the summerhouse Ben's dad had built in the backyard, a yellow wooden hut that caught the sun. It had collapsed right on top of the rabbit hutch. Two of their three rabbits had been crushed. The one that was left alive seemed sad and confused, and it died not long after. The vet didn't know if it had died of internal injuries, delayed shock, or old age. But Ben had always suspected it died of loneliness. In his defense, he'd been fifteen. He was supposed to have been emo. But his younger brother had taken the whole thing much harder than he. There had been a few weeks where Samuel suffered nightmares every night. Whimpering like Murphy, tears in his sleep. Ben had sat in his room and stroked his hair, sometimes taking him back to Ben's own bed when the crying wouldn't stop.

Murphy finally fell silent, and Ben withdrew his hand from the back of Murphy's neck. He pressed a chaste little kiss against Murphy's forehead and crept back to his bed, then collapsed into unconsciousness.

Chapter Eight

MURPHY WOKE UP from a dream about his dad just as Ben's lips met his forehead. But Ben disappeared before Murphy had processed what was happening. As he blinked into the darkness, his heart rate gradually fell back to normal. In direct contrast to the dream, the short kiss to his forehead made him feel pleased, safe, and taken care of. Every one of those feelings was unfamiliar to him. His mom was probably the last person to kiss him like that, and she'd been dead for years.

Why had Ben done that? Murphy got a sinking feeling deep in his stomach. Maybe he'd been making those stupid noises in his sleep. He'd tried to train himself out of that long ago. As a kid, if he woke people up by talking in his sleep, he got hit and yelled at or, if it was Randall, hit, yelled at, and teased mercilessly. But Ben had kissed him and comforted him. What would it have been like to grow up with people who comforted him when he was upset?

He had another long, difficult day ahead of him. Randall would be back in the morning, and Murphy would have to stay away from Ben all day. Not touch him, keep him tied up, be careful not to be nice to him in front of Randall, and let his brother poke a gun in Ben's face and not say anything. But until then there was a sweet, warm boy in the bed just three feet away. He needed to feel more of that comfort and warmth and affection, if only for a few hours. There was a magnetic pull coming from the boy on the other side of the room that Murphy couldn't ignore for one second longer.

Murphy climbed out of his bed and crossed to Ben's. But he came to a stop at his side. Why would any boy let him in his bed or want to be anywhere near him? Especially a boy who preferred Eva Marie Saint to Marlon Brando. Especially a boy like Ben. He gazed down at Ben's black hair, spread around his head on the pillow like the halo of a fallen angel.

Chapter Nine

THE FIRST FINGERS of pale morning light made Ben burrow farther under his covers. He was only half-awake but could smell Murphy all around him. Ben had been dreaming about kissing him, about wrapping his legs around him and pressing his lips into Murphy's warm neck, burying his hands in the softness of Murphy's hair, and breathing in the Murphy scent of leather and pine trees and wood smoke. Ben could almost imagine he still felt Murphy between his legs. He should stop torturing himself. It only hurt to think about kissing him. Especially now that he knew Murphy liked women.

But Ben's balls ached like hell, and he was so damned frustrated. If he could quietly get himself off without waking Murphy across the room, he could get up, have a shower, and no one ever needed to know. He was rock hard and so close already. He shifted a tiny bit, and the friction of the sheets against his cock sent sparks shooting through his entire body. He wouldn't even need to use his hands, just rut against the mattress like an animal a couple of times, and it would all be over. Damn it. He wanted to do this before he fully woke up and realized what a bad idea it was.

He grabbed a fistful of the covers and sheets in his right hand and ground his hips into the mattress. Slowly at first. Nice and slow. He breathed in the scent of Murphy, still hanging on the sheets from last night when they'd watched the film, and pretended it was him he was rubbing against. He wrapped himself in the scent and pretended Murphy was lying beneath him, his hard body pushed against Ben's, his strong arms wrapped around Ben's back, and his hands all over him. He imagined Murphy's soft pink lips parting and his tongue licking out across Ben's throat. Kissing and sucking his neck and biting him hard. Ben's hips moved faster. He was getting so close.

The bed moved. "Ben?"

Oh God, no.

His fistful of sheets was Murphy's T-shirt, and the hard mattress he'd *thought* he was grinding against was Murphy's hip. Ben looked up to find Murphy's sleepy blue eyes staring down at him. A half smile touched Murphy's beautiful face, and Ben's hips were still moving against him. It was too late. He couldn't stop. Ben gasped and came all over Murphy's stomach. Ben jumped away from him and buried his face in the pillow, cheeks scorching hot.

"Fuck. Get out."

"It's okay, Ben." Murphy touched his back, and Ben shrugged him off.

"I didn't know you were there," he whimpered.

"I know you didn't. It's all right. We've all done it before."

"I haven't."

"Well, maybe not that exactly, but forget about it. It's no big deal." Murphy paused. "It's a compliment to know I can make you come like that, though," he said, his voice softly mocking.

"Shut up," Ben shouted into the pillow.

"And that I can make you shout into a pillow."

"Fuck off," Ben said in a small voice.

"Sorry, Ben."

A cool hand touched Ben's back. He didn't shrug it off. He couldn't turn around or even lift his face off the pillow; he was too mortified. But the hand on his back was grounding. He growled into the pillow.

"What are you even doing in my bed?" Ben asked.

Murphy's shrug traveled down his arm and through the hand now squeezing Ben's shoulder. "I got cold on my own." Ben heard Murphy pull tissues from the box on the nightstand. The bed shook as he wiped himself off, and Ben's cheeks burned even hotter. Something about being in the semidarkness or Ben hiding his face seemed to make Murphy feel like talking. "Me and Randall used to share a room. Back when we were little. Well, I was little. He always seemed grown, even when he was only... Fourteen, he must have been. Dad never wanted to pay for heating, so I'd always beg Randall to let me sleep with him. He always said no at first, but he always said yes, eventually. I'd curl up by his back. I used to sleep real well back then."

Murphy had never offered up anything so personal. Ben held his breath and silently willed him to go on, but Murphy cleared his throat and withdrew his hand. Murphy couldn't have had any nightmares after he climbed into Ben's bed, or Ben would have been woken up. Ben felt a little glimmer of pleasure at the thought that he might have helped Murphy sleep better by being close to him, even if he'd been unaware of it at the time. But by the same token, it was slightly unnerving to be compared to Murphy's brother, however indirectly.

THEY EACH SHOWERED, packed up, and were ready to leave, but Randall still hadn't arrived back from his mystery appointment. Murphy and Ben waited for him, sitting opposite each other at a table for two in the café attached to the motel. Ben avoided meeting Murphy's eyes as they ordered breakfast.

"Ben."

Ben picked up the menu again and stared intently at the pictures of waffles.

"Benedict."

He couldn't help looking up at that.

"How long are you planning on being an embarrassed little bitch for?"

Ben snorted. "The rest of time."

Murphy smiled. "We got a few million years until the sun expands and time comes to an end. You think you can keep it up that long?"

Ben nodded. But he already felt better. If Murphy wasn't angry or embarrassed about it, maybe he was overreacting. Their food came, and as soon as he got some breakfast in him, Ben felt normal again.

"Do you want to go get me the ketchup from that table?" Ben asked.

Murphy scowled. "Nope."

"You wanna rethink that?"

Murphy frowned until he got it. "Jesus, that fucking bet."

He sighed and strode over to the table, bringing back the red bottle. He squirted out a huge glob onto Ben's plate and then took Ben's fork and speared some scrambled egg. He smeared it through the ketchup, picking up as much as possible, and held it up to Ben's mouth.

"That looks disgusting," Ben said.

Murphy shrugged smugly and moved the fork closer. "You asked for ketchup."

"You feeding me now?" Ben asked uncertainly.

"Looks like it."

Ben took it into his mouth and tried hard not to make a face. The next forkful was just eggs, and after each bite Murphy fed him, Ben asked a question.

"Do you think I'm more handsome than you?"

Murphy nodded.

"Am I probably the cleverest person to have ever lived?"

Murphy snorted. "Yes."

"Am I the king of all things?"

"Yes, Ben."

"Am I superior to you in every way?"

"Yes," Murphy said solemnly. Ben's plate was clear of food. Murphy dropped the fork with a clatter and looked Ben up and down. He frowned. "Are you wearing my shirt?"

"Am I?" Ben tried to sound innocent. "I just grabbed one off the floor."

He had initially picked it up by accident, thinking in the gloom from the closed curtains it was his blue shirt, but the second he'd brought it to his face to pull it on, he'd smelled Murphy on it. He'd pulled it over his head regardless. Wearing the thin cotton that had so recently been against Murphy's body filled Ben with reckless excitement.

Murphy's eyes flicked from Ben's face to his chest and up to his face again. "I've never even seen you in a black T-shirt."

"I have black T-shirts," Ben answered, sounding defensive even to himself. He might have one at home somewhere but not with him. He usually wore bright colors and white baseball shirts with colored sleeves. Some part of him was flattered that Murphy had noticed anything about what he wore. The rest of him was flushed with embarrassment.

"It looks weird on you."

"Okay, I'll take it off." Ben grabbed the hem of the shirt and pulled it up.

"No, don't. Jesus." Murphy grabbed Ben's hands away and pulled the shirt free of his fingers, then quickly ran his hands down it to straighten it out. Murphy's cheeks reddened as he got flustered again.

God, Ben loved being the cause of that adorable look on his face.

Randall chose that moment to return. He slammed his hand down on the table, rattling the plates and glasses, and pulled up the nearest chair.

"I'm back. Miss me?"

The corner of Murphy's mouth twitched. "Yes."

Randall seemed momentarily surprised. "Thanks, brother. The Chinese kid behave himself?"

"Ben is Korean," Murphy replied automatically, before answering Randall's question. "And yes."

A waitress breezed by carrying a tray of dirty plates, and Randall watched her pass. He leaned back in his chair and rubbed his hand over his crotch and upper thigh. "Goddamn. I could really do with some action. Know what I mean?"

Murphy's gaze cut to Ben momentarily before returning to Randall. "Yes."

Randall looked at Murphy strangely, obviously not used to him answering such questions in the affirmative. "You're acting weird, boy. You got something you wanna say to me?"

Murphy was clearly about to say yes, when Ben shook his head furiously at him. Murphy nodded almost imperceptibly at Ben and then said no.

"You two on your period?" Murphy shook his head. "You got a problem?" Murphy shook his head again. "Good. Then shut the fuck up."

Chapter Ten

RANDALL DROVE FOR once, leaving Murphy and Ben in the back. Randall let Murphy tie up Ben's wrists, and remembering what he'd said to Ben the night before, he did it loosely. He winked when Ben glanced up at him, and settled back into his seat, the bags piled up next to him. Murphy felt the heat from Ben's body, he was sitting so close. Murphy's leather jacket was on Ben's lap, and he watched Ben's long, slim fingers as they fiddled with the zipper.

Their yes game was verging on dangerous. Although Murphy knew he was to blame, being the one who came up with it. At first he'd kept forgetting the stupid bet. He didn't want to play. But it lit up Ben's whole face when he did. It felt good to make him smile like that. Now it had become important—practically life-and-death—to make Ben smile. He wanted to say yes to everything. He just hoped Randall wouldn't ask any more awkward questions.

"We gotta decide which way to go up here," Randall said.

Speak of the devil. Randall tossed Murphy the map.

"We're coming up on St. Louis," Randall continued.

Murphy traced the road with his finger. They were in Illinois, and a fork in the route was coming up. Both roads would lead to Canada, eventually. One went up through Minneapolis, and the other veered off to the right and took them toward the Great Lakes, heading through numerous national forests. Murphy loved forests, and he'd always wanted to see the lakes.

"The route through Minneapolis is quicker," yelled Randall over the noise of the wind whipping through his window. Murphy's heart sank. "But I ain't forgotten." Randall looked in the rearview mirror at Murphy.

"Forgotten what?"

"This is your first time out of Georgia."

Murphy bit on his thumbnail. Randall had been outside the state several times, usually for short prison stays and stretches in juvenile-detention centers when he was younger, leaving Murphy stuck alone with their dad for months on end.

"You wanna see the Great Lakes, brother?" Murphy nodded. "Then we'll go that way."

Ben smiled at him. "That was a good yes."

Murphy couldn't help smiling back.

MURPHY WOKE HOURS later to find his head resting on Ben's shoulder. Ben was asleep, his cheek lying heavily on top of Murphy's head. He smelled Ben's toothpaste and the apple shampoo from the motel. His hand felt warm, and it took Murphy a moment to realize that Ben was holding it in his sleep, under Murphy's leather jacket. His eyes snapped up to Randall in the front seat. He wasn't paying them a bit of attention, just humming along quietly to the radio. Even in his half-asleep state, Murphy knew this was dangerous, but he couldn't muster up enough energy to care. He rubbed his thumb over the soft skin on the back of Ben's hand and heard him breathe a tiny sigh in his sleep. Murphy smiled, his eyes flickered closed, and he nuzzled into Ben's warm shoulder, drifting off to sleep again.

BEN AND MURPHY fell forward in their seats, both woken by the car coming to a sudden stop. Murphy braced one arm on the seat in front and threw the other one instinctively across Ben to stop him from falling.

Randall jumped out of the car and opened Murphy's door like a chauffeur. "The lakes you ordered."

"Huh?"

"We're here, idiot."

Murphy rubbed his eyes and climbed out, leaving his jacket on Ben's lap. Theirs was the only car parked on a small circle of chalky sand. A road led back behind them through the trees and down a hill. Murphy trotted after his brother up a grassy incline, the wind whipping through his hair and blowing grit into his eyes. He heard Ben following and stopped until he caught up. They reached the top of the incline together, and the view took Murphy's breath away. He felt like he couldn't fill his lungs with enough air.

The lake was a great expanse of deep blue, nothing at all like the blue of the sky, and it stretched out all the way to the horizon. The sun made points of light that danced over the surface of the water, dazzling white diamonds, always moving. It was the most beautiful thing he'd ever seen. Even from their vantage point halfway up to the heavens, the lake seemed like an ocean. He couldn't see the other side. He'd never dreamed a lake could be this big.

"Good, huh?" Randall punched him on the arm.

Murphy nodded. Randall didn't stand for hugs, so all Murphy could do was reach out to his brother and take hold of the hem of his leather jacket in one hand. Randall batted him away but grabbed the back of his neck in one huge hand and squeezed. Murphy didn't even want to blink. He wanted to stay here and look forever with the cold wind in his face, bathing him in the fresh smell of the lake. Ben passed him the coat awkwardly, his wrists still bound, and pushed his shoulder against Murphy's. That was the most contact they could risk with Randall right there.

"I forgot how pretty this is," Ben said, almost to himself.

So Ben had been here before. It figured. He'd probably traveled all over.

There were three sailboats in the distance, not quite at the horizon. Each had a different colored sail, one yellow, one blue, and one orange. They were using the wind and zigzagging quickly, close behind one another on the flat water.

"Wish I was on one of those boats," murmured Murphy.

Ben stared at him. "You like boats?"

"Sure." Murphy shrugged. The breeze blew a lock of hair into Ben's eyes, and Murphy reflexively reached over to brush it back. "Don't you?"

Randall side-eyed them and then grabbed Murphy's arm and dragged him over to a nearby bench, keeping his eyes on Ben as he whispered hoarsely. "What's going on with you?"

"What do you mean?" Murphy yanked his arm away.

"The state of you. He's wearing your damned T-shirt, man. You were asleep in the car all over each other. All tangled up like sleepin' puppies."

"Nothing's going on, man. I just lent him a shirt. And you know sitting in the back makes me tired. It's been a long drive."

Randall hesitated, then took a deep breath. "Look, if you're..."

"What?"

"I don't—" Randall exhaled. "Not this guy, okay?"

Murphy felt a flash of heat and panic. "What are you talking about?"

"Nothing. Forget it. Anyway, man. You need to know, things might have changed."

"What things?"

Randall paused. "I owe a little money."

Murphy rolled his eyes. "Not this shit again."

Randall slapped his shoulder with the back of his hand. "Have some respect. I'm on top of it. But I need to know that you're keeping this under control while I sort shit out. Can I trust you?"

"You know you can."

Randall glanced at Ben, who was still gazing out over the lake, his hands tied together, the untethered rope pooled by his feet. "Just don't get too attached."

"Attached? What does that mean?"

Randall had always yelled at him for getting too attached to the dog. He was never entirely sure how much of an accident Nebula's death had been. Randall told him he'd hit her with the truck. Randall had dug a grave for her and buried her in his jacket. He'd seemed sad enough and about as sorry as Randall got. But Murphy hadn't been there when it happened.

"You're getting too lax with the kid. Gotta keep him tied up all the time."

"There's no need, man. He's not going anywhere."

Murphy stared at the permanent raised bump in Randall's forehead. Situated near the hairline, it was close to invisible, but Murphy knew from experience exactly where it was and exactly how hard he had to hit it to make Randall go down like a sack of bricks. One too many bar fights with random strangers had given his brother a weak spot. He'd elbowed his big brother there by accident once during a play fight, and Randall had switched off like a light. He'd thought his brother was faking it for a good five minutes till he'd realized the collapse was real and panicked. He'd never once taken advantage of his weak spot, even though he was tempted regularly when Randall was being particularly cruel or obnoxious. That was the sort of thing his dad would do. Not him.

"You're too soft, boy. When I'm not here, he stays tied to something. You hear me?"

Chapter Eleven

AN HOUR AFTER they left the lakes, Randall pulled off the road and parked outside a place called Wisconsin World of Tattoos. Its proximity to the main road gave it the feel of another obscure roadside attraction, but the line of beat-up motorcycles parked outside suggested the clientele probably weren't the curious-passing-tourist type.

"Friend of mine works inside. You can stay in the car or come in. I'll be a couple hours."

Murphy and Ben looked at each other and shrugged.

Inside, the place was bigger than it seemed from the outside. The foyer was a huge oblong room with doors and corridors leading off in all directions. Some kind of metal music was playing on the speaker system, and there were several small groups of people dotted around, mostly looking over the tattoo designs plastered over the walls and on freestanding boards in the center of the room. Randall headed to the reception desk manned by a tall woman covered in tattoos and piercings. She directed him to a door, and Randall turned, pointing at Ben.

"Keep him under control."

Murphy nodded, and Randall disappeared through the swing door.

"Is he getting a tattoo?"

Murphy laughed. "If he was gonna get a tattoo, he'd have done it by now."

"A piercing, then. Maybe a Prince Albert?"

"Ugh, Ben. Jesus."

Ben shrugged. "How many do you have, then?"

Murphy raised an eyebrow. "I think you can only get one."

"Tattoos, not Prince Alberts."

"Ah, three."

"Three? Where? I've only seen the star."

"I got a heart here." Murphy pulled down the neck of his T-shirt and revealed a tiny red heart on his collarbone. Unbelievable that Ben hadn't noticed it before. "And a dragon on my hip."

Ben's gaze fell to his hips, but Murphy evidently wasn't planning to yank his shirt up in the busy foyer and show him that one. "Wow. I don't have any."

"You want one?" Murphy smiled. "We have time to kill."

"No way."

Murphy laughed. "Scared?"

"Absolutely." Ben wasn't ashamed to admit it.

Murphy shoved his hands in his pockets and craned his head back to look at the top row of pictures. Ben glanced at the wall. He didn't like any of them so far. All mermaids, roses, butterflies, and Gothic crosses. There was a whole wall full of Chinese characters.

"I hate this kind," said Ben.

"Why?"

"They could say anything."

Murphy shrugged. "You have to do your research."

Ben scoffed. "Research. Do you know how many people have come up to me, whipped their arm or lower back out, and asked me to tell them what their Chinese tattoo means? That's what some people call research."

"You serious?"

"Dead serious."

"What do you tell 'em?"

"I got sick of explaining I wasn't Chinese. I just make stuff up now. I told one girl hers meant 'no parking.'"

Murphy laughed.

Above one of the corridors was an arrow with a sign that read VIEWING AREA.

"Wanna go and watch?" Ben asked.

"Yes," Murphy answered and winked. Ben kept forgetting the bet.

The empty corridor led to two big windows, one on each side. Each overlooked a small room with a padded, segmented dentist's chair and various tables and trays of tattoo ink and needles. All the walls inside were covered in bright, colorful posters and tattoo designs. One room was empty. The other had two people inside. Ben and Murphy watched for a while as a wiry man with a long beard and two ear gauges tattooed a man. The man lay on his front on the padded chair, his jeans around his thighs, getting what appeared to be a huge tribal tattoo on his right butt cheek.

"Do you think it hurts less or more on your ass?"

"Less. It hurts more the closer you are to bone. That's why the one on my collarbone is so small."

Ben snorted. "Thought you were supposed to be brave."

"I never said that."

"How close to the bone is your dragon? Is it big?"

Murphy checked both ways up the corridor and, finding it empty, pulled up his shirt with one hand and pushed his jeans and boxers down a couple of inches with the other, revealing smooth, pale skin and a jutting hip bone. Ben swallowed and finally noticed the dragon. It was about three inches wide and dark purple. It had curved, elegant wings and a curly pointed tail.

"It's beautiful."

"Thanks." Murphy held his shirt up under his chin and reached down to run his fingers over it, pushing his hips forward to see it better. "I hardly ever notice it anymore."

A heavily tattooed man rounded the corner of the corridor and swept toward them, holding a clipboard. He nodded at Murphy.

"Nice tat."

Murphy let his shirt drop.

"You want a tattoo today?"

Murphy's face dropped, and he looked at Ben. "Yes."

The tattooed guy grinned. "I'm free now. My name's Wendell. Come with me."

Ben laughed. "You don't really want one, do you?"

Murphy gave a half smile and shrugged. "Rules are rules. You can't renege on a bet."

"Murphy!"

Murphy just smiled and followed Wendell. The room had no viewing windows, Ben was somewhat relieved to notice. The same music that played in the foyer and corridors was playing quietly in the room.

"Do you know what you want?"

Murphy paused for a second. "I want a moon. A full moon. Realistic. With craters."

"Sure thing. Whereabouts?" Wendell turned and sorted through the pile of tattoo catalogs on the counter behind him. He passed Murphy a book of astronomy-themed tattoos and let him flick through it.

"Where should I get it, Ben?"

"I don't know," Ben whispered, not sure if he should encourage him to go through with this. He loved the tattoos Murphy already had. They were sexy, even. But the thought of Murphy covering up more of his beautiful body made Ben feel slightly panicked. "Shouldn't you think about this for longer? Shouldn't it mean something?"

"Maybe it does."

"What?"

Murphy didn't answer. "Just c'mere." Murphy showed him a page of full and crescent moons. "Which one do you like?"

This was going to be on Murphy's body for eternity. Ben had to choose the best moon possible. The full moon in the bottom corner of the page was interesting. The arrangement of the craters seemed somehow unfamiliar. It was gray and blue and looked like the moon on a cool, clear night. Ben pointed.

"That one."

"The far side of the moon. That's perfect." Murphy's smile was warm and open. His expression was full of something Ben couldn't identify. Maybe something like pride, but that didn't make sense.

"Cool," said Wendell. "That's three colors. I'll get the inks ready."

"Where should I get it? On my arm?"

Ben reached out tentatively and pushed up the sleeve of Murphy's T-shirt, trying to picture the moon there. His arms were so perfectly muscled, the skin so smooth and flawless. Ben couldn't endorse covering up even an inch of them.

"The back of your shoulder, maybe."

"Okay."

The ease with which Murphy accepted Ben's suggestions on something so permanent took his breath away.

"How big would you like it?" Wendell asked.

Murphy made a circle with his fingers, and Wendell nodded. "About three inches. I'll transfer on the outline first, and you can tell me if it's in the right place."

Murphy yanked his shirt mostly off, pulling one arm out of its sleeve and leaving his left arm and shoulder covered. To hide his scar, Ben realized. Most of his torso was on show, and Ben tried not to stare. But it was like trying not to look at the sun. He couldn't help but peek, despite the harm it could cause. Murphy didn't have any hint of a six-pack, but his stomach was flat and lean. The breadth of his shoulders and chest tapered down to a narrow waist in a delicious V shape. He was tan all over but not like he'd lain out for hours by some pool. More like he'd been working outside and got tan by accident. The light dusting of hair on his chest was blond—lighter than his hair or eyebrows, maybe bleached by the sun. He had freckles on his shoulder and a few on his chest. Ben had an inexplicable urge to taste them. He forced his gaze back up to Murphy's face, only to find him watching. Ben flushed.

"You really don't have to do this. It's just a stupid game."

"I want it."

"Are you sure?"

Murphy paused. "Yes."

"Please tell me you're not playing the game right now."

"I promise."

Murphy's eyes were clear, and Ben believed him. That didn't get rid of the butterflies in his stomach. Murphy sat on the cream-colored dentist's chair, and Wendell cleaned the area at the top of his shoulder blade with rubbing alcohol. Then he shaved it, even though Ben couldn't see anything but the finest of tiny blond hairs. He cleaned it again and then applied the transfer. He rubbed it on with water and peeled the paper away, leaving a purple outline of Murphy's moon. Wendell directed Murphy to a mirror on the wall, and Murphy jumped up and twisted around adorably in an attempt to see it.

"Yeah, it looks great. Ben?"

He was right. It was going to look amazing. Ben smiled, a little more comfortable now. Wendell adjusted the chair until the top half leaned up at forty-five degrees, and then slapped the surface.

"Okay, jump up and lean against this."

Murphy sat facing the top of the chair and leaned forward until his stomach and chest met the cushioned surface. Wendell pushed a wheeled office chair gently over to Ben and pulled another one up next to Murphy's shoulder for himself, pumping the height up a couple of inches until he was level with Murphy's shoulder. Once Murphy had gotten comfortable, Wendell shifted his chair tight up to him and wheeled the machine and all the equipment over to within easy reach. He put on latex gloves.

"You ready?" Wendell asked.

"Go ahead."

Ben sat on his chair and walked it to Murphy's side, stopping by his other shoulder. Murphy turned his head to face him and reached out his free arm, nudging Ben's knee with the back of his hand.

"You look nervous," Murphy said.

"You don't."

Murphy shrugged. "I'm not."

"Okay, for the next hour or so, don't shrug," said Wendell.

"Sorry."

Wendell chuckled softly and rubbed ointment into the transfer. "Just keep breathing steadily and stay nice and still for me." He turned on the tattooing machine, and its buzz was quieter than Ben had expected. It was drowned out by the music.

"I'm going to do the first line now."

Ben held his breath as the needle touched Murphy's back. "Does it hurt?"

"Nah." But Murphy's face said different. He bit his lip for the first few seconds. His eyelid twitched every time the needle moved, and he gave a tiny gasp as Wendell let the needle go a little deep. All Wendell's concentration was on the tattoo. He sat hunched over, inking and then wiping, staring intently at Murphy's shoulder blade. After a while, he didn't even seem to remember they were there, so Ben felt safe grabbing Murphy's hand under the chair and letting him squeeze it tight when the needle hurt him.

A long while later, Wendell wiped Murphy's shoulder off and changed the needle and inks. Then he started shading the moon with colors. Murphy stared up at Ben throughout the whole thing, hardly blinking. He winced from the pain every once in a while but never looked away. There was a little muscle in his jaw that flexed every time his eyes narrowed in pain.

Ben got so hard from holding Murphy's hand and staring at that twitching muscle he had to move closer to the chair and hope no one could see. He'd never gazed into

Murphy's eyes uninterrupted for so long or at such close quarters. A line of navy ringed the denim blue of each iris, and a starburst of gold surrounded his pupils. They studied each other for a long time until the tattoo was almost done.

Then the door crashed open, and Randall walked in. Ben swore under his breath and snatched his hand away.

"What's wrong?" Murphy couldn't see the door.

"Well, what do we have here?"

"Your brother," Ben answered. Murphy had to know that voice anywhere. Ben hoped he wouldn't have to move away from the chair too soon. It was still hiding his hard-on. Not for the first time that day—or even that hour—he wished Randall didn't exist.

"I'm all done, guys," murmured Wendell, seeming unimpressed by Randall's sudden intrusion.

Ben leaned over to see the tattoo, and Randall strode closer. The moon looked good. The colors were subtle and the lines delicate. But the flesh around it was raw and red.

"Not bad, brother. Pretty small, though. You losing your nerve?"

Ben was surprised by Murphy's self-control in neither telling Randall where to go, nor reminding everyone that Randall didn't have the balls to get a tattoo of his own. Wendell cleaned the finished tattoo, rubbed more ointment into it, and then taped a bandage carefully over the top.

"You familiar with the aftercare?"

Murphy sat up stiffly and swung both legs over the side of the chair. "Yeah, I remember."

Wendell handed him a printout. "It's all written there for you. Keep it clean and follow this, and you'll be cool."

"Thanks, man." Murphy cautiously pulled his shirt back on.

"No problem." Wendell grinned. "You pay at reception. I'll bring the bill."

Murphy paid and left Wendell a tip. Then they walked back to the Jeep. Ben was relieved that his hard-on had faded in time for their exit. "I didn't use your money," Murphy whispered to Ben as they crossed the parking lot.

"I wouldn't mind."

"I would."

They stood by the car as Randall searched for the keys. Ben found his eyes magnetically drawn to Murphy as always. He'd happily stare at him all day. Murphy was already looking at him. Warmth spread through Ben's chest, and behind Randall's back, Murphy winked at him. Ben beamed back.

WHEN THEY ARRIVED at that night's motel, Randall declared rather cryptically that he had to leave to do a thing.

"A thing?" Murphy asked.

"Yes. A thing we don't need to be discussing in present company. Let's just say I'm meeting an old acquaintance."

"The same person you met yesterday?" Murphy asked.

"Kinda."

"What does that mean?"

"Means it's none of your damned concern, brother." Randall's voice was cold, and Ben hoped Murphy would stop. "Gonna be gone a little longer this time. I'll meet up with you again in two days." He stopped Murphy's next question by holding up one hand. "We'll go get a good-bye drink, and then I'm taking off."

Two days alone with Murphy? A shudder of anticipation traveled up Ben's spine.

They found a bar a short walk from the motel for the good-bye drink. Randall untied Ben and left the rope in their room. He dragged Ben into the bar by his shoulder and shoved him onto a grubby bar stool. Randall spent most of the first hour chatting up the barmaid. She giggled and peered up at Randall through her lashes, as if she actually liked him.

As hard as Ben tried, he couldn't look at Randall and see anything other than Murphy's intimidating, violent, gun-wielding older brother. Randall leaned on the bar and flashed his teeth at the woman. He gently trailed a finger across her arm, and she giggled again.

Ben squinted at Randall. The man had an okay body. He was muscular in that barrel-chested, John Wayne way Ben had never found attractive but plenty of people seemed to. His pale-blue eyes turned Ben's heart to ice, but maybe when they were accompanied by a smile and aimed at a woman, they had the opposite effect.

Murphy stood near Randall, chewing on his thumb. No one in the bar spared him a glance. But Ben couldn't look away. Murphy's shoulders seemed even broader than usual in that shirt. It was only when he slipped the tip of a finger into his mouth and bit on it that Ben realized Murphy was craving a cigarette. At that moment Murphy turned to Randall.

"Goin' outside for a smoke."

Randall tutted and dragged his eyes away from the woman behind the bar. "Whatever, kid. Don't interrupt me."

Ben got up to follow Murphy, but Randall grabbed his wrist and pulled him back, painfully twisting his arm. He took Ben's debit card out of his inside pocket and thrust it into Ben's hand.

"While you're out there, use the ATM and get out as much money as it'll let you take," Randall rasped.

Ben nodded and yanked his wrist from Randall's steel grip.

MURPHY SMOKED HIS cigarette, bathed in the green glow of the ATM screen, while Ben tapped the buttons. All those hours he'd spent cleaning boats, rubbing his hands red raw scraping barnacles off hulls, and killing his back repainting them, all wasted and going to that lazy bastard.

"Who's he meeting up with?" Ben asked.

"Don't know. Maybe some old prison buddy."

Prison. That shouldn't have been a surprise. Ben didn't want to ask what he'd been in there for. Some things were better not to know.

Back inside, Ben handed the cash and the card over to Randall. "It wouldn't let me take out more than five hundred."

Randall stared at him hard, and Ben felt chastised.

"You can give us another five hundred in a couple of days."

"Fine," Ben said, noting that Randall had successfully made him feel like he was doing Ben a favor by letting him pay in installments. Pay for what? Randall not killing him yet? Randall ordered three shots. The barmaid placed three glasses in front of them and poured in the clear liquid, spilling some on the bar top. Randall took one and downed it.

"I'll see you in half an hour back at the motel. I gotta make a call," he said to Murphy. "And you"—he thrust some money at Ben as he left—"go to the pisser, and get me a pack of condoms from the machine."

Ben sighed, took the money, and set off hesitantly toward the men's room.

"Wait."

Ben turned to find Murphy had followed him. Across the bar, Randall slammed the exit door behind him and disappeared into the night with his phone. Murphy held out a shot glass. "To two whole days without Randall."

Ben grinned, and they downed their shots together. He handed Murphy the empty glass and pushed open the men's room door.

There were three men inside, two leaning against the sinks and one smoking a cigarette by a stall. They stopped talking when Ben entered, and he avoided eye contact as he tried to locate the condom machine.

It was on the other side of the room. He had to pass between the men to get there. He paused. Randall would not react well if he came back with no condoms, and there was no way he was going to go and ask Murphy to help him with something this simple. He had to brave it. He took a breath, trained his eyes on the linoleum floor, and walked straight through the middle of the small group.

They still hadn't resumed their conversation, and he felt each of their eyes on him as he fed the money into the machine. What the hell kind of condoms would Randall want? There were three choices: plain, ribbed, and flavored. He pressed the button for plain.

"They for your boyfriend?" One of them laughed.

Ben closed his eyes and sighed in resignation.

"Are you ignoring us?"

The machine spat out some coins in change, and as he scooped them up and put them in his pocket, Ben heard the men's room door open. *Please*, he prayed, *don't let it be more of their friends.*

"I think he's ignoring us. We asked you a polite question, bitch."

A small pack of condoms was released, and as Ben grabbed them from the slot, a hand dropped heavily on Ben's shoulder. He flinched and turned to find Murphy looking down at him.

Thank you, Jesus.

"Aw, are you his boyfriend?"

Murphy looked at the men, then back at Ben. The kiss was hard and sudden and came from nowhere. Murphy simply dipped his head and captured Ben's lips with his. Their teeth clashed, and Murphy grabbed Ben's upper arms tight and held him in place. Ben felt Murphy's tongue against his lower lip for a moment and then only Murphy's lips, crushing hot against his and scorching him into silence.

Ben froze. This couldn't be real. He kissed back quickly, before the spell broke. Murphy's hard lips softened and moved against Ben's. Ben sank further into Murphy's warm body and memorized exactly how this felt, how Murphy's chest pressed against his, and how Murphy's large hands tightly gripped Ben's upper arms.

All at once, it was over. Murphy pulled away, winked at Ben, and said, "Yeah, what about it?"

It took Ben a second to realize Murphy was replying to the man's question. The three men backed off immediately. Their hands held up, shaking their heads, and still muttering under their breath, they left. Ben knew what they were thinking. That Murphy was a tough-looking guy, and if he was this brave, he had to have the balls to back it up. They wouldn't risk getting into a fight with him. Even three against one. Ben's lips tingled.

"That was...unexpected."

"They asked me a question. I had to say yes."

"Are you fucking kidding me?"

"Kind of. But with guys like that, you gotta play them at their own game, y'know? Surprise 'em."

"Surprised me."

Murphy laughed shortly. "Bet it did."

ON THE WALK back to the motel, Murphy kept biting on his thumb. Ben couldn't concentrate. He'd only had one shot, but he felt drunk, like he was outside his body, watching them from above. His heart jumped every time he looked at Murphy. As they passed a line of oak trees, Murphy pulled Ben into the shadows underneath.

Ben panicked. "Is it them again? Are we hiding?"

Murphy shoved Ben roughly up against the tree, the bark pressing into his back.

"What's happening?" Ben asked.

"Dunno."

Murphy grabbed Ben's shirt and pulled him closer. His gaze fell on Ben's mouth, lingering there before skittering back up to his eyes. Murphy licked his lips.

"Are you gonna...?" Ben whispered, his eyes wide. "This isn't the game. You don't have to say yes."

Murphy's face moved closer and closer until their noses touched. "I'm not doing this for a bet." Ben's heart pounded. He could barely breathe with him this close. Ben held his breath until Murphy's sweet, soft mouth met his. He parted his lips for Murphy's tongue and gasped as it slipped between them, sending a hot jolt of lust through his stomach. Their tongues played lightly over each other and then pushed harder. Ben sighed at the warm, shivery feeling in his stomach and slid both hands up into Murphy's hair, pulling him close. Murphy growled, and the sound set Ben's blood on fire. All the men he'd been with in his life, and he'd never been so turned on by a kiss. He was desperate to touch every bit of him and moved his hands across Murphy's chest, down his sides, and over his jean-clad ass before pushing them under his shirt and up his back. Murphy's skin was warm under his fingers, and Ben wanted to taste him. He wasn't sure if Murphy had kissed dozens of women or no one at all. Their kiss in the bathroom had been sloppy and untidy. And wonderful. But Ben hardly had time to enjoy it. This kiss, though... This was something different.

Ben pulled away reluctantly to catch his breath. Murphy dragged his lips across Ben's jaw and slowly down his neck, and Ben whimpered as he felt the heat of Murphy's breath on his sensitive skin.

To prevent his body from surrendering completely and collapsing in a fevered heap on the ground, Ben locked his knees. He pressed his lips to the soft skin behind Murphy's ear where his unique wood smoke scent was strongest, and Murphy nuzzled farther into his neck.

"You smell so good," Ben whispered into his ear.

Murphy shivered delicately, and as if to deny that, slammed Ben into the tree harder. Ben let out a grunt and fisted his hands in the back of Murphy's shirt, tugging his warm, hard body as tight against him as he could. They kissed again, the rough stubble on Murphy's chin scratching Ben's lips. Murphy pulled back just enough to reach both hands up to Ben's face. He stared into his eyes, breathing raggedly, and stroked his thumbs softly over Ben's cheeks.

"We can't let my brother see. He'll kill both of us."

"Forget him." Ben slid a hand farther down Murphy's jeans until he could run it over Murphy's hardening cock.

"No," Murphy gasped, and Ben jerked his hand away immediately.

Murphy's hands traveled shakily down Ben's arms until he took both Ben's hands in his. He leaned his forehead on Ben's shoulder, and Ben felt him taking deep breaths as his hands trembled.

Did Murphy like him? Did Murphy like guys at all? Or was he just drunk? And if so, where could Ben get him more of those shots?

Murphy stayed on Ben's shoulder for some time, breathing hard, gripping Ben's hands, and pressing Ben back into the tree. Ben wasn't sure whether he should apologize. Maybe he'd crossed a line. He always moved too fast once he liked someone. But they were getting closer to Canada every day. He was running out of time. And Murphy had initiated this kiss. Then again, maybe Randall leaving them alone together had made Ben a bit giddy, a bit overenthusiastic. Maybe he'd misread the signals and ruined everything.

Murphy pulled Ben away from the tree and led him wordlessly toward the motel, Ben trotting to keep up. Murphy dropped his hand as they approached the lights of the parking lot, and Ben saw Randall's silhouette inside their room, moving around behind the dirty yellow blinds. Ben stopped dead, and Murphy turned to him.

"Do my lips look red?" Ben asked.

"They always do."

Murphy didn't get it. "Do I have stubble rash?" Ben rubbed his fingers experimentally over his chin.

Murphy shook his head.

"So you can't tell I've just been kissed to death?"

Murphy smiled wickedly. "Do you feel like you have?"

"Yeah," Ben whispered.

Ben saw the lust in Murphy's eyes. Ben couldn't believe it was because of him. He saw it all written out on Murphy's face even in the streetlights. In the bright motel room it would be obvious. Randall couldn't see them yet. He'd know.

Murphy agreed to smoke a cigarette before they went in.

"You want to share?" He offered Ben a cigarette from his crumpled pack.

No, Ben just wanted to watch. He hoped Murphy would take a long, deep drag on it and hollow out his cheeks again. He'd been seeing that image every time he closed his eyes for the past three days. Murphy shrugged and lit it. Ben was sure Murphy was taking tiny puffs on purpose. Ben didn't normally go for smokers, but somehow, everything Murphy did looked so damned good.

"You just gonna stare at me?"

Ben blushed and nodded. Murphy blew smoke in his face.

AS SOON AS they stepped inside the motel room, Randall grabbed his stuff, barely sparing them a glance.

"You keep the car, brother. I'll take a cab. I got the cash for it." He winked at Ben. "Call me on his phone when you get to the next motel, and I'll come meet you." Randall held his hand out to Ben, and he flinched back. "Rubbers." Ben fumbled in his pockets and eventually found them, then handed them over. Randall snatched them and handed the gun to Murphy, who took it awkwardly.

"You watch him. I don't trust him. Been acting weird today. He might be thinking of running off." Randall jabbed a thick finger into Murphy's shoulder. "It is very fucking important that you don't let him. You hear me? I'll be back before you know it." He pushed Murphy's head hard in a gesture that was probably supposed to be affectionate. "Love ya."

"Love you too," Murphy mumbled.

Randall let the door slam behind him. There was a moment of silence.

Murphy pointed the gun at Ben's head, gazed deep into his eyes, and mouthed the word *bang*. Ben was surprised to find his cock twitch in pleasure, and he swallowed hard. There was a very good chance Murphy had no idea how sexy he looked doing that.

"Is that a gun in your pocket, or are you just pleased to see me?" Ben asked.

The confusion on Murphy's face was comical, and Ben grinned. Murphy wasn't used to people flirting with him. For a second, a small part of his brain screamed at him not to flirt with an armed redneck. But Murphy was no normal redneck. Maybe there was no such thing.

"Is it loaded?"

Murphy pointed the gun carefully at the floor and opened the chamber to check for bullets. "Yeah, it is."

Well, shit. Randall really was carrying around a loaded gun. Ben watched as Murphy made doubly sure he'd clicked on the safety, and then reached out to place the gun on the TV table.

"Wait."

Murphy glanced up, his gun hand frozen in midair.

"Aren't you gonna hold me hostage or anything?"

"Whaddaya mean?"

The crooked, nervous smile on Murphy's face tugged on Ben's heart. "I'm dangerous. I'm a flight risk. I might abscond at any moment. You have to keep me under control."

"Oh yeah?"

Something flickered in Murphy's eyes. Now he was getting it. Murphy kept hold of the gun and slowly approached Ben, backing him up against the wall. Ben closed his eyes. He heard a click near his ear, and something cold and metallic pushed up against his temple. The hard muzzle slid softly across his cheek and down to his mouth.

"Like this?"

Ben nodded. Murphy ran the gun lightly across his lips, then moved it down to his throat, shoving the muzzle under his jaw. It clicked again, and Ben opened his eyes.

"Want me to take out the bullets?" Murphy whispered into his ear. Then he nipped his earlobe and slid one hand around the back of his neck, gripping hard.

Ben swallowed and ignored Murphy's question. It might have been weird and dangerous, but it was more of a turn-on if it was loaded. He squeezed his eyes shut and concentrated on the sensation of the hard pistol traveling slowly down his neck, over his chest and stomach, and past the bottom of his crumpled T-shirt. The gun continued down until Murphy pressed it hard against Ben's cock through his jeans. Ben ground his hips forward against it. Now he wondered if he'd made a mistake. The last thing he needed was his junk getting blown off before he'd used it with Murphy.

"Murph," Ben panted breathlessly. "Murphy, stop."

Murphy double-checked that the safety was on and threw the gun onto the bed. "We don't have to play with that. We've got other stuff."

"Like what?"

He shrugged. "We've got the rope."

Ben couldn't help but laugh. "Yeah. Tie me up, fuck me, and if Randall comes back, say you were showing me who's boss."

Murphy's smile froze. His cheeks reddened, and Ben realized what he'd said. They hadn't exactly addressed fucking each other just yet. Then he realized that might not even be the problem. It was Ben's mention of Randall that had made him shut down.

"Sorry," murmured Ben.

"Didn't do nothing." Murphy seemed to make his face carefully blank.

"What's wrong?"

"I wasn't joking before. Randall would kill us. Both of us. If he saw what we'd done."

"He didn't see."

"This ain't happening."

"Forget Randall. He's not here." Ben stroked a hand over Murphy's arm and made his voice soothing. "He can't control who you kiss or what you are."

A look of disgust flashed over Murphy's face. "I ain't fucking gay."

Ben pulled away like he'd been burned. "Well, I am. So fuck you."

"I didn't mean..."

It was like Murphy had morphed into Randall. Either he was disgusted by the idea of kissing a guy or by the idea of kissing Ben in particular. Ben didn't know which one made him feel worse.

"I might be gay, but at least I'm not a dumb, redneck hick."

Murphy stepped back, his face blank again. He walked into the bathroom and pulled the door shut quietly behind him.

Ben made sure he was in bed with the light off before Murphy finished in the bathroom. He rubbed a hand over his face and was disgusted to find that his eyes felt wet. Why was Murphy torturing him like this? There was nothing Ben hated more than straight boys who flirted with gay boys just to make them crazy. They thought they were being all modern and broad-minded, but they were just being assholes. The more he concentrated on his anger, the easier it was to forget he'd said something just as bad.

The light from the bathroom lit a cloud of steam that billowed out when Murphy opened the door. Ben listened as Murphy dropped his towel to the floor and then pulled on the boxer shorts he slept in. Murphy yanked off the bathroom light, and the dark fell in a comforting sweep over Ben's face.

"You asleep?" Murphy whispered.

"Yes."

"Okay."

He didn't say any more, and Ben felt guilty. Maybe he'd wanted to say something important. Fuck it. Ben turned over and tried to sleep.

BEN'S EYES FLEW open a while later. It was still dark. What had woken him up? It wasn't dawn yet. Maybe Murphy had gone to the bathroom again. He lifted his head slightly off his pillow and listened, only to hear whimpering. *Not again. Not now.* Murphy murmured Ben's name, low and sexy, and Ben's whole body froze. His heart raced. He had never liked the sound of his name so much as in that moment.

Ben stood and crossed the gap between them in seconds. Murphy was still asleep, lying on his side with his sheets pushed down to his stomach, and Ben hesitated before sitting next to him. Murphy's body was throwing off so much heat that Ben wondered if he was ill. Ben leaned close over him to press a hand against his forehead. It was warm, but nothing out of the ordinary.

He only had a second to check, because Murphy seemed to sense Ben in his sleep and wrapped his arms around him, pulling him close. Ben sighed and lay down to get more comfortable, only for Murphy to bury his face in Ben's neck. Quick, little breaths tickled Ben's skin, and Murphy's heartbeat echoed through his chest, hard and fast. Murphy tangled his legs in Ben's, and Ben pulled an arm out of the covers to stroke his dark blond hair. He whispered comforting words to him, meaningless nothings again, and Murphy's breathing slowed.

A few minutes later, Murphy's eyelashes fluttered open against Ben's neck. Murphy pulled away from him, and his hands left Ben's waist.

"What's going on?" Murphy murmured, his voice thick with sleep.

"You said my name."

When Murphy didn't reply, Ben sat up to return to his bed, but Murphy gripped him again.

"You want me to stay?"

Murphy let go. "Only if you want to."

Ben rolled his eyes. He lay back, one hand underneath his head and the other resting on his stomach. He'd stay, but Murphy could forget getting any more holding and hair stroking. Murphy didn't seem to understand, though, and snuggled up to Ben's side, annoyingly warm and soft. He laid his head heavy on Ben's chest, still half-asleep, and slung an arm across Ben's stomach. His hand collided with Ben's and stayed there.

Chapter Twelve

BEN WOKE UP to Murphy's sleeping erection against his thigh. For God's sake, this guy got hard from anything. There should at the very least have been a law against telling a guy you're not interested and then waking him up with a hard-on.

Ben started with a cold shower. They'd slept late, and it was nearing their 2:00 p.m. checkout time. He came out of the bathroom to find their motel room empty of Murphy and all his bags. A mild panic rose inside him. He grabbed up his things, filled his bag, and went searching for Murphy. Murphy wasn't outside having a smoke, nor in the motel café. Ben passed by the outdoor pool and checked the vending machine. Nothing. He eventually found him sitting on the hood of the Jeep, hugging his knees, his boots balanced on the wheel arch. Pure relief flooded Ben's stomach. He couldn't help the grin spreading over his face as he approached the car, but Murphy didn't smile back.

"What are you still doing here?" Murphy asked blankly.

"What do you mean? I'm looking for you. Where did you go?"

"To get coffee. I left you alone. Why haven't you escaped?"

Ben's stomach plummeted to somewhere near his feet. That was a good question. Escape hadn't even occurred to him. He'd found himself alone, and his first and only thought had been to find Murphy.

Murphy reached behind him, then held out a paper cup. Ben slid onto the hood, feeling the body heat radiating off Murphy.

"I brought you one, just in case."

"I don't drink coffee." But Ben took the cup anyway.

"I know. It's hot chocolate."

"Did you want me to go? Are you trying to get rid of me?" Ben hated himself for sounding so pathetic.

Murphy said nothing.

"The twenty-four hours is over. You don't have to say yes anymore."

Ben searched his blue eyes, but Murphy turned away. Ben sipped the hot chocolate, fighting sudden nausea. Why was he sticking around when Murphy had made it so clear he wasn't wanted?

"Just leave, Ben."

Those three quiet words chilled him to his soul, and it took him a moment to recover. But something wasn't ringing true. If Murphy had really expected Ben to run as soon as he was left alone, why had he bought him a drink?

"I'll leave if you come with me."

Murphy shook his head. "Stop saying that."

"I can't go if you stay. Randall would kill you. He'd never believe I managed to escape. You have a gun, and you're...you. It's not as if you couldn't catch me. I'm staying."

"Ben." Murphy still wouldn't look at him. "I don't know what he's going to do to you."

"I don't care."

"Maybe you should start caring about stuff."

"I care about lots of things."

"Like what?"

"Like you getting beaten half to death by your brother."

"Won't be the first time. You have to leave, Ben. It's the only way to be safe."

"Fuck being safe."

Murphy jumped down off the hood and slipped into the driver's seat. Ben got quickly in the back. He didn't want Murphy driving off without him, but he didn't feel comfortable sitting up front. Murphy's glowering stare directed at the steering wheel and his almost pulsating silence were pretty good indicators that the man wanted space. Ben looked up from his lap to glance at Murphy in the rearview mirror. Ben met his gaze for one hot, bright-blue second before Murphy reached up to adjust the mirror, and all Ben could see reflected in the glass was trees.

THEY DROVE FOR half a day in silence, weaving quickly along curved roads through the wooded hills of Wisconsin. Tall blurs of orange, red, and yellow rushed past the windows on either side. Ben leaned his temple against the cool window and watched the road, covered in leaves pushed like pressed flowers into the asphalt by endless heavy tires.

After stopping for gas, they passed a sign saying WELCOME TO MINNESOTA. The last state before Canada. Ben's heart raced as Murphy swore and swerved around some roadkill. Ben's eyes were drawn to it despite him wanting to look away, and he saw a flash of orange fur. Maybe Murphy looked too, because he nearly lost control of the car. He recovered quickly, but he was driving much too fast. Even if they'd been on a straight stretch of road, Ben would have wanted him to slow down.

In the cold light of a new day, Ben's repeated suggestion of abandoning Randall or handing him over to the police did seem faintly ridiculous. As the day went on, Ben's irritation at Murphy's reaction faded. Ben found he was sad rather than angry. He was finally alone with Murphy, but now they weren't even talking. Canada and the day they parted ways were growing ever closer. Murphy swerved again. Sad, with a side helping of scared shitless.

"Murph, can you put your seat belt on, please?"

Murphy merely accelerated. Ben sighed, undid his belt, and leaned forward. He reached around Murphy's body, pulled the belt across him, and clicked it into place. Ben returned to his seat and fastened his belt.

Two minutes after that, Murphy hit a pothole, and the Jeep catapulted off the road and folded around a tree.

BEN CAME TO moments later, his ears ringing. Murphy wrenched the dented driver's door open and jumped out of the car. The electronic beep started to sound. Nice that it was still working. The rest of the car was smashed to bits. Ben's door didn't seem damaged, but it nearly came off its hinges when Murphy ripped it open. He stared down at Ben, his eyes wide and panicked.

"Are you okay?"

Ben licked his lips but couldn't speak.

"Where does it hurt?"

There was a sharp pain throbbing in his wrist, and his whole body ached from his hips up to his chest.

"Everywhere," Ben croaked out.

"Shit." Murphy kneeled beside him.

"You gotta turn off the engine." Ben couldn't stop focusing on the beeping, even though there were bigger things to worry about.

"In a second. Don't worry. Can you move?"

"I'm fine. It's just my wrist." He moved forward and hissed in pain. "And my ribs."

Murphy took his arm and held it softly. Blood seeped through his sleeve.

"Can you move your fingers?"

Ben wiggled them and his toes while he was at it. Everything worked. Murphy rolled Ben's sleeve up gently to reveal a two-inch-long cut across his forearm. Murphy pulled a small pocketknife from his jeans and cut through some of the stitches on the shoulder of his plaid shirt and then ripped the sleeve off. The material tore loudly, exposing one defined muscular arm. He wrapped the long piece of fabric over the cut.

"It's not too deep. It'll be fine. I can stitch you up myself."

"We're not going to call an ambulance?"

"Do you want to? We can."

"But you don't want to involve the police."

Murphy paused. "Not really. C'mere." He put one arm behind Ben's back and his now bare arm under Ben's knees.

"What are you doing? You don't have to carry me."

"Shut up."

"I can walk."

"I said shut up."

Murphy picked Ben up like he weighed hardly anything, which hurt his pride somewhat, but being clutched tightly against Murphy's chest felt so damned good he decided not to let it bother him. He let his head fall onto Murphy's shoulder and hooked his uninjured arm around Murphy's neck.

The car was now hidden from the road by a good fifty feet of trees and bushes. It was a miracle their car hadn't hit any trees before the one it was currently wrapped around. Ben didn't know if that was luck or Murphy possessing some kind of superhero ability to dodge obstacles at high speeds.

Murphy carried Ben away from the car, the beeps getting quieter and quieter, and picked his way through more trees. They found themselves in a small, grassy glade surrounded by thick forest, and Murphy set him down on a huge tree root.

"Do you feel like you're gonna pass out or throw up?"

Ben shook his head.

"Okay, I'm gonna go back to the car and get some stuff. I'll be right back. Don't move."

Their little glade was quiet and secluded. It was protected from the breeze, and the sky was a rough circle of blue beyond the tall treetops. Ben sat back against the tree trunk. The bark was warm through his shirt, and he tried not to look at the blood. He couldn't even look at a paper cut and not get nauseated. Thank God he wasn't on his own. Murphy would have to fix him up, 'cause he'd be no good at it. He sighed. He should have told Murphy to get the first-aid kit from the trunk.

Murphy appeared through the trees looking like a Sherpa. He dumped bags and blankets and God knew what else on the grass in front of Ben.

"I brought everything, just in case. It's not like we can lock the car anymore." Ben opened his mouth to answer, but Murphy interrupted him "And yes, I killed the engine." Murphy turned all businesslike. "I'm gonna fix you up. Then I'm gonna put up your tent."

So that's what else he was carrying.

Murphy kept his eyes on the bags and continued. "I don't know how far we are from civilization. But you can't go traipsing around the forest injured. And I'm not leaving you alone to go looking. We'll sleep in the tent tonight, and tomorrow, when you're feeling better, we can hike to the next town. Or maybe even hitch a lift back at the road." He looked at Ben for the first time. "Sound good?"

"Whatever you say, boss."

Murphy dug out Ben's first-aid kit from one of the bags. It was a green plastic box with a red cross on it that his mother had bought him before the trip. Ben had taken out the bug spray on the first day and thought that was all he'd use. Murphy sat in front of Ben, legs crossed. He took out disinfectant, antiseptic cream, cotton wool, a roll of white gauze, medical tape, and a sterilized needle and thread and set them all out neatly on the upturned lid of the box. He soaked the cotton wool in disinfectant and held Ben's hand; he wiped the cotton wool over Ben's wound gently, shushing his hiss of pain. His arm had stopped bleeding already, and Murphy carefully wiped away the dried blood that had crept down toward his elbow and the streak of blood over the back of his hand.

Murphy stopped, still holding Ben's hand. "I'm sorry about your car."

Ben laughed. "I don't care about the car, Murph." He was surprised to find that he didn't. He loved that car, but the fact that Murphy was okay—with not even a scratch on his perfect face—filled him with such profound relief that he hadn't given the car a second thought.

"Oh yeah..." Murphy pushed his hair out of his eyes with the back of his hand. "And thanks for the seat-belt thing. I guess I would have been lying in a ditch in two or three pieces if you hadn't done what you did."

Ben pictured that, and it sent a chill through him. "Don't think about it."

Murphy's hair fell back over his eyes. He scrunched up the used cotton wool and dropped it on the ground. "Now that I've cleaned it, I'm gonna sew you up. It won't hurt much. I promise."

"You sure?"

Murphy frowned. "I'm sure. You never got stitches when you were a kid?"

Ben shook his head. "Never been to a hospital in my life. I was even born at home."

"I never really been to hospitals that much either, but I was always falling out of trees and shit. You were really born at home?"

"Yeah, in my mother's bedroom. They still have the same bed. Which is kind of gross, now that I think about it."

Murphy smiled. "So you never even broke your arm or nothing?"

"Nope. I'm too boring."

Murphy laughed. "I don't think it's boring to stay in one piece."

"I dunno. Maybe I should have been climbing more trees. Having more adventures."

Murphy let go of Ben's hand and placed it on his knee so he had both hands free and a steady surface to work on. The denim of Murphy's jeans was rough and cold underneath Ben's palm.

"Well, you're having one now."

That he was. Murphy threaded the needle and tied a knot in the end. He paused with the sharp point at one end of Ben's wound.

"I don't have any numbing gel. So it's gonna hurt a bit, but relax and concentrate on something else. You'll be fine. You ready?"

Ben searched for something to concentrate on and chose to focus on Murphy's heart tattoo, just visible above the neck of his T-shirt. Then he watched the way Murphy's hair curled into his neck below his ear. It stung when the needle went through his flesh, but he bit his lip and refused to let the whimper out. He would not give Murphy the chance to think Ben was any more of a wimp than he did already. Ben breathed in and out deeply and stared at the tiny red heart. His eyes wandered, and he found the scattering of freckles at the junction where Murphy's neck met his shoulder. Who did the heart commemorate? A friend? A partner? His mother? Murphy had never mentioned her.

"Relax," Murphy whispered and touched the back of Ben's hand.

Ben hadn't realized he was gripping Murphy's knee. He relaxed his hand and tried to distract himself from the hot point of pain threading in and out of his arm.

"How do you know how to do this?" Ben asked.

"Had to do it for myself a few times growing up."

Ben pictured a younger Murphy—blonder hair, smaller frame, and still lanky but without any of the muscles he had now, wearing scruffy, oversize clothes passed down from his big brother. Murphy getting hurt by the kids at school, Randall, or maybe even his dad. Never being taken to the hospital, never having any help, and always having to fix up his own wounds. Ben felt his heart crack a little bit. He gripped Murphy's knee again, but this time, Murphy didn't stop him. He tied off the thread, then bit off the tail end. Then he rubbed antiseptic cream over the wound and wrapped gauze around Ben's arm, covering the stitches with a clean white bandage. He trimmed it off the roll with his pocketknife and taped the end firmly.

"There. How does it feel?"

Ben stared down at what had once been a gaping gash. Now it was clean, sterile, and neatly bandaged. But Murphy misunderstood his awed silence.

"Maybe I should take you to the hospital. Leave you with some real help and then get going."

Panic swelled deep in his stomach at the thought that Murphy might leave. Ben had only been with him for a few days, but it felt like a month, and the idea of never seeing him again made him feel sick.

"No, you've done an amazing job. As good as any doctor."

Murphy scoffed.

"What would Randall do to you if you left me at a hospital?"

Murphy shrugged. "Nothin'."

It was Ben's turn to scoff. "He'd beat the crap out of you."

"What do you care?" Murphy seemed to regret how harsh that sounded. "I mean, you shouldn't worry about that. I can take care of myself."

"I'm not going anywhere. I want to see Canada. I want to see the snow."

Murphy put the tent up while Ben rested in a comfy spot against the tree. It was a two-man tent but still pretty small and had only been used once. Last summer, Ben and his friend Nina had had the regrettable idea to camp at a music festival. It had rained for forty-eight hours straight, and they'd gone home covered head to toe in an inch-thick layer of mud. He hadn't used the tent since then.

Murphy found a flat piece of ground on the opposite side of the glade beneath a place where two trees met, meaning even if it did rain, the pine branches should keep the rain off. The tent was up in three minutes. Ben was sure it had taken Nina and him an hour of giggling and falling over poles, getting entangled in the groundsheet and redoing it from scratch at the festival. Murphy picked up everything else he'd brought from the car and deposited it just inside the flap opening of the tent. He disappeared inside for a minute and then strode back over to Ben. He managed to slip one arm under his knees before Ben pushed him away with his good hand.

"You are not carrying me again."

Murphy put his hands up, palms facing out in a gesture of surrender. As much as Ben enjoyed being held close by Murphy, there was only so much babying his pride could take. He did let Murphy help him up, though. His knees felt wobbly, and as Murphy pulled Ben's arm around his neck and supported him under his other armpit, he was grateful for the help. Maybe it was delayed shock, but all he wanted to do was lay down and sleep.

Murphy folded him through the flap and lowered Ben onto the sleeping bag he'd already unrolled. He passed Ben a bottle of water from the cooler and held out two small pills in his palm. One was flat, powdery, and oval-shaped, and the other was a white capsule with a shiny surface. Murphy picked up the capsule.

"You can take some acetaminophen, which was in the first-aid box." He put it down and picked up the other pill.

"Or you can have this. It's from Randall's jacket. It's a lot stronger, and it'll be better for the pain. You're not planning to operate any heavy machinery in the next few hours, right?"

Ben smiled. "Is it safe?"

"Sure. It's not ecstasy or something. Just some kind of superstrength painkiller."

"Will it make me sleep?"

"Probably."

"I'd like that." Ben took the oval pill and swallowed it down with a few gulps of water. He took his shoes off with one hand, tucked his legs into his sleeping bag, and settled down.

Murphy grabbed his leather jacket and after folding it up, he placed it under Ben's head as a pillow.

"Thanks. What are you going to do? There's only one sleeping bag."

"I don't need one. I'm gonna make a fire."

"What? How?"

Murphy shook his head. "You are such a city boy. It's easy." He hopped out of the tent. "Get some sleep."

Ben snuggled down farther into Murphy's leather jacket. It smelled phenomenal and just like Murphy. He was sure there was something he was supposed to remember. Something he was meant to be anxious about, but he couldn't quite place it. He felt very relaxed. It seemed as if the walls of the tent were getting far away, and he was sinking deep into the soft ground. He closed his eyes and surrendered to sleep.

Chapter Thirteen

MURPHY WANDERED AROUND the clearing, picking up sticks and fallen branches for firewood. He smiled, remembering the awe on Ben's face that he could make a fire. Something so simple. He and Ben were so different they shouldn't get along at all, but there was something about Ben that was incredibly easy to like.

The pill he'd given Ben was powerful, but he needed to sleep to heal properly. And that arm was going to hurt once the shock wore off. If Murphy's experience with his brother's pain pills was anything to go by, Ben wouldn't remember a thing that happened between then and the next morning. Generally, Murphy avoided drugs and medication altogether. He'd dipped into his brother's stash once or twice when he'd been really hurt, and the painkillers had made him pretty delirious before he fell into a deep sleep. With any luck, Ben wouldn't get too out of it, but even if he did, Murphy would be there to look out for him.

Ben could take another of Randall's painkillers later, or he could switch to acetaminophen if he wanted. There was plenty of that in the box. If Murphy could get Ben to rest up for one night, he'd probably be fine to travel the next day, and they could walk to the nearest town. Murphy had suggested hitching as a possibility, but he wasn't too eager to try it. He wasn't willing to take the risk that anyone could pick them up—someone dangerous, someone just like Randall.

Murphy cleared a space free of fallen leaves, and then piled up the wood he'd found. He balled up some paper torn from the back page of the map and placed it at the base; then he lit the paper with his cigarette lighter, and it crackled into flames. He sat by the fire for an hour or so, warming his hands and listening to the evening birds sing high in the trees. He and Ben didn't have much food on them, so after checking on Ben and finding him fast asleep, he took a walk on a hunt for some berries. The sun was starting to set, flooding the forest with orange light. He didn't find any berries.

He broke out through some trees and found a thickly forested green valley. The cozy yellow lights of a small town spread out below him, twinkling among the pines. It looked like a picture on a Christmas card. It was probably only an hour or two's walk away. They could easily manage it tomorrow, when Ben felt better. More relaxed now that he had a concrete plan, Murphy headed back to the tent. He stopped outside and stared at the flickering fire, not sure whether it would be more uncomfortable to face Ben or to be on his own and be forced to think.

He'd been trying to avoid thinking all day, but the embarrassment that he'd kissed the first guy to come along the second his brother was out of the way wouldn't leave him. Before his brother had even gone, Murphy had had his tongue down some guy's throat. Pathetic. Pathetic and desperate. That was what he was. Just the thing to impress someone like Ben. Jesus.

But Ben wasn't anything as insignificant as the first guy to come along. He might even be the first man Murphy had ever wanted to do more than kiss with. He'd tried kissing a couple of men before. Maybe had a few dumb crushes. But the only sex he'd had was with women at the command of Randall. He'd admitted to himself he preferred men years ago, but that didn't mean he had to admit it to anyone else. Living that life wasn't an option. He was always with Randall, and Randall was the last person who'd be able to deal with that kind of crap. So he'd chosen his brother over being happy a long time ago.

Not everyone got to be happy. Most people didn't, in fact. Some people got stuck with kids they didn't want, some people with an illness they never asked for, and others with a life that meant they didn't get to have love and sex and all that bullshit. At least that was the story Murphy had told himself. But recently, he was getting to a point where ignoring that part of his life was becoming too fucking exhausting. Spending time on his own and having time to think had turned from the one thing that gave him a little bit of comfort into something that was slowly driving him insane.

He opened the flap of the tent and found Ben lying awake and staring up at his hand, moving it back and forth in front of a flashlight. Ben noticed Murphy after a moment and sat up. His eyes were huge and unfocused.

"My hand has a tail."

Maybe Randall's drugs hadn't been such a good idea. Murphy squinted into the glare of the flashlight and grabbed it from him, clicking the off switch. The sinking orange sunlight brought out the true shade of Ben's eyes— honeyed gold hiding behind the brown, his long eyelashes casting sooty shadows over his cheeks. Ben's bandaged arm rested outside the sleeping bag on top of an open book. Murphy carefully lifted his arm, moved the book out of the way, and sat down cross-legged next to him, wondering what to do with a Ben who was high as hell. He gently pushed Ben back onto his leather-jacket pillow and kept a calming hand on his warm chest. Ben must have taken off his jeans at some point. They were strewn over the bags in the corner of the tent.

"You okay there, kid?"

"You're so pretty."

"What?" Murphy recoiled, yanking his hand away.

"I think you're the most handsome man in the world."

"Shut up, man." Murphy squirmed. He couldn't think straight, because no one had ever told him that before.

"Your eyes are so blue." Ben gazed up at him, eyes wide. "They're like a wolf's eyes."

Murphy scoffed, feeling his cheeks redden. "Go back to sleep. You're talking crazy."

"I'm not. You smell like magic. Like rain and fire and the forest."

"No, you can just smell rain coming and the campfire I made, and we're in a fucking forest."

Ben shut up for a while, and then he rolled over on his side and his eyes tracked slowly up Murphy's body, making him feel hot and exposed.

"Your shoulders are so wide. I can't believe you're real."

Murphy chuckled quietly and shook his head. This was getting ridiculous.

"No, it's not funny, Murph. You're perfect. I've never seen anyone so beautiful in my whole life."

"Cut it out. I ain't perfect or beautiful." Quite the fucking opposite.

"No, no, you don't get it. You're the kind of person that..." He seemed to struggle for words. "When Michelangelo made the statue of David, he did it because he'd met someone like you and couldn't get him out of his mind."

"Shut up, Ben." Murphy put an edge in his voice that usually worked to intimidate people.

"You think your scar is ugly, but it's not." Ben pointed vaguely at him with his good arm. He looked sad and sleepy but determined to get this out before he lost consciousness.

"Jesus, Ben. Give it a rest." Murphy fidgeted. This was beyond uncomfortable.

"The person who put it there is, but not you." Ben mumbled so quietly Murphy barely heard him. Ben relaxed his arm, and his hand landed on Murphy's knee.

"Okay, quit it." Murphy slapped his hand away and then regretted it as a hurt look flickered across Ben's face. Murphy knew it was the drugs talking, and he was the one who'd given them to him. Of course, he was also the one who'd hurt him in the first place. He sighed. Yet again, he'd proved to be every bit the asshole everyone thought he was. Everyone except Ben. Murphy glanced down at Ben's sweet, open face, and every ounce of irritation flooded out of him. He'd only just met the boy, but Ben had already said more kind words to him than anyone else had in his whole life. Ben was high right now, but he probably meant every word he was saying. Ben might be wrong about him, but Murphy wasn't about to refuse any of those words just because they embarrassed him. Unfortunately, though, it seemed like Ben had run out of things to say. Murphy felt Ben's forehead. It was feverishly hot.

"D'you have a headache? Huh?" Murphy whispered.

Ben seemed to have tired himself out. He mumbled something unintelligible and closed his eyes. Murphy crawled around until he was sitting behind Ben's head and reached down to massage his forehead with cool fingers.

He carefully avoided eye contact. Ben licked his lips, and the sight of his tongue made Murphy's stomach flutter.

He couldn't believe he'd kissed Ben. Fucking kissed him. Twice. That kiss in the men's room was only meant to be a quick peck on the lips to shock those guys into leaving Ben alone. But once their lips met, Murphy couldn't stop. Then later, when it seemed like Ben might want to reciprocate properly, Murphy had lost his nerve. Just imagining what Randall would say about him kissing a guy—wanting a guy—made him feel ice-cold and nauseated. So he'd done the easy thing and played repulsed by the whole thing. Ben had seen Randall in him. He knew it. Seen the real him: full of hate and fear. Murphy was crazy to think he had any right kissing someone like that. He didn't deserve something special like Ben. Murphy's dad hadn't passed down much wisdom, but he'd taught him that.

Murphy had ruined everything. Even Ben. He hadn't only totaled the guy's car. He'd cut his arm open. His flawless body, which had never been beaten or broken like Murphy's. Ben's body that fascinated him in its perfection. Murphy had fucked that up too. Nothing as good as Ben could last. He'd probably hate Murphy in the morning. Ben's eyes snapped open, and he stared up at Murphy adoringly. But he didn't hate him right now. Murphy gazed into his eyes.

"How're you feeling?"

Ben tried to reach under his bandage and scratch his arm, but Murphy stopped him.

"Let it heal."

He tried to let go of Ben's hand, but Ben wouldn't let him. His left hand closed firmly around Murphy's, and he picked up his book carefully with the other.

"Murphy gave me a head massage," Ben whispered quietly and flicked through the pages.

Murphy wasn't sure if Ben knew he'd spoken out loud. Murphy noticed his bottle of water was empty. Good, he'd kept hydrated while Murphy was out making the fire.

"I'm gonna get you another drink. Don't move. I'll be back in a second."

Murphy yanked his hand from Ben's grip and reached over to the cooler.

"Ben won't go anywhere," Ben murmured, attention still on his book.

While he was by the door to the tent, Murphy checked that the fire was still flickering safely. It was nearly dark outside now and freezing cold. At least Ben wouldn't remember a thing about all this in the morning. Those pills of Randall's were strong. Shame similar couldn't be said for Murphy. He'd be remembering all this in great detail. Murphy set down the new water bottle within easy reach.

"You still talking in the third person?"

Ben seemed confused and didn't answer.

"Never mind. You thirsty?"

"Lie down." Ben patted the ground next to him. Murphy dragged their biggest bag level with Ben's head, then sat down beside him on the groundsheet, his back against the bag. Ben shuffled over to give him more room and held out his book. "Read me this. I'm on chapter two."

Murphy automatically took the book. "You want me to read to you?"

"Yes, please." Ben stared up at him, his brown eyes wide. He looked strangely young and hopeful, and Murphy couldn't say no to him. He pulled the sleeping bag tighter around Ben and opened the book to the right page.

"Murphy's tucking me in," Ben whispered to himself.

Murphy chuckled softly and started to read. "'Not until it was twilight did Gregor awake out of a deep sleep, more like a swoon than a sleep...'"

Ben sniffled quietly. A strand of Ben's hair was lying across his face and brushing his nose. Murphy pushed it gently away from his face and behind his ear.

"Keep doing that," Ben said.

Murphy wasn't sure he understood. "Doing what? You want me to stroke your hair?"

Ben nodded.

"You regressing or something?"

Ben blinked.

"Your mom used to do that?"

Ben nodded again. Murphy curled his right arm around Ben's head and stroked his fingers through Ben's hair a few times, but he found the angle awkward. So Murphy settled for stroking back and forth over Ben's scalp with his thumb, holding the book in his other hand. He leaned back against the bag and moved his legs closer to Ben's warm body, crossing his ankles. Ben tucked his head into Murphy's side and closed his eyes, puffing warm breaths into Murphy's T-shirt. After ten minutes of listening to Murphy's soft, comforting voice, Ben breathed slower and more evenly, and Murphy fell silent.

Ben's nuzzled his face farther into Murphy's side. "Why'd you stop?"

"Thought you were asleep."

"M'not."

"You in any pain? It's been a while. You can have more pills soon."

Ben shook his head against Murphy's side, tickling him. Murphy flinched. Ben leaned up on his arm and touched Murphy's waist.

"Didn't know you were ticklish."

Murphy paused. "I ain't."

Ben's eyes narrowed, and a flash of mischief darkened them. He reached his bandaged hand across Murphy's stomach, both hands bracketing Murphy's waist.

"What are you doing?" Murphy asked slowly.

Ben maintained eye contact and smirked as he jabbed his fingers into Murphy's side, making him jump in the air and exclaim loudly. All the breath rushed out of his lungs in a panic.

"You shriek like a little girl," mocked Ben as he continued to tickle him mercilessly.

Murphy literally couldn't breathe. "Shut up! Stop. This ain't fair. Stop."

"Stop me."

"I can't," Murphy forced out. "You're an invalid."

"Pussy."

"Ben, for Christ's sake, stop it. I'm gonna piss myself."

Ben sniggered. Murphy finally managed to catch one desperate breath and grabbed Ben's upper arms firmly, pinning him onto his back and putting most of his weight on him until he stopped squirming. Murphy panted down over Ben's smirking face.

"Behave."

Ben stared back up defiantly. "I am behaving."

"You're being a huge pain in the ass. And you've probably messed up your arm even more."

Ben glanced down at it, seeming surprised to find it bandaged. "It doesn't hurt."

"Good. Let's keep it that way." Murphy jumped off Ben and the sleeping bag to grab the box of acetaminophen from the first-aid kit in the corner. He kneeled down at Ben's side and held two out to him.

Ben leaned up on his elbows, opened his mouth, and waited.

"I'm not gonna feed 'em to you."

Ben didn't move. Murphy sighed and reached across Ben's chest for his untouched bottle of water.

"Just take the damn pills." He pushed them one at a time into Ben's mouth, and when Ben refused to take the bottle, Murphy tipped it carefully, spilling water between Ben's lips. He dutifully swallowed them down. "Ah, so you will actually swallow them yourself? I don't have to stroke your throat like I'm forcing worming pills into a cat?"

"I'm an invalid. You have to take care of me."

"You're a drama queen," Murphy mumbled.

This was as lucid as Ben was going to get tonight. In a little while the new pills would take hold, and mixed with the previous pill, Ben might be higher than ever until Murphy got him to sleep. He left the bottle standing by Ben's head and took a steadying breath.

"I'm sorry I hurt you," Murphy said.

"Doesn't matter."

"'Course it does."

Ben pushed up onto his good hand and twisted around. He attempted to neaten the leather jacket behind him. Murphy helped him, bashing it into shape before he shoved it back behind him.

"I'm just sorry. It's all my fault," Murphy said.

Ben shook his head and frowned. Maybe trying to remember what had happened.

"I totaled your car. I hurt your arm. And I know I offended you with what I said before. I'm always trying so hard not to be Randall. Or my dad. But I'm starting to think maybe it's unavoidable."

Ben's focus sharpened, and he seemed to manage a moment of lucidity. "You're nothing like them. You hurt me by accident, not on purpose."

Ben didn't know anything.

"I shouldn't have reacted like that." Murphy pulled away. "Whatever you are, I am too."

"Forget it." Ben fell back into his newly plumped leather-jacket pillow.

Ben didn't seem to understand what Murphy had just revealed. Good. With any luck he wouldn't remember in the morning.

"Anyway. I wanted to apologize. If there's anything I can do, just let me know."

They sat in comfortable silence for a while. Ben's gaze followed the dust motes floating in the light from the fire outside.

Ben opened his mouth to speak and then paused.

"Anything?" Ben asked.

"Sure. What do you need?"

Ben held up his bandaged hand. "It hurts now," he said quietly.

"Yeah?" Must have been the tickling. Murphy hoped he hadn't pulled any stitches.

"Make it feel better," whimpered Ben.

"I already gave you more medicine. You'll feel better soon."

"No. No, do it like my mom used to."

"How'd she do it?"

"She kissed it better," Ben whispered.

Murphy marveled at the fact that Ben's cheeks flushed slightly. This he was embarrassed about? After everything else Ben had done so far tonight? Murphy sighed. Poor bastard had had a tough week. He just wanted some looking after. He was the closest thing Murphy had to a friend right now, so however embarrassing this was, surely Murphy could do this for him. Murphy hesitated once and then pressed his lips carefully against Ben's bandaged wrist.

"More," pleaded Ben, and moved his fingers slightly.

Murphy took the hint and kissed Ben's fingers. Ben's skin was hot against his lips. "Anywhere else hurt?" Murphy asked, mostly kidding.

Ben pushed down the sleeping bag with one hand, stopping at his waist, and pulled his T-shirt up, revealing angry red bruises all down his side. Shit. Murphy hadn't expected them to be this bad. The edges were turning blue. They'd be a rainbow of colors in a day or two.

"Hurts," Ben whispered.

Murphy felt a little silly, but Ben sounded so sad. And if it made Ben feel better, who was he to argue? It wasn't much to ask in the grand scheme of things. Murphy's knees ached on the ground, so he shifted onto the edge of the sleeping bag, planted one hand down on either side of Ben's body, and leaned over him. He glanced up at Ben to check that he still wanted this, and found him staring lazily down at Murphy, his eyes half-closed.

Murphy started with the largest bruise covering the side of Ben's chest and kissed it softly. He heard his father's voice calling him ugly names as he pressed his lips to Ben's hot flesh. Next, Murphy worked his way down to Ben's waist and kissed the center of the bruise there.

Then he finished with the smallest bruise. He had to pull the sleeping bag down a little farther to see it properly. The bruise covered Ben's hip bone in a heart shape, and as he kissed it, Ben gasped quietly.

"Sorry. That hurt?"

Ben shook his head and touched Murphy's hair. Ben sighed as if he didn't know what to do. Then he pulled his hand away and yanked his shirt off over his head.

"Do it again," Ben said.

In for a penny.

This time, Murphy went the other way. Three more soft kisses against Ben's heated skin. He ended with a kiss near Ben's chest. Murphy licked his lips and glanced up, finding Ben's face unexpectedly close. His hands now rested on Ben's body instead of the sleeping bag—one hand splayed out over his uninjured hip, the other wrapped gently around Ben's upper arm to keep him steady. Ben swallowed audibly and stared at Murphy's mouth. He felt Ben's hot breath on his face. He wanted to straighten his tousled hair again—hair that still carried the smell of that damned apple shampoo from the motel bathroom.

Ben inched forward, and before Murphy could think, Ben's lips were on his. Murphy's heart raced. Was this too much? Did Ben know what he was doing? Was it just the drugs? Should Murphy stop? Did he care?

Ben's lips parted slowly, and his tongue brushed across Murphy's lower lip. His mouth opened in surprise, and Ben groaned softly as their tongues met. Murphy's whole body buzzed in mild panic. He heard his father's voice again in his head, but he pushed it away. Then he stopped thinking entirely as Ben clutched the back of his neck and forced their faces closer so he could lick into Murphy's mouth. Ben's soft lips moved over his, and he sucked hard on Murphy's tongue. Murphy moaned into Ben's mouth.

He stroked Ben all over, trying somehow to slow his breathing and calm him down with gentle touches. He dragged his fingertips soothingly all the way up Ben's arms, down over his shoulders, and lightly across his chest, coming to a stop on his lower stomach. But it made the boy beneath him shiver and pant harder. As Ben squirmed, Murphy looked down to check his injured arm, only to catch sight of something unexpected. He'd somehow made Ben rock hard.

Murphy gasped as Ben buried his face in his neck. Ben dragged his lips across Murphy's throat, sucking and nibbling at his skin, sending shivers through his body. Ben licked a long line up his throat to his ear and then nipped at Murphy's earlobe.

Murphy pulled away. "Ben," he panted. "We should stop."

Ben whimpered and squeezed his eyes shut. "Can't."

"Ben?" Murphy reached out for Ben's jaw and tilted his face with one finger till Ben was facing him. Ben opened his eyes, and they glistened, his pupils huge and black. "Why don't I leave you alone," Murphy said softly. "And you can take care of that." He glanced back down at Ben's crotch.

"I can't," whispered Ben again and held up his bandaged hand.

Oh, right. It was his right wrist. "So use the left one. Variety's the spice of life."

"Murph?"

The plea was right there in Ben's eyes. *Oh, you have got to be joking.*

"Please? So I can sleep?"

Ben's eyes looked so desperate. Desperate and sad at the same time. Murphy couldn't leave him like this. Murphy knew Ben wouldn't remember a thing about it tomorrow. He didn't have to worry about Ben being embarrassed in the morning because he'd let Murphy touch him. No one would ever know but Murphy, and Ben seemed like he'd lose his mind if someone didn't touch him soon. Murphy took a deep breath and reached under the sleeping bag.

Ben breathed out a long, shaky sigh as Murphy's fingers crept under his boxers and closed around him. Murphy's hand felt immediately at home. It might have been an unfamiliar angle, but Ben's cock felt much like his, if longer and not quite as thick. Ben was hard as iron, with hot, taut skin that was satiny soft.

Ben grabbed at Murphy's back with his uninjured arm. He clawed at Murphy's shirt and held it tight in his fist. His breath hitched as Murphy squeezed him firmly and started to move his hand up and down Ben's length.

Ben moaned, and Murphy pressed Ben's face into his shoulder to keep him quiet. He felt Ben's racing heart beating through his chest as Ben thrust upward into Murphy's hand. Murphy didn't think Ben would last long. He whispered words of encouragement into Ben's ear.

"That's it. Such a good boy." Murphy was embarrassed at the words coming out of his mouth, but they seemed to work. "Come on, Ben. Nearly there."

Ben's body shuddered up against him as Murphy stroked faster and faster, and Murphy felt a familiar warmth growing inside him. He was getting hard too.

Ben came quickly with a loud groan, but Murphy kept pumping his hand, milking out every last drop until Ben pushed him away. He wiped his hand on his T-shirt and then yanked it off over his head to wipe off Ben's stomach. He balled it up and dropped it on the ground. Ben breathed heavily, flat on his back. His face was utterly relaxed. Murphy smiled and ran a thumb over the beads of perspiration on Ben's cheekbone, moving damp strands of hair from his face.

"You can sleep now, buddy." Murphy got up, intending to check the fire.

"No." Ben held tight on to Murphy's hand, the hand that moments ago had been grasped around Ben's cock. "Stay."

Murphy sighed before lying down and carefully tucking Ben's body into his arms, Ben's face against Murphy's neck. Murphy's brief hard-on was forgotten about entirely, but despite that, Murphy was satisfied. He couldn't remember the last time he'd felt so accomplished. Like he'd actually made a difference to someone. He'd have to sneak away sometime and check the fire, but he'd just stay here for a while. Ben's body was so soft and warm against his. Their legs tangled together, and Ben was soon breathing tiny, satisfied snores into Murphy's chest.

MURPHY CREPT AWAY a little later and kicked dirt on the fire, his breath clouding up in front of his face. He checked that everything was safely stored away inside and then closed up the tent. He shivered as he pulled down the zip on Ben's sleeping bag and crawled half inside, pushing his body up against Ben's sleeping form for warmth and using his softly rising chest as a pillow.

He'd just given his first hand job, and the recipient would probably never remember it.

Maybe that was for the best. He might have been terrible at it. Although Ben seemed to enjoy it well enough. Murphy took a deep breath, and his shoulder twinged. He knew he should rub something on his still-healing tattoo, but the pain was comforting somehow. Grounding.

In the silence of the tent, Murphy's thoughts inevitably turned to his brother. He'd been acting strangely even for Randall, creeping off to meet random people every day and never revealing who they were or what he was doing with them. Maybe he was being extra secretive because Ben was around. If he was up to something shady—which was a pretty safe bet—Randall wouldn't want Ben hearing any details.

To be honest, Murphy would be happier not to know either. Something still didn't feel quite right, but he was too tired to think straight and was sick of thinking about his fucking brother in any case. Right now, in the afterglow of what had happened with Ben, Murphy didn't give a shit if Randall disowned him. Maybe if he did, this could even happen again. Murphy enjoyed that liberating concept for about thirty seconds before he remembered.

An empty feeling of dread gnawed at his stomach. If Randall found out his secret—and he would; he always did—Randall wouldn't just disown him. He'd be confused, overwhelmed, and hurt, and he'd want to hurt Murphy in return. He would explode in anger and violence, and it wouldn't stop at Murphy. But Randall wasn't the only reason nothing could happen between Murphy and Ben. Ben was too clever and too good. And in Murphy's experience, good things were like shooting stars. Beautiful, breathtaking, and over quickly, leaving behind just the burned image of something special.

Murphy listened to Ben's heart beating. Slow, steady, and alarmingly reassuring. God, fate, or whatever else had given him two days alone with Ben. And yeah, Ben probably wouldn't want to kiss him again. And this certainly wouldn't happen again. But they would be together, and he intended to make the most of it. He vowed not to even think about Randall for the next forty-eight hours.

Chapter Fourteen

BEN WOKE FIRST. His stretch and yawn knocked Murphy awake, and they extricated themselves from each other's sleepy arms and tangled legs.

"I feel like I've been asleep for days," Ben said, rubbing his eyes.

Murphy cleared his throat and shifted back as far as he could in the small space. His face seemed a little red, but maybe he was hot.

"How's your arm?"

"Aches, but the pain's better."

"I gave you some pills for it last night. You probably don't remember." Murphy's gaze flicked around the tent, settling anywhere but on Ben.

"Vaguely. Can I have some more?"

"You can have acetaminophen." Murphy finally met Ben's gaze. "Safer that way."

"Safer for who?"

Murphy didn't answer. He just popped them out of the foil square and handed them to Ben. Then Murphy opened the tent flap and unwrapped the bandage in the light to check Ben's wound.

"Looks good. No swelling or infection."

There was no hand-holding this time. Murphy was even more businesslike than he'd been the day before. He wrapped Ben's arm with a clean bandage and taped it up but knocked him with the first-aid box as he turned to pack it away.

"Shit, sorry. It's too early to be coordinated."

"I don't know. Your hands seemed pretty capable last night," Ben shot back with a wicked smile.

Murphy's gaze snapped up. He opened his mouth, then shut it again. He looked mortified. "Do you... What do you remember from last night?"

"Everything." Of course Ben remembered. It was burned into his brain. He grinned. "I don't know why you're embarrassed. I'm the one who begged for a hand job."

Murphy's cheeks darkened even further. "Shit."

Ben hesitated. Although he hadn't meant last night to happen, he didn't regret a second of it. But if Murphy did, Ben had to offer him a way out—a way to save face.

"It's okay, Murph. I know it didn't mean anything. To you."

Murphy took a deep breath. "Feel like I took advantage or something."

"If anyone took advantage, it was me. Unless you drugged me on purpose so you could get some."

"I...I didn't. I..."

"I'm kidding." Ben grabbed Murphy's arm and squeezed it. "Thank you for taking care of me."

Murphy blinked at him. "Can't believe you remember."

A grin spread over Ben's face. "Who could forget a hand job as good as that?"

Murphy rolled his eyes. "It lasted about five seconds."

"Hey! That's my sexual stamina you're talking about." Ben reached outside and threw a handful of dry leaves at him.

Murphy froze, leaves showering down from his hair and settling on his shoulders. He stayed still long enough for Ben to wonder if throwing the leaves had been a mistake. Then Murphy launched at Ben, rolled him out of the tent, and straddled Ben's lap. He was careful not to touch Ben's injured arm and ribs but sure to rub plenty of leaves and dirt into his face. He laughed and rose, leaving Ben breathless and spitting leaves from his mouth.

Murphy packed up the tent alone after waving Ben away and saying it'd be quicker without his help. Ben hovered close by and watched, trying not to get in the way. His stomach was cramped with nerves. It was all very good being the smug, sexually satisfied patient, but where the hell did things stand now?

"Murph?"

Murphy didn't look at him but stopped folding the tent rods and waited patiently for Ben to continue. Ben swallowed. He had no idea what to say.

"Are we okay?" Not massively eloquent, but it would have to do.

Murphy's hesitation felt like torture. But a moment later, he answered. "We're good."

Did "good" mean he wanted to do it again? Or did "good" mean that in these extenuating circumstances of drugged-up delirium, he forgave Ben for getting physical? Ben didn't ask. One more day of not knowing was infinitely better than rejection. While he could retain some tiny hope of Murphy touching him like that again, he would keep his mouth shut.

They divided the bags between them, and Murphy set off toward the town he'd seen the night before. He led the way, walking quietly and efficiently, never wasting a movement. Ben tried to follow his exact footsteps through the thick-layered leaves but still managed to find the odd muddy spot. He slipped several times, but each time he fell behind, Murphy slowed down until he caught up.

AFTER NEARLY TWO hours of steady hiking, the bags were starting to get heavy, and Ben's feet ached. But the lights were getting closer.

"It's through these trees." Murphy lit a cigarette while he waited for Ben. The smell of smoke comforted him as he walked closer, pulling him in and reminding him of warmth, safety, and Murphy. Just as Ben reached him, something landed softly on his eyelashes. Ben squinted up into the trees as snowflakes fell down onto his face and hands.

"Awesome," Ben said.

"Is it? Guess we're lucky it held off till we got here."

"I'm always ready for snow. Don't care where I am."

"You would have welcomed three feet of snow, sleeping in that tent?"

Ben shrugged. "Would have been cozy. Could have made a killer snowman."

They finally broke out of the trees and found themselves in an empty playground. A stream lay to their right, and a couple of big wooden houses sat behind a low hedge to their left.

"You think there'll be a place to stay? It doesn't look like that big a town," Ben said.

"There's gotta be something."

They found what seemed to be the main road and wandered down it, passing large wood-clad houses on both sides. Each was painted a different pastel color and set back from the road by a wide, leafy garden. At an intersection, they found a gas station and a couple of stores.

"Guess this is the center of town," Murphy said.

The bell on the door of the general store clanged quietly to signal their arrival. Ben headed automatically to the candy aisle and gazed at the chocolate.

"Can we buy all of this?"

Murphy smiled and brushed the snowflakes from Ben's hair. His hand lingered, and Ben held his gaze for a few long seconds. Murphy glanced down, brushed the snow off Ben's bandage, and then carefully pulled his sleeve down to cover it. Ben watched Murphy's eyes as they drifted over to the elderly woman at the counter. Murphy's gaze hardened. He quickly stepped back—well away from Ben—and inspected the shelves of chocolate. She was watching them. Ben left him there and shook the snow off his shoulders as he approached the counter.

"Is there a hotel anywhere around here?" Ben asked.

"Sure is!" she answered brightly. "The big new one is a couple miles up that road, and there's a small one just around the corner. I'd recommend the small one for you two." She winked. "Very romantic in this kind of weather."

Murphy's mouth opened and closed like a guppy's, and Ben snorted out a laugh.

"Thank you," Ben said.

He gathered up a bunch of the chocolate Murphy had been staring at so intently and grabbed a couple of drinks from the refrigerator in the corner. Then he remembered he was effectively penniless.

"Do you have any money, Murphy?"

Murphy came back to life and scrabbled in his pocket. "Yeah, Randall left us some." He grabbed two pairs of navy-blue winter gloves from a display near the counter and passed them to Ben along with a fifty pulled from a roll of bills.

THEY FOUND THE hotel easily. The snow was heavier now, and it fell softly on red and yellow trees and settled thickly on the ground. The woman in the store had not been kidding about romantic. The trees framed a winding one-lane road that headed under a hand-painted sign reading PEBBLEDASH LANE HOTEL and on toward a grassy clearing. A handful of wooden cabins sat between the trees, each with a covered veranda and mossy roof. Two had smoke puffing from the chimneys, suggesting warm open fires inside. Uneven stone paths led between each cabin, and trees grew all over, coloring the scene with vivid fall shades. There was even a rabbit hopping around and grooming an ear in the snowless grass under a tree.

"Holy crap. We're in a Disney movie," Ben said.

They walked past neat piles of covered chopped wood, stacked ready for fireplaces, and made their way to a small cabin marked RECEPTION.

LATER ON, ONCE they'd warmed up, Ben took a good look around their cabin. They'd been shown to the one in the far corner, and the guy on reception had lit their fire for them even though Murphy had protested that he could do it. The wood smoke was already filling the large room with its delicious scent. A small red sofa faced the fireplace. Behind that were two single beds, both covered in soft wool blankets and tons of pillows. There was also a bathroom with a shower, bath, and two sinks. The cabin was well stocked with antique books, and there was a shiny coffee machine and a room-service menu by an ornate vintage telephone in the corner.

"Did Randall really leave you enough money for all this?"

"Probably not on purpose, but yeah. He just thrust a roll of bills at me. I'm guessing he thought they were ones." He looked out of the window at the snow—now at least an inch thick—covering everything in sight. "How about that snowman?"

Ben smiled and rushed to the door, but Murphy pulled him back.

"Wait. Here." He picked up a pair of the gloves they'd bought at the shop and yanked off the label that tied them together. He held each glove open, and Ben shoved his hands inside. "Slow down. Don't mess up the bandage."

"You gonna wear the others?"

"Don't need 'em. Don't have a bandage to keep dry."

"Trust me. You'll need them."

Murphy rolled his eyes but pulled the gloves on gruffly. Ben hid a smile. He loved that Murphy insisted on trying to seem tough even when making a snowman was the issue at hand. Their breath clouded up as soon as they stepped outside, and the bright white over everything made Ben squint. The snow still fell. A little from the sky but most came from the trees above as the breeze moved through the leaves. It covered Murphy's hair within seconds and clung to his eyelashes, making him blink. He walked out onto the fresh blanket of snow, then turned around, twisting his hands awkwardly.

"So what do we do?"

"Get building."

Murphy hesitated and stood looking like he'd never done this before. Maybe he hadn't.

"We have to make two big balls of snow for the body and head. You make the body. Just gather some snow up into a big snowball. Then roll it along the ground."

"Roll it?"

"Yeah, it'll pick up all the snow and get big."

Murphy shrugged and kneeled down, seeming to take Ben's word for it.

"It's not gonna be huge. There's not enough snow, but we can make a decent one."

Murphy grunted and started work on his part of the body. A few minutes later he stood, breathing heavily, wet patches on his knees. "Is this okay?"

He'd managed to make a huge, oval-shaped mound. It stood level with his waist and was perfectly clean and white. Ben's head was smaller and spherical but had dirty brown patches here and there where he'd worn through the layer of snow on the ground and gotten too close to the dirt underneath.

"That's perfect." Ben hefted his heavy head into his arms and swung it up, then deposited it on top of the body. He twisted it so the dirt faced away, and then packed handfuls of snow around the snowman's neck. "This'll stop his head from rolling off." He smoothed down the edges with his hands, and Murphy copied him.

"I wish we had all the stuff to make him a classic snowman," said Ben.

"Yeah, well, I don't got any coal with me. What else can we use?"

If Murphy had never done this before, Ben wanted to give him the full snowman experience. That included a hat, a scarf, and a face. Ben shrugged.

Two kids in matching red woolen hats and scarves tumbled down the steps of one of the other cabins and ran into the snow. They threw a few snowballs at each other, missing every time, and then ran off giggling toward the trees.

"I need a smoke break," Murphy said, breathing heavily.

Ben smiled. "Smoke away. I'm gonna head back to that store. I want to make hot chocolate later. I'll be two minutes."

Murphy handed him the whole roll of bills, and Ben heard the click of his lighter before he'd even gotten three steps away. He flicked through the bills as he wandered up the winding road to the store. There were a couple of hundred dollars there. More than enough for what he needed.

BEN RETURNED TO find Murphy standing in the snow still smoking. The smoke mixed with the mist his breath made in the cold air and hung around him like a cloudy white halo. Both kids were twenty feet away trying to hit him with snowballs, but most of them weren't making it anywhere near him. The few that did, he sidestepped casually, hardly moving and never missing a beat as he took a drag. He held the cigarette between his teeth, scooped up some snow, and packed it into a ball in his ungloved hands. He threw it with deadly accuracy, hitting one kid full in the face. The other one laughed, and the kids pushed each other over, then started to make snow angels.

"Making friends?" Ben asked.

Murphy scoffed and put out his cigarette on a log. "What you got?"

"Finishing touches." He'd picked up two sticks on the way back and a pocketful of tiny, smooth black pebbles. He dropped the sticks and handed some pebbles to Murphy. "You do his face. I'll do his buttons."

Ben crouched to press eight buttons into the snowman's front while Murphy hesitantly pushed in two eyes and a happy smile. He was about to press one in for a nose when Ben pulled his hand away and grabbed a carrot out of his pocket.

Murphy barked out a laugh. "What the fuck?"

"If we're doing this, we're doing it right!"

"That store sold vegetables?"

"Not exactly. She had to go upstairs and get me one from her kitchen."

Murphy smiled. "I dread to think what she reckons we're doing with that."

"Gross." Ben pushed him out of the way and screwed the carrot into the snowman's face.

"Pretty cool," said Murphy.

"Not done yet." Ben grabbed up the sticks, slid them in for arms, and then wrapped a scarf around its neck. The store only had one for sale. It was dark orange and about twice as long as any scarf Ben had ever seen before. He had to wind all eight feet of it around the snowman's neck three times to keep it from reaching the ground.

"Long enough?" Murphy asked.

It was a shame the store had sold out of hats. "He needs something on his head, but unless we steal one off those kids, we're out of luck."

"I reckon I could take 'em." Murphy rubbed his hands together and shivered. His hands looked red raw.

Ben grabbed them in his gloved hands and rubbed them. "You must be freezing."

Murphy shrugged. "Took off my gloves to light up."

Ben brought them up to his mouth and blew on them, trying to warm him up. Ben caught Murphy's small smile before he ducked his head and let his hair cover his eyes. Once his hands returned to their normal pink color, Ben risked kissing them lightly and let go.

"Eww." The two kids were standing behind a tree, watching them.

Ben tensed. He hadn't known the kids were still there. "Get lost, brats."

But they just giggled, and Ben relaxed. It was the same reaction they'd give any couple kissing. They whispered something about cooties before they ran off and started to build a snowman, Murphy and Ben already forgotten.

"You know, traditionally after making a snowman, you have hot chocolate."

Murphy made a face. "I'd prefer coffee."

"Stop being so grown-up."

"We are grown-ups."

"We just spent an hour making a snowman."

"True. But there's a coffee machine in there that looks like it cost a thousand bucks. I've been dying to try it out."

"Aw, come on. Sometimes you have to be brave and try something new."

Murphy's cheeks seemed to redden further at that for some reason, and Ben hoped he hadn't somehow embarrassed him.

"You can make coffee if you don't like my hot chocolate. I promise."

Back inside the cabin, Ben peeled off his gloves and coat. They both admired their snowman through the window as Murphy redressed Ben's arm. He'd gotten the bandage wet despite trying not to, but it was healing nicely and barely even ached anymore. It was a little hard to judge, though. Being outside had numbed it up completely. Along with the rest of his body.

"What should we name him?" Ben asked.

"The snowman?" Murphy's eyebrows pulled together as though he'd never heard such a crazy question.

"Yeah."

"Randall?"

"No! God."

"Sorry. Bad idea." Murphy frowned.

"That's not even funny," Ben mumbled. Couldn't they forget he existed for five minutes? But Ben couldn't help smiling at Murphy's stricken face. "Let's get warmed up."

Ben pulled out the hot-chocolate powder and bag of mini marshmallows he'd bought at the store and set the mostly intact roll of money on the side table. As the coffee machine boiled some water, Ben darted outside in his T-shirt to grab the scarf from the snowman's neck. He made up the hot chocolate in two mugs and sprinkled pink and white marshmallows generously over the top.

"Here."

Murphy leaned forward on the sofa and took it reluctantly. "Ain't this for kids?"

"Just drink it and shut up."

Ben joined him on the tiny sofa, the size of which required them to snuggle up close. Murphy blew on his drink and sipped it. Ben waited quietly for his response.

"Went a bit light on the marshmallows, didn't you?"

Ben snorted and passed him the bag. "Go crazy."

Murphy held the bag of marshmallows up above his head and tipped some into his mouth.

They watched the snow, bundled up on the sofa under a blanket, pressed together arm to arm and thigh to thigh with the long scarf wrapped around both their shoulders.

Chapter Fifteen

AS IT STARTED to get dark, without actually discussing why, they pushed the two heavy beds together and overlapped the blankets.

Ben lay on his side, propped on one elbow, and read his book by the light of the bedside lamp. Murphy lay beside him, sneaking looks at his back. Listening to Ben's soft breathing made him feel comforted and horny at the same time. He was strangely envious of the book. He wished Ben would study him that intently but, at the same time, was scared of what Ben might see. This moment of silence—this moment of nothing—seemed somehow deathly important. Profoundly full of possibilities. It felt as if the whole day had led to this moment. If he didn't do something significant, the moment would pass, and he would never get it back.

With a sudden burst of courage, Murphy rolled over on his side and curled up close behind Ben. He waited for the time when Ben would move away, but it didn't come. Before Murphy lost his nerve, he reached out and trailed a hand slowly from Ben's knee up his thigh. Ben froze, and when Murphy reached his hand higher, Ben drew in a long, shuddering breath. Murphy took that as a good sign. He found Ben's hand and held it, stroking a shaky finger over his palm and admiring the shiver that coursed through Ben's body.

"What are you doing?" Ben asked.

Murphy paused. "Being brave. Trying something new."

Ben pushed his book away and shuffled closer. Murphy trailed his fingers lightly down Ben's bare arm and watched, fascinated, as goose bumps appeared in their wake.

"I keep expecting Randall to burst in," Ben whispered.

For one weird second, Murphy wasn't sure if he meant his brother or the snowman.

"Don't think about him. He don't even know we're here," Murphy whispered. His lazy touch reached Ben's hip, and he circled his fingers around Ben's hip bone. "And the door is locked." God, he really didn't want to talk about his damned brother right now, or all this bravery would fly right out the window.

"Oh, please don't stop," Ben murmured.

"Stop what?" Murphy asked, working his hand slowly underneath Ben's jeans.

Ben gasped. "Touching me there."

"Where?"

"Oh fuck," Ben whispered.

Murphy brushed his fingers softly across Ben's stomach, making him shiver again. "Here?"

Ben arched back into Murphy's chest, and Murphy brought his fingers up to trace over Ben's nipple.

"Here?" Murphy couldn't believe what he was doing. He let his hand drop lower and graze briefly over Ben's hardening cock through his jeans. "Or here?"

"Oh God, please."

Ben rolled over to face Murphy. As soon as their gazes met, all Murphy's confidence left him, and he couldn't think of anything other than the fact that he'd never done this before. That he would be terrible. That Ben would feel embarrassed for him. But Ben leaned over, burrowed his face into Murphy's neck, and kissed him. Ben's cold nose sent shivers of pleasure through Murphy's body before he paused.

"You okay?" Ben whispered. He must have noticed that Murphy had reached his limits as far as being brave went.

Murphy pulled Ben closer. Ben pressed endless kisses all over Murphy's throat and the sides of his face, and Murphy had never felt anything so fucking overwhelmingly blissful. Ben stopped his assault on Murphy's neck only long enough to push Murphy's shirt off over his head and drop it to the floor.

They kissed on the mouth now. Their tongues entwined as Ben ran his hands down Murphy's body and tugged off his belt and unbuttoned his jeans. Glad that Ben was taking control, Murphy lifted his hips, let him drag his jeans down to his knees, and then kicked them off. Murphy opened his eyes to find that at some point Ben had removed his jeans too, but he still wore his shorts and T-shirt. It was embarrassing to be so naked, especially when Ben wasn't.

"What do you want?" Ben whispered.

Murphy shrugged, too shy to put it into words.

"Tell me. Tell me what you want, and I'll do it."

Murphy took a deep breath. It was now or never. "Want you inside me," he forced out.

A sweet smile spread over Ben's face, but his eyes seemed doubtful. "You sure? We can start slower if you want."

He'd told Ben what he wanted, and now he wasn't going to do it? "Fuck you. I know what I want."

Ben smiled. "Okay, but this is your first time, right? With a guy, at least?"

Murphy flushed and glared but gave a tiny nod.

"I want this to be good for you. I want you to want to do this again. So stop me anytime it hurts, or if you change your... Just stop me, okay?"

"Stop treating me like some girl. Just do it." Ben still hesitated. This was infuriating. "I ain't gonna break."

Ben laughed. "Okay, okay. I'm sorry. But let's take this slow.

"I want it now," he growled.

"Demanding, aren't you?" Ben grabbed Murphy's wrists and raised them over his head, holding them both in one hand against the mattress. "Just this once, I'm in charge," he whispered.

A shiver ran through Murphy's body, and he gave in willingly. Ben stroked down over his ribs and stomach, and Murphy arched into Ben's touch. Murphy's body betrayed him by trembling from a mixture of adrenaline and nervousness.

"God, look at you. You're so gorgeous, Murphy."

"Shut up. I ain't."

"You are."

It was easier not to argue, and Murphy stopped talking to concentrate on how good everything felt. Ben's tongue began a slow journey down Murphy's body. He licked all the way down his neck and then across his chest and trembling stomach to his hip bone. Then he bit Murphy, making him gasp. Ben smiled and kissed the red mark on his hip before licking it better. He kissed across Murphy's stomach and dragged his lips lower until at last his mouth reached the place Murphy wanted it most of all.

Murphy froze as he felt Ben's hot breath on his cock. With no warning, Ben licked it all the way from base to tip and then sucked the head into his mouth. Murphy gasped and grabbed Ben's head, tangling his fingers in the soft silk of his hair and trying like hell not to come right there and then. Ben wrapped his hand around the base of Murphy's cock and sucked him into his soft, hot mouth. He bobbed his head up and down, sucking hard, and Murphy did his best not to thrust up into his throat.

Ben pulled his lips off Murphy with an audible pop, and Murphy's cock slapped obscenely against his stomach.

"Is that good?" Ben asked breathlessly.

Murphy moaned an answer, unable to form words. Ben smiled, caught his breath, pulled Murphy's cock back into his mouth, and kept sucking. He slowly worked his lips farther and farther down each time he bobbed his head, flicking his tongue across the underside of Murphy's cock until his nose pressed into Murphy's stomach. Murphy felt himself hit the back of Ben's throat, and Ben swallowed around him.

Jesus Christ. Murphy gazed down in awe. He stared at Ben's jaw stretched wide, his cock completely out of sight buried down Ben's throat, and he'd never seen anything so insanely sexy. Ben swallowed on his cock again.

"God. Ben, 'm gonna..." Murphy couldn't help but hitch his hips harder into Ben's throat.

Ben choked around Murphy's dick, and Murphy came explosively. His hips thrust beyond his control through his climax, and his back arched so hard he almost threw Ben off him. He'd never come so hard in his life.

Ben sat back, gasping for breath. He smiled and wiped his mouth with the back of his hand.

"You liked that?"

"Jesus fuck, Ben." Murphy whimpered. "What the hell are you doing to me?"

Ben stroked a hand over Murphy's sweaty chest, soothing him as Murphy panted hard. He remembered Ben's arm and caught sight of the blue bruises on his chest.

"I didn't hurt you, did I?"

Ben shook his head, smiling, and kissed Murphy's stomach. Murphy felt weak and boneless as Ben leaned closer to stroke his fingers across Murphy's sweat-slicked face. Murphy kissed him and faintly tasted himself on Ben's tongue.

"Touch me now," Ben whispered into Murphy's mouth.

Murphy moved his hands obediently to Ben's shorts. He eased them down, and Ben's rock-hard cock sprang free. Murphy took his first look at it. It was a shade darker than the rest of Ben's body and so, so hard. As he had felt inside the tent, Ben had more length than Murphy. He licked his lips nervously as he imagined how it might feel inside him. Ben grabbed Murphy's hand and licked his palm. He knew what Ben wanted him to do. He just wasn't sure how. He didn't stand a chance of making Ben feel as good as he just had, but he was desperate to try.

He wrapped his hand around Ben's cock and concentrated on touching it the way he would touch his—the way he had in the tent. He did his best while Ben reached over to his bag and searched for something. Ben sat up, having magicked a small tube of lube and a foil-wrapped condom from his bag. He pulled Murphy's hand gently off his cock and up to his mouth. He kissed it. Then he ripped the foil open and pinched the tip of the condom as he rolled it down over himself.

"Are you ready?"

Murphy made to turn over and get on his hands and knees, but Ben grabbed him.

"Don't. I want to see your face."

Murphy had always imagined that guys did it doggy style. He didn't know what to do otherwise or how on earth it all worked. Ben pushed Murphy down onto his back, and he let Ben position him. His limbs were pliant. Ben pulled one of Murphy's legs up and hooked Murphy's knee over his shoulder. He kneeled between Murphy's legs and maintained eye contact as he kissed his way from knee to inner thigh.

Staring into Ben's eyes was too overwhelming as Murphy's arousal deepened, so he gazed up at the ceiling. He stared at the textured white swirls as Ben squeezed out some lube and slid a slick finger slowly inside him.

"Fuck, Ben."

Ben slid his finger into Murphy deeper and deeper and then moved it out and in again. He leaned his forehead down on Murphy's.

"You're so good. So tight, Murph." He slipped another finger in. The stretch was uncomfortable, but something made Murphy push up, wanting more. Ben moved his fingers, stretching Murphy around them. As Ben curled them, he hit a certain spot inside Murphy that made him buck and gasp, seeing stars. Ben chuckled softly and did it again. An electric shock jolted inside Murphy, jerking through his cock and knocking the breath from his lungs. He shut his eyes as those wonderful fingers stroked inside him, gently stretching him out. Ben's hardness dug into his leg where they were pressed together. Murphy's cock was already hard again and heavy against his stomach, and he moaned at the overstimulation.

"More. I need more. Please, Ben."

"Soon."

Ben moved his free hand up to Murphy's mouth and roughly pushed two fingers between his lips. Murphy automatically sucked on them, and Ben added a third—both in Murphy's mouth and in his ass. He felt filled at both ends. He needed this, needed all of Ben right now, and Ben seemed to know he'd pushed him far enough.

"You want me inside you?"

Murphy groaned around Ben's fingers.

"Want me to fuck you?"

Murphy nodded, biting Ben's hand. Ben pulled his fingers from Murphy's ass and squeezed more lube onto them. He pumped his hand over his cock a few times, covering it with lube, and then held it at the base, lining himself up with Murphy, and pushed in.

Murphy gasped. Ben felt impossibly big and impossibly wide. But he kept going, slowly, steadily. Murphy gazed down to watch Ben's cock gradually disappearing inside him. Murphy's cock twitched on his stomach, and he wrapped his legs around Ben's back, yanking his body closer and opening up more. He felt the stretch, the burn, and the tightness. Then Ben stopped. He'd bottomed out deep inside him, buried as far as he could go. He paused, letting Murphy adjust, and they held each other tightly. Murphy pulled Ben as close as he could. He breathed hard and got used to the feeling until pain became pressure, fear became want, and want became hot, urgent need.

Murphy rocked his hips up greedily to show he was ready for the next step and tried to force Ben farther inside him with his heels.

Ben didn't hesitate. He pulled almost all the way out and then thrust back inside him in one fluid move. It was painful and perfect, and Murphy couldn't help but growl in delight as he was filled so perfectly. Ben fucked him harder as he cried out, groaning on every thrust.

Ben's fingers found their way back into his mouth, and Murphy held them between his teeth, trying not to bite down too hard as Ben pounded into his ass over and over. Murphy's cock was trapped between their bodies, and it rubbed against Ben's stomach each time their hips ground together.

Murphy writhed on Ben's cock, squirming beneath him, feeling all Ben's body weight pressing down on him, and wanting more. He held on to Ben tightly, moving with him as their slick bodies rocked together. His face against Ben's chest, Murphy reached forward and sucked on Ben's nipple until it got hard. He nibbled on it and moaned at the noises Ben made in his throat. He sucked harder on it, before Ben slapped him lightly away and gripped Murphy's hips.

As Ben held Murphy in place and drilled into him, fucking him into the mattress, Ben stared down, his eyes blazing with hunger, and Murphy couldn't look away. Ben kissed him and started to climax, raw guttural noises coming from within his throat as an orgasm ripped through him. Ben pushed deeper than ever into Murphy, hitting that spot inside him one more time, before Ben's cock pulsed and shot his load. He reached down quickly for Murphy's hard-on, but it was unnecessary.

Murphy's whole body tensed, and he came there and then just from the noises Ben had made, shooting onto Ben's hand and both their stomachs. Ben collapsed onto Murphy, apparently unconcerned with the mess between them.

Ben kissed him so softly and carefully that it brought tears to Murphy's eyes. He felt sore and stretched out. It hurt, but the pain was good. It felt like the ache Ben had put inside him would be there for days. And he wanted that. Murphy wrapped his arms around Ben's sweaty back and held him as tightly as he could, burying his face in Ben's shoulder. His body twitched with aftershocks as he caught his breath, and Ben pulled back and smiled at Murphy. He was kind of beautiful, his face flushed and his brown eyes bright and sparkling.

So that was what sex was supposed to be like. The way the whole world was so obsessed with it, Murphy had suspected he might have been missing something, and this was planets apart from any kind of experience he'd ever had. Granted, he'd only had sex with women before, but even the few fumbling kisses he'd shared with men had been empty and meaningless. He'd wondered if sex just wasn't for the likes of him. He'd never really known what to put where and when. Never known what he actually wanted, let alone how to ask for it. He'd always wanted to need something as much as Randall needed women. Wanted to know how it felt to have that much passion—a passion he'd risk everything for.

And now he wanted to touch Ben with every piece of his soul and never let him go. Just for one moment, he allowed himself to believe that Ben might feel the same way. He could sense that Ben had enjoyed it as much as he had. He felt it through every touch and every quiet sigh into his chest. Maybe he'd never get to do this again as long as he lived. But it'd be worth it. He could think of this one time for the rest of his life. It could be enough. It would have to be.

Chapter Sixteen

"YOU WANT TO clean up together?" Ben asked.

"Huh?"

"Share a shower?"

"Nah, I dunno, man. You can go first."

"Come on. Let's take a quick shower together. Then we can eat. I'm starving."

Murphy didn't seem too enthusiastic.

Ben pressed a light kiss to the tip of his nose. "You don't have to be shy with me," he whispered. "Not anymore."

Murphy let Ben pull him up by the hand. He wanted Murphy to feel relaxed with him, but that wasn't something that could happen overnight. He was willing to spend forever getting Murphy to trust him if that was how long it took. What could he say to make Murphy feel safe? *I want to marry you and have your tiny redneck babies* wouldn't really cut it. Even if that was what he desperately wanted to say.

Murphy kept his back angled away as Ben tugged him gently into the bathtub and turned on the shower. He soaped himself up, enjoying the way Murphy just watched as he ran his soapy hands over his chest and stomach. But soon his hands were itching to touch Murphy, so he reached out and gathered him closer, kissing Murphy's neck experimentally. He licked, sucked, and bit, leaving marks and enjoying the adorable whimpers Murphy made in his throat.

They kissed under the spray. Murphy's fingers played with Ben's nipple again. Ben dragged his hand away from the sore spot and brought it up to his throat. Murphy followed Ben's lead and loosely wrapped his large hand around Ben's neck as they kept kissing deeply. Close, but not quite what Ben wanted. He moaned into Murphy's mouth and pulled Murphy's hand tighter against his neck. Ben's cock jerked with pleasure as Murphy held him tight around the throat, not squeezing but holding him firmly against the cold tiles, and Ben almost purred. Now he was getting it.

"You like that?" Murphy murmured.

"I like it rough," Ben whispered. Murphy shivered in response.

They kissed hard, and Ben gasped as Murphy's other hand reached down between their bodies and found his slick, soapy cock. Murphy held it under the water, rinsing the bubbles off. Then he gulped audibly and kneeled down, gazing at it for a second before taking the tip of it into his warm mouth. Ben thrust both hands out to grab something, colliding with the shower wall and the shelf of shampoo. This man was full of surprises and had the ability to make his knees weak with just a touch of his tongue.

Somewhere through the thick haze of arousal, he realized that his was the first cock Murphy had ever had in his mouth.

Somehow, the idea that he was corrupting this older man—this tough guy who in every other walk of life held an air of masculine experience—was sinfully hot. Just like his lips. God, the way it felt to sink deeper and deeper into the velvety warmth of his mouth. He watched as Murphy tried to take him farther down his throat and gripped the shelf hard as Murphy sucked him down. Murphy choked and pulled away coughing but gamely jumped back on Ben's cock as soon as he caught his breath.

Ben's fingers brushed against a shampoo bottle. He grabbed it and squeezed some out onto his shaking palm, then reached down to fist both hands into Murphy's wet hair. He lathered it up and massaged his fingers through the silky strands, washing his hair and encouraging his head back and forth gently as he sucked on Ben's cock.

Murphy's blue eyes squinted up at him, and Ben ran his fingers across Murphy's forehead, wiping white suds away and being careful not to let any soap bubbles slip into his eyes. He had an overwhelming urge to take care of Murphy. He wanted him to feel just how much he desired him. He wanted to pour every bit of the affection he was feeling through his fingers and into Murphy's heart. Murphy was the first man he'd ever met whom he wanted to fuck into oblivion and then, afterward, tell him to put his feet up while he made him his favorite sandwich.

He did his best not to thrust his hips into Murphy's mouth. He didn't want to choke him again, and Murphy was sucking his cock so well and moving his tongue so beautifully that even though he wasn't taking more than half of Ben into his mouth, Ben was close to coming anyway. Murphy's cheeks hollowed out around his cock— just like they had around his cigarette—and Ben gasped.

"Murph," he warned.

Murphy hummed questioningly on his cock, and Ben gulped hard, taking a second to recover from the extra vibrations before he could speak again.

"Murph, I'm gonna come." Ben expected him to pull off, but Murphy just sucked harder and let Ben come in his mouth. "Oh God, baby. Fuck."

Murphy swallowed it all down and sat back, wiping his mouth with the back of his hand. He looked so proud that Ben felt his heart swell.

"You did so good, Murph. So good." He pressed his hands to the sides of Murphy's face and pulled him up, then kissed him softly and slid their tongues together. After a long, searching kiss, Ben reached up, grabbed the showerhead, and pulled it down. Then he tilted Murphy's head back and carefully rinsed the last of the shampoo from his hair.

Murphy stayed still and quiet under Ben's hands until Ben was finished. Then Murphy grabbed the soap and lathered it up in his hands before soaping up Ben's smooth chest and stomach. He ran his soapy hands over Ben's arms and pulled him closer to do his back. Murphy's cheeks went adorably red as he quickly soaped up Ben's spent cock and reached around to run his hands over Ben's ass. Ben gladly did the same for Murphy, and they stood under the spray together until all the suds were gone. And for quite a few minutes after.

Ben climbed out of the bath and leaned across the two wide sinks to the neat pile of fluffy white towels. He passed Murphy a towel and grabbed one for himself, then wrapped it around his waist. Murphy copied him, and once the towel was knotted at Murphy's hips, Ben grabbed him by it and pulled him forward through the steam until their stomachs bumped each other.

"So how was your first time?"

Murphy frowned. "I ain't some virgin."

"Your first time with a man, I mean."

"Oh." He smiled ruefully. "It was..." He scratched his head and seemed vaguely perplexed. "I don't have the words."

"I wouldn't have guessed I was your first if I hadn't known." Ben spoke so earnestly it made Murphy laugh. "You were amazing."

"You don't have to say that," said Murphy. "I'll get better."

"I don't want you to change anything. I'd be happy doing exactly that every day for the rest of time."

Murphy snorted, and a mischievous look flashed across his eyes. "Nah. There's some things I want to try."

Ben's eyes widened, and he let out a laugh. "What kind of things?"

"None of your business," Murphy said shyly.

"I'd like it to be my business," Ben said. He reached out—fascinated—to touch the tiny bruises on Murphy's neck where he'd nibbled and sucked on him. Murphy looked past Ben's head and wiped the mirror behind him with a *squeak*. He turned his head to the side and inspected the marks in the reflection.

"Sorry." Ben winced.

Murphy stared at them, seemingly as fascinated as Ben had been. "I like them."

They'd be hard to explain to Murphy's brother when he rejoined them, but the last thing Ben wanted to do was bring Randall up. So Ben kissed the bruises better instead.

"Hope they don't hurt," Ben murmured into his neck.

"Nah," Murphy said, his voice breathy.

Murphy's skin was hot against his lips. If Ben wasn't careful, he was going to push Murphy to the floor and fuck him all over again. He cleared his throat and, hard though it was, moved Murphy softly away, holding him at arm's length.

"Where do you want to eat?" Ben asked.

"Where is there to go?" Murphy's pupils were big, and he stared at Ben's mouth as if trying to focus.

"I don't know. Maybe nowhere. Maybe that other hotel has a restaurant."

Murphy paused and gazed at the floor, shy and hesitant again. "Do you mind if we stay here?"

"We can do anything you want. Staying here sounds fun." Ben took Murphy's hand and after leading him into the bedroom, he grabbed the menu from behind the phone. "Let's order in. Have a bed picnic."

"Is that a thing?"

"We'll make it a thing."

THEY SAT CROSS-LEGGED on the bed and spread Chinese food out over the blankets between them. Ben had phoned the order through to reception, and they ordered it from a local takeout place, which drove it over. Then the hotel put it on fancy plates, added a complimentary bottle of wine, and delivered it—somehow still hot—to their cabin.

Ben brought his chopsticks to his mouth and nibbled on a dumpling. "So, I assume Randall doesn't know you're bisexual."

Murphy's face was a picture of astonishment. "Who the fuck's bisexual?"

"What are you saying? I think today kind of proves beyond a shadow of a doubt that you're into guys."

Murphy speared a dumpling with one chopstick and stuck it in his mouth. "I ain't denying that," he said with his mouth full.

"Oh." He didn't like women at all? "But that prostitute..."

"Been trying to forget about that. Thanks for bringing it up."

"Sorry." Ben smiled.

Murphy shrugged. "I did what I had to do to keep Randall off my back. He does that all the time. Brings some woman home. Tries to pair me off with her. Forces me in the end." He smiled, but it didn't reach his eyes. "I should be safe for a while now." He scooped up some egg fried rice with his hand and ate it. "I'm sorry you even had to see all that. I bet you've never met a hooker before, huh?"

Ben's heart hurt for Murphy. "Let's just say this whole trip has been an eye-opener." Ben watched as Murphy bit nervously on his thumb. He probably didn't know he was doing it. "Did you have to think about guys while you were having sex with her?"

"I thought about you."

Ben's stomach plummeted to the floor, and his mouth fell open. Murphy had thought about him like that, even way back then?

"And I did not have sex with her. She just used her hand on me."

Murphy carried on talking as though he hadn't said something monumental and life changing. Ben tried to force his mind back to the present, still wondering if she'd been better at touching him than Ben.

Murphy drank some wine from the bottle. "And no, I don't think Randall has a clue. I ain't exactly tried telling him. I don't know what he'd do."

Ben grabbed the offered wine bottle and took a sip. "Beat the gay out of you?"

"I doubt he'd quit before I stopped breathing."

Ben sensed Murphy getting melancholy. It was time to change the subject. But before he had a chance, Murphy changed it for him.

"So, what you said earlier. About liking it rough."

Ben waited for him to go on. Murphy stared intently at a spring roll and opened his mouth to speak, but nothing came out.

"Yeah?" Ben prodded gently.

Murphy swallowed. "How rough, exactly, do you mean?"

"I dunno. I don't want to get punched in the face or anything. I just..." Ben shrugged. "I guess day to day, excluding kidnappings, I'm pretty much in charge of my life, so sometimes in bed, I like to be controlled by someone else. Maybe feel a bit...used."

Murphy seemed to be breathing a little heavier, and he was still staring at that spring roll.

"Like how?" he whispered.

"Held down, maybe. Pushed around. Get my hair pulled a bit. Fucked so hard it hurts." Ben shifted position uncomfortably. He was getting a hard-on just talking about it.

"You want it to hurt?"

"Well, that's the thing. When I'm turned on, nothing seems to hurt. If my dick's hard, anything goes. Within reason. Maybe my pain threshold goes up when I'm aroused or something."

"So everything needs to be harder so you can feel it?"

"Maybe. Or maybe I just like getting good and fucked."

Murphy's Adam's apple moved as he swallowed.

"No one's ever really gotten it right, though. They're either too gentle or too hard."

"Like Goldilocks and the three bears."

Ben smiled. "Yeah. I guess I'm waiting for Baby Bear's porridge."

Murphy snorted, and Ben made a face.

"That came out really wrong."

Ben piled up their plates on the tray and left it by the door. Then he crawled into bed next to Murphy. Murphy was lying on his stomach, limbs spread out like a starfish and face pressed into the soft pillow, and when Ben disturbed the covers, they slipped down to reveal Murphy's shoulders and back. It was a testament to how much Ben had tired him out that he didn't pull them back up immediately to cover himself. Ben eyed his scar and reached out to stroke lightly across his back from the scar to the new tattoo. Murphy flinched but didn't pull away. Not for the first time, Ben wanted to ask what had happened, but he kept his mouth shut. He didn't need to know until Murphy needed to tell him.

"I know it's disgusting."

"No, it's not," Ben said truthfully. He crept closer and kissed the scar where it crossed his shoulder blade.

"My dad did it."

"You don't have to tell me."

"When I was a kid."

It seemed that was all Murphy was going to say. Then Ben kissed his back again, and it all came out in a rush of quiet words.

"He only attacked me once. He did it with a fire iron. Rest of my life he just ignored me. Never said nothing to me that wasn't about how ugly I was or useless or how he wished he'd punched my mom harder when I was inside her."

Ben felt a slick kind of shock at his words, but Murphy wasn't telling him anything he didn't already suspect. He kissed the scar softly one more time and rested his chin on the small of Murphy's back, running his thumb over

Murphy's healing tattoo. He felt the vibrations of Murphy's voice rumbling through his body.

"After my mom died, he left us for a long time. Randall had to work or steal so we could buy food and stuff. Dad would be gone for a year, then turn up again, acting like nothing was different. When he started on me, Randall would get between us, say something, make Dad forget about me and go after him. He always took it for me. Every time. No one else ever put us first, so we did it for each other. But when he started going to jail and Dad came back, well, he wasn't there to save me anymore. But he'd tried, you know?"

Ben nodded even though Murphy wasn't looking.

"I know you can't see it in him. I can't see it myself most of the time no more, but he was a good brother. Protected me. It's not his fault, what he's like. He just never had an older brother, not like I did."

Maybe he was right. Without Randall, Murphy wouldn't have had the chance to be the sweet, sensitive man he was now. Randall could have been just as good as Murphy if he'd had a big brother, but he'd had to stay hard to protect Murphy. Ben remembered Randall's permanent frown lines. As cruel as he'd seen the man be, Ben wasn't sure he could hate him anymore. Randall's threats and intimidation paled now that he knew for sure who the real monster was. After all, whatever horrible things had happened to Murphy had probably happened to Randall too—maybe worse. Randall was just Murphy gone wrong, Murphy a few years down a different path. An older version of Murphy who'd had the kindness beaten out of him.

"If I saw your dad hurt you, I'd kill him," said Ben, his voice taking on an unfamiliar hardness.

Murphy raised an eyebrow and twisted around to study him. "Never heard you say nothing like that before. You're too late anyway." Murphy rolled over onto his back and whispered at the ceiling, "About a week too late."

Ben's heart raced as he realized what Murphy was saying.

"Randall always said if he touched me again, he'd kill him. And then a week ago he did." Murphy pushed the covers down and showed Ben a scar he hadn't noticed—a thin red jagged line across his hip. "He used a pocketknife. I was asleep."

Ben's stomach filled with ice. "Why the hell did he do that?" Ben hated asking such a stupid question. There was no why. No reason for anyone doing that.

"He was high. He hadn't touched drugs for a while. Couldn't afford 'em," said Murphy. "But I dented his truck, and he got so angry he went out and got some stuff to calm down."

"Doesn't sound like it worked."

"I woke up to find him crouched over me with a knife, cutting me open."

"Shit."

"I yelled out, and Randall heard. He ran in and pulled him off me. He beat his head into the floor. Just kept doing it. Didn't stop. And he was just gone."

There was a long silence. "I don't know what to say. I guess at least you don't have to be afraid anymore." Ben held his breath. Maybe saying nothing was better than saying the wrong thing.

"Oh, I ain't scared of my dad. Only thing I ever been scared of is turning into him."

Ben wrapped his arms around Murphy and rested his head on Murphy's chest. Ben listened to his heartbeat, and enjoyed the rise and fall of the warm body underneath him. Ben stroked his thumb over the soft skin of Murphy's hip for a long time until Murphy's breathing was regular and quiet. Ben leaned up on one elbow and watched him sleep. Murphy really was the most beautiful person he'd ever seen in real life. He wasn't sure he'd ever be able to look away.

Ben wished there were words he could say to fix everything. But he wasn't a knight in shining armor, and Murphy didn't need rescuing. He just needed to know he deserved something better and that he could save himself, simply by walking away. Murphy's legs twitched in his sleep like a puppy's, and Ben smiled. He sighed. If he was getting sentimental over leg twitches, he really was well and truly lost.

Chapter Seventeen

MURPHY WOKE BEN with a sugary kiss and a doughnut in a white paper bag. "The lady at the store says hi."

Ben laughed sleepily and stretched, pulling Murphy down for more kisses.

"I called Randall. Told him where we are."

Ben frowned, and he sat up, rubbing his eyes. "Why'd you go and do that?"

"Huh?"

"I mean, where is he?"

"He was playing poker somewhere nearby. He knows people everywhere. He can get in on a game whenever he needs to."

"Poker? Seems kind of tame for your brother."

"You don't know what he bets." Randall had lost a truck, his motorcycle, and even Murphy once before. Murphy shook his head. He didn't want to think about that.

"How long do we have?"

Murphy felt as sad as Ben looked. "Not long."

"You should play with the coffee machine while you can."

Murphy glanced at it and then back at Ben. Even after everything they'd done, he couldn't tell him what he really wanted to do in their last minutes alone.

Ben bit his lip. "You want to share this doughnut?"

Murphy smiled and climbed into bed, pushing up against Ben's warm body. He took one bite and let Ben eat the rest, watching as he got sugar all over his face like a little kid. Murphy tried to enjoy being with Ben, but he couldn't stop feeling anxious. He should have told Randall about the car crash on the phone. Not because his brother would have given a shit about how they were or even asked if Murphy was all right, but because they no longer had transportation. He just hoped Randall would bring another car with him and not come by cab from wherever he was.

As Murphy reluctantly packed up their stuff, he passed the back window and caught sight of their snowman. It sat in a shaft of strong sunlight. Its head had rolled off onto the ground, and its body was half-melted. Murphy couldn't stop a disappointed sigh. Ben jumped up and followed his gaze through the window. They both took in the fallen carrot and the disarrayed buttons in brief silence, before Ben smiled and flung his arms around Murphy's neck.

"Aw, don't be sad. That's what they do," said Ben.

"Just thought it'd last longer."

Ben paused. "What day is it today?"

"Thursday."

"Already?" There was a full minute of silence before Ben spoke again. "I inherit my dad's business today."

"You what?"

"It's my birthday. I'm twenty-one. Well, technically I was born at midday, so I'm still twenty for a few more hours."

Murphy was mortified. "Why didn't you say?"

Ben shrugged and blushed.

"Well, no shit. Happy birthday." Murphy hugged him tight.

"Thanks."

"So, why don't you want your dad's business?"

"How do you know I don't?"

"You've been putting off going home for months. You ain't in no hurry to get home and claim it."

Ben shrugged. "It's not that I don't want it. It's been the plan since I was born. When I turn twenty-one, Dad retires, and I take over. I guess that's why I went so far away to college. I thought there must be something else out there in the world I should be doing instead."

"Like what?"

"I don't know. I never did find anything. But you're not meant to do what your parents want, are you? You're supposed to rebel, join a band, convert to some weird religion. At least get a tattoo."

"You wanted to rebel so much you've been hanging out with a couple of gun-toting criminals."

Ben laughed. "True. I just didn't feel ready for the next step. I was almost relieved when you kidnapped me."

Murphy snorted. Ben ducked his face and pressed it into Murphy's shoulder. Murphy's heart swelled at Ben's sudden shyness, and he stroked a thumb over the soft skin of Ben's neck.

"This family business must be something pretty fucked up if it's worse than being stuck with us. What is it? Human-waste management? An abattoir? Illegal puppy farm?"

Ben laughed. "We sell yachts to rich people."

Murphy scoffed. "Sounds like hell."

"I've helped out there every summer since I was a kid. But as soon as I get back and sign the papers, I'm gonna be the boss."

"And that scares you?"

"Maybe not as much as it did. I've gained a bit of perspective on what's scary. Staring down the barrel of your brother's gun is. Selling boats, not so much."

"Glad to be of service. Cruella is pretty scary," Murphy admitted.

Ben smiled. "I forgot he called it that."

"When were you supposed to sign the papers?"

"Tomorrow morning. We were meeting my dad's lawyer at nine."

"Shit. There's no way we can drive to Florida by then."

Ben seemed baffled.

"Florida," Murphy repeated.

"Oh. No, I lied about Florida. I was never headed there. I live right on the shore of Lake Michigan."

"For real? Why'd you lie?"

"I don't know. I didn't want to tell you anything too personal after you'd just kidnapped me. Nearly didn't even tell you my real name."

"Why Florida?"

Ben shrugged. "I was coming from Florida when you found me. That's where I went to college. My mother wanted me to fly home, but I wanted to drive. That's what I was doing when I ran into you. But listen, what are you talking about, driving me home?"

"You're really from the lake we saw on the way here?" It felt like weeks ago.

Randall flung open the door and swooped in, letting in a burst of cold air. Ben jumped back, putting several feet of space between them.

"Could you have picked a more difficult place to find?"

The mood changed from relaxed to volatile in as long as it took for the door to close. Murphy mourned it like a death and sank back against the edge of a table. Everything felt wrong now. Randall didn't belong here. Not in the place where he and Ben had spent the most perfect day of his life. His brother was like a great white ape in a library. Murphy didn't even notice what Randall was doing until Ben yelped in pain. Murphy automatically jumped up.

"What're you doing?" Murphy asked.

"We gotta truss this bitch up like a turkey."

Murphy felt his cheeks flush as Randall put his hands all over Ben's body. Sacred places Murphy's lips and tongue had been only hours before.

"Stop, Randall. You're hurting him."

"So what? I told you I'd figure out what to do with the Chinese kid."

"What? What have you done?"

"I lost all his money and all of my money too. Damn near lost the privilege of breathing. But I had insurance. A backup plan. Old Randall always has a backup plan. My acquaintance, the one I been meeting up with all week, he knows a guy with a liking for"—he gestured at Ben—"for guys like him."

Murphy stared at him, uncomprehending.

"Use the brain our mama gave you, boy."

Murphy did, and as the truth became clear, it stunned him that he hadn't worked it out sooner. "You can't fucking sell him."

"It's a bet. You can't renege on a bet."

Ben grunted in pain when Randall pulled the rope around his ankles too tight, and a sharp crack sounded as Randall's palm met Ben's cheek hard. Ben slumped to the side, his hair over his face.

Randall shrugged. "What's the problem here? I got no other use for the kid. Do you?"

Everything was falling apart. Murphy's hands shook in frustration and panic. He blinked and tried to breathe as he pictured himself saying yes.

Yes, I do have a use for him. I want to kiss him, hold him, fuck him, and love him.

Then he pictured Randall making him watch as he killed Ben like he'd killed their dad.

"No, Randall. I don't have a use for him." Murphy kept his face blank but glanced at Ben as he said it. The boy's cheek was still red from Randall's hard slap. The sweet understanding in Ben's eyes nearly broke Murphy in two.

"Cheer up, man. I got you to thank for this," said Randall.

"For what?"

"You picked the car with the hidden gift inside." Murphy felt sick. "Where is the car? I didn't see it outside."

Shit. Murphy knew he should have told Randall over the phone. His brother would have shouted and cursed at him but might have cooled down by the time he got here.

Murphy took a deep breath. "I crashed it. It's gone."

Randall didn't make a sound and stepped closer. "I'm sorry. What?" he asked quietly.

Murphy's hands started to tremble again, so he stuffed them in his pockets. If Randall saw that he was scared, it made him even angrier. "I crashed the car."

"Are you stupid? As well as fucking useless?"

Murphy kept his eyes on the floor.

"I crashed it. It was my fault," Ben piped up from the corner. His voice wavered, contradicting the bravery it had probably taken to say it.

Ben was trying to help, but it would just make things worse. God, why did he even care when Murphy had betrayed him?

"You let him fucking drive?" Randall's gaze darted down to Murphy's neck, and Murphy slapped a hand up to cover his bruises. Then Randall's gaze drifted across to the bed. The bed very obviously made from two beds pushed together. The two beds they'd forgotten to push apart. Murphy didn't even see the fist coming. Just found himself facedown on the soft rug. His ear and the base of his skull throbbed with white-hot pain.

"Get up, boy." Randall kicked Murphy in the ribs.

Murphy winced but didn't cry out. It would only anger Randall further. He got up on his hands and knees and shook his head like a wet dog. He staggered to the bed and dropped onto it, wiping a hand across his face. Blood came away on the back of his hand.

Randall stared at Murphy for a long minute. "I'll find us another car. Watch him." He rifled through their bags and handed Murphy his gun. "I'll be back with it as soon as I can, and then we can exchange. Might be a while, though. Gotta get somewhere less public first on foot." He paused. "This has to go smooth, you understand? My acquaintance don't play nice. I'm dead, and you are too unless we deliver this boy."

Randall knocked his bag off the table and swore as he picked it up. His gaze darted all over the room, and his chest heaved from how hard he was breathing. Murphy rubbed his eyes and focused on his brother. He'd never seen Randall like this. He'd completely sidestepped the bed issue and what it meant, like he had something more important to sort out first.

Murphy blinked. This was what Randall looked like when he was nervous. He really was scared this time, scared he might get killed. Murphy's chest tightened. He couldn't lose his brother. Randall was the last piece of family he had left in the world. The only one who'd ever done anything for him. It was Murphy's job to put him first, whatever it took. He couldn't abandon him like every other person in their lives had.

"Can I rely on you, brother?"

Murphy nodded, and Randall pushed his head affectionately as he left. Murphy swayed back, then forward again in his seat on the bed.

Chapter Eighteen

RANDALL DISAPPEARED IN a whirlwind, and the room fell silent. The only sounds were Ben's fidgeting, as he tried uselessly to work his hands free, and Murphy's wet breathing through his thick lip.

"I don't know what to do," Murphy said.

"You don't have to do anything."

"M'sorry."

"It's fine."

"Fine? Course it's not fine."

It was. Ben stopped struggling. He'd never been in a life-threatening situation before, but he'd had dreams about them. Dreams where his plane was crashing or his elevator was plunging down fifty floors, and it always felt like this. Panic followed by calm acceptance. Whatever happened, he was going to be fine. Murphy would never risk his brother's life, and why should he? Randall was family. Ben knew how that felt. He would do anything for his siblings. He didn't expect Murphy to care more about a guy he'd just met than the brother he'd known all his life. In their own ways, Randall and Murphy were each just looking out for their brother. As soon as Randall handed Ben over to the freak in question and as soon as Murphy was safe and out of the picture, Ben was going to escape. He was going to run. Jump out of a moving car if he had to. Maybe Murphy would let him take Randall's gun.

"I can't just walk out on him, Ben. You know I can't."

"It's okay." Ben carefully looked away from Murphy's beautiful face. "I don't mind. We both knew this wasn't forever. It's no big deal." The lies fell from his lips and then disappeared into silence like snow falling on the ocean.

Ben glanced back at Murphy and flinched at the tears running down Murphy's cheeks. He was sure Murphy didn't know he was crying.

"Thing is," Murphy said quietly, "if I do what Randall wants, I'm abandoning you. And that's just as bad."

"I'm not family."

"Yeah, y'are."

Ben's chest tightened. "You're not your dad, Murph. He wouldn't be upset like this. He wouldn't give a shit. Even if you do this, you're nothing like him."

"Why the hell are you comforting me? I should be comforting you."

"But I'm not upset," Ben whispered.

Murphy moved nearer. Up close, the blood on Murphy's face looked a lot worse, and Ben winced in sympathy.

Murphy saw his expression and misinterpreted it. "Please don't be scared of me."

"I'm not, stupid. Look, untie me, and I can clean you up."

Murphy sniffed and immediately started to work on Randall's knots.

BEN PUSHED MURPHY softly onto the sofa. Kneeling by the open first-aid kit, he was reminded of how their roles had been reversed only days ago and wanted to do as good a job as Murphy had for him. He wiped the drying tears off Murphy's cheeks with one hand and then held a wad of tissue to his earlobe until it stopped bleeding. He cleaned the cut with antiseptic and covered it awkwardly with a Band-Aid.

"How's your lip?"

"Just sore."

"I don't think it's cut. Hopefully you won't get a bruise." Ben ran a finger lightly over Murphy's lower lip. "He's gotta stop hitting you, baby."

"He don't mean it."

Ben paused. "I know he's the most important person in the whole world to you."

Murphy met Ben's gaze pointedly. "Maybe not."

Ben's stomach flipped. "Don't say that." He couldn't take hearing those words if Murphy didn't mean them.

After Ben cleaned him up, Murphy pressed tiny, soft kisses all over Ben's face. Ben counted them. Ten.

"If that's what happens afterward, you can agree to sell me more often."

Murphy smiled for a second before it was replaced by anguish. "I don't know how else to apologize."

"Just give me ten sorry kisses every night until you're not sorry anymore." Ben's words were a harsh reminder that he wouldn't be spending any more nights with Murphy.

They moved closer together on the sofa, and Murphy pulled Ben's head onto his shoulder. One hand stroked his shoulder in little soothing circles. The other played with his hair.

Chapter Nineteen

BEN'S HAIR FELT silky under Murphy's calloused fingers. Murphy's heart raced at the surreal turn everything had taken, and he tried not to think about what was happening. He concentrated on the things he trusted. On real, solid, and reliable things that were always there, even if they hurt. Like family. Like his loyalty to his brother. But somehow that wasn't enough anymore. He couldn't stop thinking about the boy next to him curled up by his side, warming him. The boy who had never once hurt him. The boy who wasn't asking for anything and wasn't demanding Murphy pick a side or make any difficult choices. The boy who was a little smaller than him, a few years younger than him, but about ten times stronger.

"Sorry for ruining your birthday."

Ben took his hand. "You haven't."

Murphy raised an eyebrow. "I kidnapped you, crashed your car, cut your arm open, and agreed to let my brother sell you to pay off his debts. In what way is your birthday not ruined?"

Ben smiled. "The most beautiful guy on the planet is playing with my hair. I'm good, thanks."

Murphy scoffed, and his cheeks flushed. "You still relieved we kidnapped you?"

Ben laughed shortly. "Well, I never thought *this* was going to happen. Worst-case scenario, I thought I might get beaten up a bit and dumped in the forest."

"By me?"

"By Randall."

"You really thought that?"

"I heard him say it! That first night in the motel."

Murphy sighed as he remembered. "And yet you still stuck around. Even when I told you to go."

Ben shrugged shyly. "What're we going to do?"

"Just let me think," Murphy whispered. They sat in silence for a moment.

"Whatever happens, I'm glad I met you," Ben said quietly.

Murphy held Ben's hand and stared down at their interlaced fingers. He'd caught a glimpse of what life was like with someone who cared about him. Someone who soothed away nightmares instead of throwing them in his face or trying to beat them out of him. Maybe he didn't need time to think after all.

"I can't do this. I'm not going to let my brother sell someone I like to a psychopath."

Ben smiled. "You like me?"

"You're all right."

They beamed at each other.

Randall burst back into the room a moment later, the door hitting the wall with so much force that a table lamp fell over. Murphy didn't flinch but jumped up, standing between his brother and Ben.

"I got us a pickup. And this time I checked the backseat," Randall said.

Murphy watched as his brother realized Ben wasn't where he'd left him.

"Why'd you untie the kid, ya idiot?"

"His name's Ben." Murphy calmly reached into his back pocket and pulled out Cruella. He pointed her at

Randall's confused face. He thought about every time Randall had hurt Ben, every cigarette he'd flicked at him, and his solid hand slamming into Ben's sweet face. White-hot rage pooled deep inside his belly and spread up through his chest. He remembered every act of violence that Ben should never have experienced, everything Ben should never have seen, and everything from Murphy's dark life that had polluted Ben's bright one. His gun finger twitched.

Randall tilted his head like a curious dog. "I know you ain't shooting my own gun at me, brother."

"Correct." Murphy's heart thudded so loud and fast he was surprised Randall couldn't hear it hammering. He waited for his brother to step closer, then brought the barrel of the gun down hard over the weak spot in his forehead. Randall dropped to the floor like a rock.

Ben was by his side immediately. "Holy shit. I thought you were gonna shoot him."

"Would have been hard. I took the bullets out."

"Is he okay?"

Murphy kneeled down and felt the back of Randall's head. "Yeah. He's not even bleeding. Just unconscious. He's got a weak spot on his big fat head there. He's always getting knocked out."

"Like an Achilles' heel. But...in his head."

"Right." Murphy pushed him over onto his back, into a more comfortable position, then shoved a pillow from the bed under his head.

"What do we do now?" Ben asked.

"Leave him here. Pack up our stuff. Get you home." Murphy grabbed his bag and started collecting up all their belongings.

"Wait," said Ben. "I should be able to take more money out now. If we leave it with Randall, would that help him with whatever trouble he's in?"

Murphy's heart swelled. "Maybe. Might buy him more time, at least." Murphy tied Randall's wrist to the bed with Ben's blue rope. "Just in case he wakes up before we get back."

"Do it tighter."

Murphy looked up at Ben. "You're enjoying this part, huh?"

"Can't say revenge doesn't taste a little sweet."

Murphy took Ben's debit card from Randall's inside pocket, and they made a quick visit to the ATM in the wall outside the general store. Ben emptied his account.

Back in the cabin, Murphy left the money fanned out neatly on Randall's chest, hoping it would serve as both a sorry note and a good-bye.

"I'll pay you back someday, Ben." He wasn't sure how, but he would.

Murphy rooted around in Randall's shirt and found his pocketknife. He left it within easy reach and silently said good-bye to his brother. His dangerous, infuriating, crazy-son-of-a-bitch big brother. He'd always love who Randall used to be, but now he was everything dark and poisonous from their old life. Murphy couldn't let that control him anymore, not now that he'd found Ben's brightness.

Randall grabbed Murphy's arm in a viselike grip. "What the fuck do you think you're doing?"

Murphy tried to jump away, but Randall's hold was too tight. Randall squeezed so hard Murphy thought his arm might break.

"Let me go," he said, pulling at Randall's fist.

"No chance."

Randall lunged forward to grab Murphy around the neck with his other hand but came to a sudden stop when the rope tying him to the bed reached its limits. He stared down at his tied wrist as though he couldn't believe what he was seeing.

Randall and Murphy both went for the pocketknife at the same moment, but Ben scrabbled to the floor and grabbed it first. Ben pointed the blade at Randall, his hand trembling.

"Let go of him," Ben said. Randall snorted with laughter. "Do it!" Ben continued. He got a better grip on the knife and strengthened his stance. He brought the blade closer to Randall's face but kept it out of his reach.

Randall leaned back slightly and raised an eyebrow. "So you do have balls after all. Where've they been up to now?" Randall pushed his brother away roughly, and Murphy ended up sprawled on the floor on his back. Randall caught Murphy's eye and pointed at Ben. "I don't know what this toxic little bitch has done to your mind while I been gone. I don't know what bullshit he's been whispering in your ear. But you need to tell him to give me my knife right now."

"He's not toxic. He's my friend," said Murphy.

"Aw, you made a friend. Congratulations," Randall said, sneering.

"He's more of a friend to me than you've ever been."

"I'm your damn brother," Randall shouted.

"Only by blood. And blood ain't thicker than water." Murphy got to his feet. "I'm sick of living like this. Always looking over my shoulder. Always braced for the next attack."

Randall's gaze faltered. "I just been trying to keep you tough. Keep you a man."

Murphy sighed. "I'm leaving. With Ben."

"It figures you only had the guts to do this after sucker punching me and tying me up," Randall growled. "You always been a coward, boy. It makes sense you two would hit it off."

"You haven't even noticed, have you?" Murphy asked.

"Noticed what?"

Murphy gestured at the bills scattered all over the floor. "That's from Ben. His idea. His last five hundred dollars. He wanted you to have it. Thought it might help you out. God knows why after what you've done to him."

Randall frowned as he studied the money. "So what do you want? Why you tying me up? Is this payback?"

"No! Of course not. But selling people ain't right. And you know it. So we're leaving. Going somewhere you can't hurt him." Murphy reached over to squeeze Ben's shoulder.

Randall frowned. "Why haven't you just set the kid free?" He dropped his gaze and continued in a strained voice. "Why the hell are you leaving too?"

Murphy swallowed. "I just... I think I can do better than staying here with you."

Randall looked back and forth between Ben and Murphy, his forehead creased. "Fuck you." Randall twisted his body and kicked out at Murphy's legs, but Murphy hopped out of the way. Randall stopped kicking and lay still, panting. "Oh, go ahead and leave. Just like Dad did."

Murphy felt like he'd been punched in the stomach. But he didn't feel destroyed by guilt like he'd thought he would. He was angry.

"Don't try and manipulate me. I ain't like him. This is your damn mess, and it's time you fixed it without involving me or innocent fucking bystanders."

There was a long moment before Randall sighed, as if all the fight had been knocked out of him. "I always knew you could do better than me, kid." Randall sat up and rubbed a hand over his head. "I just been waiting for you to figure it out."

Murphy gazed at Randall. His brother stared back, unblinking. For the first time in a long time he felt like they were really seeing each other. Like Murphy was with the brother who used to look out for him. The one who let Murphy sleep cuddled up to his back when he was cold.

"If you ever find the old Randall again, you let me know, okay?" Murphy said.

"I won't know where you are."

"I'll be in touch."

Randall looked hard at Ben before turning back to his brother. "He'll hurt you."

"He won't," Murphy answered.

Randall shook his head and blew out a breath. "Fine. Go on, then. Get outta here." Murphy and Ben exchanged a wary look. "I ain't gonna follow you," he said wearily. "You do what you gotta do." He glared at Ben. "Even if it is this Korean kid."

Murphy wasn't sure whether to laugh, run, or pass out.

"What about the money you owe?" Murphy asked.

Randall glanced down at the bills on the floor. "This might keep them off my back for a while." He shrugged. "I'll look at my portfolio. Sell my stocks and bonds. Move some shares around."

Murphy smiled. That meant he'd be stealing cars and selling them. He took the knife from Ben's hand and passed it to Randall. "Don't hurt anyone, okay?"

Randall nodded once.

Murphy smiled and hurried Ben out of the motel room, before turning back to his brother at the door. "Bye," Murphy said quietly. "Love you."

Randall exhaled and gave a half smile. "Love you too."

Murphy and Ben jogged through the trees back up to the road.

"Bet he still wants me dead," said Ben.

"Are you kidding?" Murphy asked. "He finally called you Korean. He's practically welcomed you into the family." Ben snorted. "It's about as close to his blessing as we're ever going to get."

"Then I'll take it," Ben said, and kissed Murphy on the lips.

They found the pickup Randall had hot-wired, and Murphy dug the map out of one of their bags.

"Wish I still had my GPS," said Ben.

"I left it in your car. You said it didn't work."

Ben winced. "I didn't tell the truth about that either. Didn't want it announcing my destination if I was going to lie about where I was going."

Murphy rolled his eyes and then took a deep breath. "I'm gonna get you home for your birthday." He didn't know quite why, but it suddenly seemed imperative that he get Ben home safe by the end of the day.

"Oh yeah?" Ben said. Murphy nodded resolutely. "Well, then, we've got about five hundred miles to cover." It was a lot, but it was doable. "I'll take the first shift."

"You?"

"Yeah, I can drive, you know. Not that you would think so based on the past few days. I feel bad about taking this car, though."

"I know." Murphy chewed on his lip. "But we need to travel fast, and it's not like there's a bus around here we can catch headed straight for your house."

"Maybe we can return it later."

"Sure." Murphy shrugged. "I'll drive it back or something."

"You'd really do that?"

"Got nothing better to do."

Chapter Twenty

THEY STOPPED AT the small gas station to fill up, and Ben ran into the general store to get a drink and look for some more of his favorite potato chips. At the checkout, the elderly lady smiled at him and patted his hand.

"How did the snowman turn out?"

"Amazing. Mostly thanks to your carrot, of course."

"Oh, I'm sure. Is your boy with you?"

His boy. He liked the way that sounded. "He's outside. We're just leaving."

"Well, then, you can have these on the house. If you promise to come back soon."

"Seriously?"

She nodded.

"I promise," Ben said solemnly. He hoped he wasn't lying.

A FEW HOURS passed before Ben yawned loudly. Murphy stirred from his sleep.

"Sorry." Ben smiled. "I'm gonna fall asleep at the wheel in a minute."

Murphy wiped the drool off his face and cleared his throat. "Let me drive. It's my turn."

"I think we should stop somewhere. Get a few hours of real sleep. Then you can have your turn afterward."

Murphy sighed. "It'll be the last motel we stay in together."

"You make it sound like a momentous occasion."

"Maybe it is."

"Wish we could have stayed at that last one. It was pretty perfect."

"Until Randall," said Murphy.

"Until Randall." Ben paused. "Do you think he'll be all right?"

"He's always all right."

Ben drove with one hand on the steering wheel, the other resting in his lap. He watched from the corner of his eye as Murphy reached a tentative hand toward his. He seemed to change his mind and tucked his hand between his thigh and the seat. Ten minutes later, he tried again and, this time, succeeded. Ben turned his hand palm up to meet his, and Murphy held it tightly, neither of them saying a word.

Chapter Twenty-One

THEIR MOTEL ROOM had a big bathroom with a wide sink and long, marble-effect countertop. Above the sink was an oblong mirror with bulbs all around it like some 1950s film star's dressing room. Murphy pulled the bedroom curtains shut and switched the lamps off, so the only light came from the bulbs around the mirror, covering Ben in a soft glow like candlelight.

Murphy watched from the bed as Ben pulled his shirt off over his head and threw it on the floor. Ben dropped his head to inspect the healing cut on his arm, and Murphy felt a familiar stab of guilt. As Ben ran water into the sink, he flicked his hair out of his eyes and stared into the mirror. Then he bent over and splashed his face. Water ran in rivulets over his flawless skin. A water droplet trickled slowly down his neck, over his shoulder, and down his finely muscled arm. Murphy licked his lips, instantly thirsty.

Ben had said he was tired, and up until a minute ago, Murphy had felt the same. The adrenaline rush of escaping Randall had left him exhausted. The long car journey had made him sleepier still, but seeing Ben like this had him wide-awake. He rubbed a hand over his crotch, wincing at the hardness already in his jeans. His gaze traveled down Ben's body, over his toned shoulders, and over his back, and he watched the muscles move under Ben's skin as Ben buried his face in the hand towel and then rubbed it over his hair. As Ben swapped his weight from one leg to the other, Murphy watched his perfect rounded ass and had the sudden urge to grab it. Murphy couldn't resist any longer. He left the bed, wrapped his arms around Ben's waist from behind, and hugged him close. Ben gasped and dropped the towel.

"It's my turn," whispered Murphy into his ear.

"What?"

"You heard me."

When Ben had talked about liking it rough, his words had gone straight to Murphy's cock. He'd shuddered with anticipation and stored that information away for later. For now. All Ben wanted was someone to dominate him, and all Murphy wanted to do was try. He buried his nose in Ben's soft hair and melted into the scent of apples, soap, and the heat from his body. Ben made a noise in the back of his throat, and something about it caught Murphy's heart on fire. He could do this.

He knotted his hand into Ben's hair, and he tugged hard, yanking Ben's head to the side to reveal his pale, elegant neck. He held Ben tighter around the waist, licked at the remaining water droplets, and then sucked hungrily at his warm throat. He felt Ben's pulse under his tongue and lightly bit the point where Ben's throat met his shoulder. Ben whimpered, and molten heat coiled low and urgent in Murphy's stomach. He flipped Ben around so they were facing, Ben's limbs completely malleable in Murphy's hands. Ben gazed up at him, his pupils so big his brown irises were almost hidden.

They kissed hard. Then Murphy ran a thumb over Ben's swollen lips and pressed down, pushing his thumb between them and invading his mouth. Ben sucked on Murphy's thumb, his mouth hot and wet. Murphy moved his body against Ben's and found they were both hard as a rock.

Murphy rubbed his palm over the bulge in Ben's jeans, and Ben cried out softly. Murphy fumbled at Ben's button and fly, but his hands were shaking so much that Ben had to help. Ben's jeans finally hit the floor, and Ben made quick work of Murphy's jeans and shorts. He stepped out of them, kicked them both away, and then reached his trembling hand inside Ben's shorts.

Ben moaned as Murphy pulled out his cock. Murphy wrapped his long fingers around both of them and stroked them together in his fist. Ben's eyes snapped shut, and he thrust up into Murphy's hand, whining desperately, but Murphy just watched with fascination as their erections rubbed together. The friction of Ben's cock against his felt amazing, but it looked even better.

Murphy spun him back around, shoved him up hard against the sink, and bent him over it. Their eyes met in the mirror, Ben's hooded, lustful gaze meeting Murphy's predatory one. Murphy might never have been with a man before Ben, but he'd seen enough porn to learn a few things. Mostly in tiny clips on late-night TV. He remembered flashes of images: sucking, fucking, and thrusting. He was desperate to try them now that he had the chance.

He kneeled behind Ben and grabbed his perfectly rounded ass, kneading it. Ben sighed and pushed back for more. The fact that Ben wanted this to happen gave Murphy another burst of confidence. Murphy spread Ben's buttocks apart and hesitated for just a second before leaning in and darting out his tongue at Ben's clean pink hole. Ben jerked forward and gave a surprised yelp. Murphy liked the reaction and did it again. Then he flattened his tongue out and licked a firm stripe from Ben's balls all the way up the crease of his ass.

"Fuck, Murphy."

Murphy pressed his face against Ben and dived his tongue at Ben's hole over and over, trying to push his way inside. Ben gasped and reached back with his uninjured hand to pull Murphy's face closer.

After a minute, Murphy pulled back. "Where's the lube you had at the cabin?"

Ben gestured desperately to his bag on the corner of the bathroom counter, and Murphy tried to repeat what Ben had done to him. He prepped Ben slowly, first with one slick finger, then two, and then a third. Ben's ass felt so good clamped around Murphy's fingers, he almost didn't want to pull them out to find a condom.

"Hurry up. And don't use too much lube. I want to feel it."

Murphy bent Ben over farther. "Who said you could talk?" he growled. Ben groaned and shoved his ass back hard.

Murphy rolled on the condom and wrapped his hand around his cock, pumping it and spreading out the lube on his fingers. Ben's ass had been unbearably tight even around the first finger; he couldn't imagine being able to push his cock inside. But he grabbed Ben's hips roughly to angle them, took a deep breath, lined himself up, and then slipped the tip of his cock inside, feeling the unimaginable tightness envelop him. He gasped and stilled, hesitating.

"Please, Murphy," Ben whined softly. "I'm ready."

Ben's plea woke the dark coil of lust in his stomach, and a hot jolt of arousal shot up Murphy's spine. He knotted his fist into Ben's silky hair, and he shoved him down face-first, pushing the full length of his cock inside him in one brutal thrust. Ben grunted in a mix of pain and pleasure. Murphy had never felt anything clamped so deliciously, mind-blowingly tight around him, and the thought that he might come right away—just from that— filled him with fear. He froze, both willing himself to calm down and waiting for Ben to signal he was ready for more. Ben breathed raggedly into the sink for a minute, then lifted his head and nodded at Murphy, his breath fogging up the glass.

Feeling a little more in control, Murphy pulled almost all the way out, then thrust back inside him until he bottomed out. He pushed his hips forward experimentally once, twice, three times before settling into a rhythm, grinding deep inside Ben on every thrust. He gripped hard on to Ben's slim hips, digging his fingers into Ben's soft flesh, fingertips leaving tiny red marks, and pounded into him mercilessly.

"Ah, fuck," Ben cried out.

Murphy slowed. "You okay?" Now he saw why Ben had been so annoying earlier about stopping for him. The last thing he ever wanted to do was hurt Ben.

"Don't you dare fucking stop."

"I don't want to hurt you."

"You won't. Come on. I'll stop you if it hurts, I promise. Just fuck me. Please. Hard, as hard as you can. I'm yours. Use me."

If that was what he wanted. Murphy pinned Ben down with both hands on his lower back, held him in place, and fucked him. Ben squirmed beneath him and spread his legs wider. Murphy set an even pace, fucking Ben hard and fast, letting Ben slam his hips back for more, and writhing desperately beneath him. Panting hard, Murphy licked his dry lips and watched Ben's reflection.

Ben's mouth hung open, his eyes closed. Then Ben bit his lip hard, as if to keep from shouting out.

As Murphy changed the pace and rolled his hips into Ben, he leaned over and covered Ben's back with his chest, melding their slick bodies tightly together. He moved his hands down the length of Ben's arms to entwine their fingers and held both his hands tight. He slowed further and ground into him, fucking him deep and steadily. It felt so good to have this beautiful, strong boy underneath him, submitting completely to his cock, his mouth, and the slow grind of his hips. Murphy licked Ben's neck as they both enjoyed the slower pace and the chance to catch their breath. Ben moaned underneath him as the angle of Murphy's thrust changed, and the sound sent another jolt of lust through him. Murphy latched on hard to Ben's shoulder with a bite to hold him in place as he quickened his thrusts again, pounding harder and deeper into him. Ben's head shot up, and he arched his back, groaning loudly in surprise.

The hint of pain in Ben's moan sent sinful sparks shooting through Murphy's body. He kissed the bite mark and then licked it, soothing away the hurt. He remembered what Ben had asked for in the shower and wrapped both hands around Ben's neck. He held Ben firmly by the throat and pounded even harder into him.

"Shit, fuck, yes," Ben choked out. He stretched out his arms, bracing them against the wall, muscles straining against the brutal onslaught from Murphy's relentlessly thrusting hips.

Murphy looked in the mirror and saw the lust in Ben's fuck-drunk eyes. His chest heaving, he grabbed Ben's leaking cock and matched the strokes of his hand around Ben to the rhythm of his hips. His heart pounded, and blood rushed in his ears. As he increased the speed of his hand and hips, Murphy had the unspeakable pleasure of watching Ben come.

Ben's whole body stiffened as he climaxed, his back arched, and every muscle in his body contracted. His ass clamped down even tighter on Murphy's cock. The sudden tightness made Murphy's orgasm rip through him. He gripped Ben hard around his neck and cock and drove deep into him with a strangled cry, convulsing from his climax. As he emptied inside him, Ben whimpered, and Murphy saw his hand reflected in the mirror, covered with Ben's release. As it ran down his wrist, Murphy forced his grip to loosen and pulled out of Ben carefully, only to collapse onto Ben's back, slick with sweat and his knees weak. He rested all his weight on Ben, feeling utterly boneless and a little alarmed by the intense, slightly filthy sex he'd just initiated.

As he slowly came to, he became aware that Ben was squashed between him and an uncomfortable sink. He pushed his hands underneath Ben's chest and raised him up, nuzzling his neck.

"You okay?"

Ben just groaned, apparently unable to speak. Murphy laughed and twisted Ben around, lifting him to sit on the counter facing him. Ben seemed surprised to be so close to Murphy all of a sudden and reached out to his face. All his motions were languid, as if he were moving through molasses. His eyes half-closed, he caressed Murphy's cheek with one hand and, with the other, stroked tiny reverent circles over his neck. He wrapped his legs round Murphy's waist and pulled him in for a long, breathtakingly tight bear hug.

"Thank you. Thank you. Thank you," Ben whispered into Murphy's ear. His breath, hot on Murphy's neck, made him shiver.

Ben had made him lose it. The second he'd said in that sweet breathy voice that he liked it rough, Murphy had felt something hot and molten deep in his belly. He'd wanted to give Ben what he wanted—what they both wanted—and then was scared he'd gone too hard, been too rough. But he felt Ben's genuine gratitude in those words. Murphy hadn't pushed it too far. He hadn't ruined everything. He hadn't been too hard or too gentle. He'd done it just right.

"Take me to bed, Baby Bear," Ben whispered between soft kisses.

Still kissing, Murphy hoisted Ben up, gripped him firmly under his thighs, and carried him into the bedroom, then threw him onto the bed. Ben bounced a little from the impact and then stared up at Murphy, his gaze traveling solemnly over Murphy's naked body like he was something special. Murphy darted back into the bathroom, pretending to tidy up but really just needing a minute to himself. He stared hard at his reflection. He didn't look any different. But he felt it.

When Murphy returned to the bed, Ben switched off his phone and put it down on the nightstand. His face lit up with a smile.

"Just so you know..." Ben said.

"Yeah?"

"That was the best sex of my life."

"Shut up."

"You shut up." Ben threw his arms back over his head and sank into the pillow. "I have never felt so thoroughly fucked, nor come so hard."

Murphy rolled his eyes but couldn't help smiling. "Whatever."

Ben moved onto his side and pushed Murphy's hair out of his face so he could make eye contact properly. "I'm not kidding, Murph."

Murphy swallowed hard and felt his cheeks redden, but he couldn't look away. Ben smiled, kissed his shoulder, and lay back down, entwining his fingers in Murphy's and holding his hand.

"We'll be at my house in a few hours."

Murphy's stomach flipped. "What's gonna happen then?" Would today be his last day with Ben? This thing had to end sooner or later. He pushed that thought to the back of his mind and concentrated on the here and now, listening to Ben breathe and feeling his soft, warm hand enveloping his.

"You'll meet my family."

Panic washed over him. Ben seemed to sense it and wrapped his arms around him, resting his head on Murphy's chest and finding his hand again.

"What are your parents gonna think?"

"About what?"

"You know what."

Ben glanced up at him. "They're gonna love you."

Murphy snorted.

"Are you nervous?"

Murphy didn't answer.

"Don't be. It'll be amazing. I can't wait to get you home and show you around." Ben paused. "Wow."

"What?"

"I've been dreading going home for so long, it feels weird to actually want to be there again."

Murphy stared at the shadows on the ceiling. "Am I gonna..."

"What?"

"Should I find a hotel or sleep in the car or what?"

"Murphy, no." Ben held him tighter. "You're going to stay in the house with me, as a guest. We have tons of room. I just texted my mother to tell her I'm bringing you home."

"You did?"

"Yeah. While your brother had my phone, I got about twenty missed messages. I guess she was worried about me after all. Had to tell her I wasn't dead, at least." Ben squeezed Murphy's hand. "Do you want to go to the beach?"

"Sure." Murphy hesitated. "But then what?"

"What do you mean?"

Murphy didn't want to push Ben into answering all these questions. He didn't want to ruin Ben's good mood with logistics and shit, but Murphy couldn't just wonder anymore. He'd been following his brother around his whole life, not knowing what he'd be doing the next day, the next week, or six months in the future. Just knowing it'd be whatever Randall said it was.

"What am I gonna do? I can't go back home." He didn't have a home anymore. Randall was the only thing that had kept him in one place, and now he was gone.

"Oh. You mean big picture."

Murphy waited.

"Well, I don't want you to go back home."

"That makes two of us," Murphy murmured.

"But I don't know what you're doing big picture. I don't even know what I'm doing big picture. I just want to be with you. If you'll let me."

Murphy's whole body tingled. Maybe he didn't have to know exactly what was coming. Maybe knowing he would be with Ben was reassurance enough. But when had he ever been that lucky before? The other shoe had to be about to drop.

"How do you feel about boats?" Ben asked.

"Boats?" Murphy tried to concentrate. "I like engines."

"Boats have engines."

Murphy elbowed Ben softly. "I know that."

"Well, that's a good start."

Before they slept, Murphy kissed Ben again. Ten soft kisses pressed against his cheek. Ben's delight showed on his face, and Murphy added another one for luck.

"I'm still sorry," he whispered.

Chapter Twenty-Two

EARLY THAT EVENING, just as it was getting dark, they pulled off a tree-lined road onto a long gravel drive. The driveway curved after a quarter of a mile, and as they passed the biggest oak trees Murphy had ever seen, he noticed a stone fountain and a building behind it.

A wide three-story home sat on top of a small, steep hill. The lawn was landscaped with well-kept rosebushes and neat rows of winter flowers hugging a pathway of steps that led up to a huge front door. Half the windows were lit with a cozy orange glow from within. There were two smaller buildings on either side of the house. One was a double—maybe triple—garage, and there were two cars parked on the wide driveway.

"Okay, stop here," Ben murmured.

"This isn't your house."

"It is."

"All of it?"

"Yep."

Holy shit. Murphy pulled up by the stone fountain and switched off the ignition. "Do I smell like cigarettes?"

Ben sniffed the air. "No, why?"

"I made sure I finished them all off so I wouldn't smoke here. I don't want your family thinking I stink."

Ben laughed. "You smell good."

As soon as Ben climbed out of the car, a tall woman wearing jeans and a tiny red cardigan ran down the steps, tying her black hair back in a messy bun as she reached the gravel drive. She wrapped Ben in a huge hug. As she kissed him and wished him a happy birthday, Murphy stayed on the far side of the truck and shoved his hands in his pockets. She gave the pickup a puzzled glance.

"Where's your Jeep?"

Murphy stared at the ground, praying Ben wouldn't mention yet that he'd crashed it. The chances of her liking Murphy were slim enough already without destroying them from the very beginning.

"Oh, I swapped it with a friend."

She frowned. "You've had that car since you were sixteen."

"It's just a car."

"We'll discuss it later," she said and then grinned widely. "I owe you about six months' worth of feeding up and invasive hugging. Let's get started." She pushed Ben up the steps ahead of her and turned to Murphy, holding out an arm. "I hope you're hungry, Murphy."

Murphy bit his lip, approaching her around the pickup. She laid her arm casually across his shoulder, and he only flinched a little. If she noticed, she didn't let on and squeezed his shoulder lightly.

"I'll send the kids out to get your bags in a minute."

"S'okay. I can get 'em," said Murphy.

"Not at all. You're our guest. And I have five children to use as slave labor. We're about ready to eat. You made it in perfect time."

She swung open the double front doors to reveal a large, well-lit hallway. A wide staircase sat in the far corner; an open archway led to a big room with a lit fireplace, table, and chairs; and several other dark wood doors led off to who knew where. Patterned tiles covered the floor, and a circular persian rug the size of Murphy's entire house sat in the center. Ben dropped his coat on a small table and shrugged at Murphy, as if to say *this is it*. It was surreal to see Ben in his world.

A little boy ran up to them as soon as they shut the front door. He wore a blue-and-white cap just like one Murphy had seen in Ben's bag and stared up at Murphy.

"Hey, Joseph." Ben pulled off the cap and ruffled the boy's hair. Joseph pushed his hand away, grabbed the cap back, and smoothed his hair back into place, his face serious.

"Are you Ben's new boyfriend?"

Murphy was stunned into silence and shocked further when Ben's mom giggled softly. After one glance at Murphy's face, she dragged Ben's little brother gently toward the dining room.

"Come on, Joseph. Let's get you sitting at the table."

Murphy couldn't believe this was real. Before he could say anything, a teenage girl appeared at the top of the curving staircase. Murphy recognized her from the photo in Ben's book, slim and pretty with light-brown hair and big brown eyes. She descended the stairs and scrutinized him.

"Who's this guy?"

"Polite and welcoming as ever, Grace." Ben smiled as he gazed at Murphy. The look in Ben's eyes made him feel hot. "This is Murphy."

His sister looked from her brother's face to Murphy and smiled, raising an eyebrow. "He's much cuter than Jimmy." She hopped down the last two stairs and held up her hand at shoulder height. "Good work."

Ben seemed to panic for a second, then rolled his eyes and reluctantly high-fived her.

"Who's Jimmy?" Murphy managed to croak out.

"Just his ex. He was an idiot. None of us liked him." Grace stepped past Murphy and into the dining room to join everyone else, leaving Murphy and Ben alone in the quiet hallway.

"How many...boyfriends have you had?"

"Only that one." Ben reached out and pulled gently on Murphy's sleeve, walking them into the dining room.

There were two empty seats around the oval dinner table, and Ben steered the way toward them. They were in a big room with floor-to-ceiling french windows. The rear garden was decorated with soft white lights hung in the trees. Lake Michigan sat below the sloping hill of the back garden, the lights of other far-off coastal properties twinkling in the distance and curving their way around the lake.

There were several sofas and armchairs spread around the edges of the room, haphazardly dotted with cushions. Piles of books and newspapers and magazines were scattered over the side tables and floor.

"Don't mind the mess," said Ben's mom.

Murphy liked it. The room could easily have been intimidating, but the slight untidiness made it feel cozier despite how grand everything was underneath. Ben pulled his chair a little closer to Murphy's under the guise of moving it toward the table, and Murphy appreciated the comforting warmth. Ben's mom passed out plates of food, and Ben poured water into Murphy's glass.

When Murphy finally worked up the courage to look at the people sitting around the table, he found he could see a tiny bit of Ben in each of them. His three younger brothers were shorter, skinnier versions of him. His mom and sister only shared his smile, but his father was Ben plus thirty years and a lifetime outdoors. He had a kind face, but he still looked like he could beat the shit out of a bad influence.

None of them were staring at him like he'd feared. They all chatted over one another as they ate spaghetti and meatballs, and Murphy enjoyed being silent and listening in.

"So, are you ready to be lord of the manor, Ben?" his sister asked, smirking.

Ben licked tomato sauce from his knife, and his mom tutted. "I'm ready. You ready to be my lowly serf?"

"You wish."

"Don't tease him on his birthday."

"Thanks, Mom."

"Save it all up for tomorrow, and then really give it to him."

His mom disappeared to the kitchen and then returned a while later holding a birthday cake, lit with twenty-one candles. His family sang cheerfully off-key to Ben. Murphy was too shy to join in, and Ben blew out the candles after some insistence from his mom.

"Don't you think I'm getting a little too old for this sort of thing?"

"Never. Now make a wish and behave." She brought a stack of plates to the table and cut everyone a piece. Murphy shifted his arm an inch closer to Ben's until they were touching. It worked to get his attention, and Ben leaned closer.

"What's up?"

Murphy moved his hands to his lap. "I didn't get you anything."

Ben smiled widely. "You didn't know."

"I know, but I wish I coulda got you something."

"I know what you can give me later." Ben winked.

Murphy's eyes widened. "Don't," he whispered. "Are you trying to get me murdered by your dad?"

Ben's smile disappeared, and he grabbed Murphy's hand under the table. Murphy glanced over at his parents and tried to pull it away, but Ben held tight until he gave up the struggle. Ben's parents paid them no attention at all, and Murphy finally relaxed.

"It's okay here. We're safe," Ben whispered in his ear.

Murphy wanted to believe him, but he was still waiting for everything to go wrong.

"I'm glad you got back in time to sign those papers tomorrow." His dad's voice was deep and gravelly, unlike those of the rest of his family. It made Murphy jump. Only Ben seemed to notice, and he squeezed Murphy's hand under the table before letting go and spearing a piece of chocolate cake on his fork.

"Oh yeah. I forgot to say happy retirement, Dad."

His dad smiled.

"Do you think it will hurt, Ben?" Grace piped up.

Ben rolled his eyes. "What?"

"Squeezing your big head through the door tomorrow."

Ben tossed his screwed-up napkin at her head, and she ducked, laughing, knocking her fork from her plate onto her mom's lap with a clatter.

Ben's mom sighed and picked it up, trying to wipe the chocolate from her clothes. "I said no teasing."

"I've waited as long as I can, but where the hell are my presents?" Ben said plaintively.

"The family business isn't enough?"

"We got you a few little somethings," said his mom. "But you can open them later. Right now, I think you should give Murphy a tour of the house. He could probably do with a break from the Lee family en masse." She sighed. "I know I could."

Ben jumped up and pulled Murphy from his chair and out of the dining room almost before Murphy knew what was happening.

"Don't linger too long in the bedrooms," called Grace.

"Hush," Ben's mom said.

Chapter Twenty-Three

BEN WAS STRUCK by how intuitive his mother was, knowing just like he did that Murphy needed some time to be quiet. All this was new to Murphy. Ben's family was big and boisterous. That alone must have been overwhelming, but Murphy still seemed to be getting used to Ben. Murphy had said the word "boyfriend" like it was a foreign word. Like he'd never said it before.

Ben wanted to show him the whole house. Introduce Murphy to every room so he'd be part of Ben's home. Ben pulled Murphy all over the ground floor, showing him the kitchen, the utility room, the conservatory, the library, and ended up in the kids' lounge room where his younger siblings could watch TV, play video games, and leave their toys all over the place without their dad making a fuss. Ben leaned back on the arm of one of two sofas.

"Mom says Dad's not allowed in here. He gets upset when he finds us all busy staring at screens."

Murphy gave a sidelong glance at the sixty-inch plasma screen on the wall. "You have enough of 'em."

"Yeah, too many." Ben reached for Murphy's hand and squeezed it. "There's better stuff to look at."

Murphy smiled, squeezed back, and then shoved his hands in his pockets as the tips of his ears turned an adorable shade of red. "Does your mom work with boats too?"

"Not really. She spends most of her time looking after us. Plus it takes a lot of dedication being a full-time eccentric."

Murphy looked back at him curiously.

"She makes bad furniture out of driftwood she finds on the beach and collects art by men on death row."

"Seriously?"

"Yeah, it's all in her study. I'll show you."

Ben led Murphy by the hand up two flights of stairs and into his mother's large study. He'd always liked spending time in this room, mainly for its whole wall of windows facing the lake and the views of orange sunsets rather than for the odd, spiky, whitewashed furniture.

"Don't sit down. It's all liable to collapse at any moment."

Murphy snorted. "It don't look that bad."

Ben opened a window, letting in cool air and the soft sound of waves on the shore. They gazed out over the bay together, and Ben remembered his younger, more obedient days when his mother would send him down to the sandy beach and point out pieces of driftwood for him to fetch and bring back up to her. Her head would poke out of the study window, binoculars up to her eyes and windswept hair whipping across her lips.

Ben turned away from the window. There were several misshapen chairs and a couple of side tables as well as a sculpture that looked like a giant octopus in the throes of an epileptic fit.

"Guess what that's meant to be," Ben said.

Murphy appraised it solemnly from all angles. "Is it a dolphin?"

Ben stared at him. "No one's ever guessed that close. She's gonna love you. It's a killer whale."

There were seven paintings and a framed pencil sketch hanging on the wall opposite the windows. "They're mostly self-portraits by murderers. Mom was a psychology student for years. She's into a lot of weird stuff." He pointed to a painting of a bearded man surrounded by a night sky full of stars. "That's by a man who hasn't seen the sky for twenty-five years."

Murphy studied each painting carefully. Ben joined him as he reached the farthest one. "That one's rumored to be by Jeffrey Dahmer, but there's no definite proof. I think it's creepy even having it in the house. I just tell myself it's by someone else."

Murphy took Ben's hand and entwined their fingers. "'S only paint."

Chapter Twenty-Four

BEN'S DAD STEPPED through the open door and patted Murphy's shoulder. "Benedict showing you the gallery of psychopaths?"

Murphy stiffened, panicking for a second, and Ben stroked a soothing hand over his forearm. "Hey, hands off the merchandise, Dad." He pulled Murphy gently toward him, and his dad let go.

"Sorry, son. Didn't mean to make you jump."

"'S fine," Murphy spluttered. No one had ever called him "son."

"I have to pee," said Ben. "I'll be back in one second."

"Too much detail, Benedict," said his dad.

Murphy tried desperately to communicate with Ben using just his eyes to please not leave him alone with his dad. But Ben squeezed his arm one more time.

"I'll really just be one minute, promise."

Murphy bit his thumbnail and followed Ben's dad to the open window. Here it was, time for the other shoe to finally drop. His chest tightened. He knew what was next. It was inevitable. Now that they were alone, Ben's dad's expression would change from friendly to blank, and he'd push Murphy against a wall with one strong arm across his neck and whisper for him to leave, tell him he was disgusting, and tell him to keep his filthy hands off his son.

Ben's dad sneezed loudly. "It's a beautiful night." He sniffled. "Unless you have allergies." He closed the window and pulled a tissue from his pocket. "There's an eclipse in a couple of nights. We're planning to take a boat out to the middle of the lake and watch it from there. You don't mind the water, do you?"

Murphy's eyes widened, and he missed a breath. He was invited? "Sure. No, I like it. Thanks."

Ben's dad smiled. "Good, good."

Murphy's tentative smile grew as they both admired the lake in silence. He was oddly tranquil. The man next to him was so relaxed and so much quieter than the rest of his family that it had some kind of sedative effect on him. Ben's dad spoke after a moment.

"The crayfish is always drawn to the crab."

Murphy frowned up at Ben's dad, and he smiled at Murphy's consternation. "Benedict seems happier."

Murphy blinked. Ben's dad looked back out at the lake and didn't seem to need a response. Which was lucky, as Murphy couldn't think of one.

"You get back and join the throng. I think I'll enjoy the peace for a few minutes more." Ben's dad smiled. "It can get a bit much, you know?"

Murphy knew, all right. He left Ben's dad in his wife's study and set off in search of Ben. He didn't know where the bathroom was that Ben had used, or where any of the bathrooms were. Or how many there were to choose from. Probably fifty, judging from how big the damned house was. He was glad he hadn't known how wealthy Ben's family was from the beginning. He probably would have been too intimidated to even talk to him.

Murphy wandered through the house slowly, every room warm and bright. He scanned the now occupied lounge as he passed, but Ben wasn't in there. He stood and watched for a second, unnoticed, as one of Ben's brothers stood, pointing the remote at the TV. He changed channels repeatedly, only giving each one three seconds to impress before moving on. Little Joseph batted at the boy's leg with a plastic sword and was roundly ignored. Murphy heard Grace laughing hysterically in another room, and he smiled. He was watching and listening from the sidelines, but he didn't feel like an outsider. He'd been embarrassed, awkward, and shy most of the evening, but despite that, these people had made him feel more accepted in one evening than his family ever had. As he moved on down the corridor, he heard Ben's voice and was drawn to it. His feet moved automatically toward Ben.

Murphy found him on the balcony with his mom, both leaning against the wooden railing and looking out over the lake. The moon hung in the night sky, reflected in the inky water below. Murphy stared at the way Ben's arms flexed as he leaned on the railing. His eyes traveled up Ben's arm and on to his lips as he spoke. All Murphy had to do was look at Ben's sweet, innocent face and remember the filthy things they'd done together, and his cheeks flushed. Murphy stood at the sliding doors for a few seconds more before Ben's mom turned and noticed him.

"There you are! Told you he'd find us. I hope my husband didn't bore you rigid talking about his allergies."

Murphy shook his head and bit on his thumb.

"I hear I have you to thank for Benedict's arm."

Damn. Murphy's brain scrambled to think of a way to apologize enough for breaking her son with his shitty, careless driving.

She pulled up Ben's sleeve and stroked a finger over the fading scar. "He told me you patched him up all by yourself? You did such a beautiful job."

Oh. She wasn't being sarcastic. She was actually thanking him.

"Least I could do." Murphy shrugged.

"Are you okay? You weren't hurt?"

"Nah, 'm fine."

She rubbed his upper arm. "Thank you, Murphy. For looking after him."

"Jeez, Mom, why don't you just adopt him? You obviously like him better than me already."

"Benedict Wolfgang Lee, I did not raise you to be so impertinent."

Murphy snorted involuntarily. "Wolfgang?"

Ben's cheeks reddened, and he stared at his feet.

"He's our little Wolfie," said Ben's mom and kissed him on the temple loudly. "I'll leave you to it. Don't stay out too long. You'll get cold. Use the blanket," she shouted over her shoulder as she joined the rest of the family inside.

Ben grabbed the soft blue blanket, and they huddled under it together on the swing seat. Ben drew him close.

"I'm really sorry. Mom grabbed me after I went to the bathroom and wouldn't let me go. I was going to make a break for it in a second, I swear. Were you okay?"

Murphy smiled. "I was fine. Your dad is cool."

"Sorry about my family."

"Are you kidding?"

"They're so embarrassing."

"No. They're like Christmas."

"What?"

"This house, your family. Anyone that woke up here on Christmas morning would have to be the happiest person alive."

Ben blinked at him and then squinted up at the full moon, silent for a moment. "It's just like your tattoo." Ben reached under Murphy's shirt and touched it gently. "Does it hurt?"

"Not anymore." Murphy paused and rubbed the back of his neck. "I never told you why I got it, did I?"

Ben shrugged. "I know you like space. And stuff. You called your dog Nebula."

"How the hell do you remember that?"

"Easily."

"Well. I do like space. And stuff." He smiled. "And that's how I know there's a crater on the moon called Benedict. It's right by the lunar equator on the far side of the moon."

Ben blinked at him. "You got it for me?" His voice squeaked.

"And now that I know your middle name, it's even more perfect. Wolfie."

"I'm not going to howl at it."

"Maybe I can get you to later."

Ben smiled and touched it again, like he couldn't bear not to. His low voice, so close to Murphy's ear, spread warmth all through Murphy's body. "That is one hell of a birthday present."

Chapter Twenty-Five

"COME SEE MY room," said Ben.

They climbed up another flight of stairs to the attic floor. There were three rooms up here: Ben's, a guest room, and a bathroom that only Ben used. All the walls were at an angle heading up to the roof, but it was light and airy, like the rest of the house.

It was warm in his bedroom, and Murphy pulled off his outer shirt, leaving him in just a black T-shirt. His lean, muscular body filled it to perfection. Ben reluctantly pulled his gaze away and glanced around his room, checking for anything majorly embarrassing. He hadn't spent much time in his room since he left for college, so it was still full of a lot of his teenage things.

He suddenly felt self-conscious about the posters on the wall. Adults had framed pictures, not posters. He half hoped Murphy wouldn't notice the shelf of mint in-box action figures. As usual when he hadn't been home in a while, the carpet looked bluer and the walls seemed brighter than he remembered. Ben sank onto his bed and patted the blanket next to him.

Murphy hesitated, wringing his hands together. "Don't wanna get it dirty."

"You're not dirty." Ben shrugged one shoulder as he reconsidered. "Outside of motel bathrooms."

Murphy laughed shyly and sat down next to him. Ben's heart raced with nerves but happy nerves, not the anxiety he'd been feeling over the past week. He'd made it home alive, and he'd brought Murphy with him. He couldn't stop the goofy smile covering his face.

Murphy narrowed his eyes. "What?"

Ben stood and maneuvered himself onto Murphy's lap. He wrapped his legs around Murphy's back and pulled him close. He played with the hair at Murphy's nape as he soaked up the warmth from his body.

"I'm just really happy."

"You're always happy."

"No. I'm always smiling. There's a difference."

Murphy bit his lip and stared at Ben's mouth.

"I know it's not easy, and you just got here," said Ben. "But I want you to feel at home. I want you all relaxed and leaving your stuff around and walking dirt in from outside and wearing your shoes on the bed."

"You want that?" Murphy seemed doubtful.

"More than anything."

Murphy awkwardly reached over, his lap full of Ben, and grabbed his shirt. He raised it above his head and tossed it onto the floor. "Better?"

"Much." Ben grinned.

"Don't tell your mom I did that."

"Why not?"

"She likes me better than you right now, and I want to keep it that way."

Ben laughed and pushed Murphy back onto the bed, not to ravage him but to tickle him senseless. Relief flooded his heart. Murphy wouldn't joke around like this if he weren't feeling at least a little secure and comfortable. The tickling soon dissolved into kissing. Not scorching, lustful kisses that would inevitably lead to sex but something just as enjoyable. Sweet, slow, and shy kisses into which Ben tried to pour every bit of what he felt for Murphy. Murphy moved his hands up and down Ben's body. Soft, endless touches with his fingertips that made Ben feel worshipped. Murphy's hands ended up in Ben's hair and then moved to cup his face, tracing over his cheekbones and down to his neck as they kissed. Ben shivered and melted into his touch before finally pulling away, breathless.

"Do you know how amazing you are at that?"

Murphy shrugged shyly and buried his face in Ben's neck.

"I have something for you. But I have to go get it."

"What is it?" Murphy sounded worried.

"You'll like it."

Ben forced himself off the bed and away from Murphy, who in turn scooted back across the mattress to lean against the wall. Murphy picked up a book from a pile by the bed and flipped it open.

"Anime porn?" Murphy asked.

Ben smiled. "Don't judge me." Murphy leaned over the book, frowning as he concentrated. God, he looked cute reading. He looked cute doing anything. Ben jogged out of the room, calling out over his shoulder.

"Bye, back in a second."

Murphy didn't look up from the book. "Bye, love you," he called casually, the door swinging shut between them.

Ben turned back and froze, staring at the door. A moment passed, and then he heard a noise that sounded suspiciously like Murphy banging his head against the door.

"Did you hear what I said?" Murphy asked, his voice muffled.

Ben stared at the closed door, then swallowed. "It's okay. I know it didn't mean anything. It just came out by accident."

Murphy flung open the door. "Shut up, Ben. You always do that. I said it 'cause I fucking mean it, okay?"

"Okay," Ben whispered, completely undone.

Murphy met Ben's gaze, a small smile playing over his lips, and then grabbed the door handle. "Now go get me the thing."

Ben took a couple of seconds to recover, before resuming his mission. That wasn't quite how he ever imagined that happening, but he would take it.

HE SLIPPED BACK into his bedroom five minutes later to find Murphy peeking into his wardrobe. He looked guilty at being caught.

"You can look. And you can use anything you want. I know they're not really your kind of clothes, but if you need anything..."

"What are my kind of clothes?"

"I can't really carry off the James Dean thing like you do."

Murphy raised a quizzical eyebrow, wrinkling his forehead, and ran a hand through his hair, leaving it endearingly rumpled.

"Yeah, just like that."

Murphy rolled his eyes.

"I got you this." Ben held up a single cigarette. "My dad used to smoke. I know where he hides his emergency pack."

Murphy's eyes lit up.

"I kind of wish you didn't smoke. I don't want you to get sick. But you look like you need one." He passed Murphy the cigarette.

"Thanks."

Ben yanked up his stiff bedroom window, and they climbed out to sit on the wide windowsill, hanging their legs outside.

"I have matches too." Ben scrabbled to get one out and struck it against the box three times before it lit, swearing under his breath until he was successful. Murphy leaned back against the window frame and sucked on the cigarette, letting out a quiet sigh of ecstasy. He raised his chin and blew a perfect white smoke ring.

"Wow."

Murphy gave him the smuggest look Ben had ever seen, and Ben burst out laughing. Murphy pushed Ben away and then, with the same hand, grabbed his sleeve and pulled him closer. Murphy hung his arm over Ben's shoulders and smoked the rest of the cigarette. Ben reached out and hooked one finger in the pocket of Murphy's jeans.

"My mom said we have to sleep in different rooms."

Murphy's eyes clouded with disappointment, but he nodded.

"I wish you could stay here with me," Ben added quickly. "They're open-minded. And totally cool with the boy thing. But I don't think they want to think of me having sex with anyone till I'm either married or thirty-five."

"They'd do the same if I was a girl?" Murphy asked, a slight smile on his face.

"They'd be sitting me down and asking me what the hell was wrong if I'd brought a girl home."

"Well, I don't mind at all. This is their home, man. I'll do whatever."

"I know. You're such a gentleman."

"Shut up."

He loved it when Murphy told him to shut up. Murphy always got that sulky, flustered look on his face, like he didn't know what else to say. They climbed back inside, and Murphy pulled the window back down with a grunt. Ben took Murphy's cold hands in his and pushed him toward the bed. When the backs of Murphy's knees hit the mattress, he sank onto it, and Ben crowded him, his hands on Murphy's shoulders and his body pressed between Murphy's parted legs.

Murphy spread his hands over Ben's back, making him tremble. He stroked his way down to Ben's waist, pushed his hands beneath Ben's shirt, and smoothed his thumbs over the soft skin of Ben's hips, leaving goose bumps. Murphy kissed the raised flesh, then stared up at him. Ben returned his gaze, smiling, his hair falling over his eyes, and Murphy pushed it back.

"I like your eyes," said Murphy.

"I like your everything."

Murphy looked so natural and so good sprawled over the end of Ben's bed. It felt like he'd always been there. Ben wanted to kiss him, hard. He wanted to cover Murphy's body with his and give him enough warmth that it would last him all night until they could be together again. Ben reached out one hand, twisted it into Murphy's hair, and pulled him close. Then his mother knocked on his bedroom door.

She poked her head in, then stepped inside, holding a towel over her arm. "Come on and get settled in your room, Murphy."

Murphy pushed him off and jumped up obediently. Ben sighed. It was stupid, but he felt physically sick as Murphy drew farther away. This was the first time they would really be apart in days. Or ever since they'd met. Ben's mother put a hand on Murphy's arm and pulled him away.

Murphy turned back in the doorway. "Night, Ben."

"Night." The word came out in a whisper.

BEN COULDN'T SLEEP. He retrieved Murphy's shirt from the floor and curled up in bed, pressing the shirt against his face. The fabric smelled of leather, wood smoke, and spearmint. He felt like they were in the tent again, or in the car, holding hands under his jacket, or in their forest hotel, alone with the snowman outside and only Chinese food between them.

He lasted twenty-eight minutes. It was the thought of the kisses that did it. Murphy might feel bad if he couldn't give Ben that night's ten sorry kisses. Ben didn't want Murphy to feel bad. He couldn't let Murphy feel guilty or sad one more second in his whole life.

So he stepped quietly out of his room and crept into the dark, feeling ridiculous sneaking around the house at his age. Everything was silent. He checked the closest spare room down the corridor from his bedroom and found it empty. The next two bedrooms he checked one floor down were empty too. He cursed their stupidly big house. Nobody needed this many rooms. He tried to ignore the fact that when both sides of the family came to visit at once, they always ran out of beds, and a couple of cousins always had to sleep on the floor.

As he opened another door and found no Murphy, panic slowly bloomed in his chest. Where the hell was he? There was only one possibility left, the nicest guest room they had, right next to his mother's study, with its own balcony, an en suite bathroom, and the best view of the lake.

He found Murphy inside, curled up in bed with blankets right up to his chin and his back to the door.

"Finally, the right room," Ben muttered under his breath.

Ben kneeled at the side of the bed, relieved to have found him, and enjoyed being able to just stare. The moonlight flooded in through the window, bathing Murphy's face in soft white light, the shadows accentuating the sharp cheekbones that made Ben's heart swell. Murphy was so beautiful. And the best thing of all was, he was fast asleep and totally quiet. No whimpering, no sweating, no writhing, and no nightmares.

This beautiful boy had actually chosen Ben. He still couldn't believe it. He never would have asked him to choose between Ben and his brother, however much he might have wanted to, but Murphy had done it anyway. Ben's dad had always told him people come and go. He said that some of them were cigarette breaks and others were forest fires. Ben had thought it was another one of his dad's old Korean sayings that sometimes got lost in translation. Or one of those things people say that don't really mean anything. But Murphy flooded it with hot, bright meaning. Like it was written for him.

Ben stroked Murphy's face as gently as he possibly could and pressed their foreheads together. He breathed in Murphy's familiar scent and enjoyed the feel of Murphy's soft, sleeping breaths on his lips.

"Can't believe I almost lost you," Ben murmured.

"It's only a room. You woulda found me eventually."

Ben's eyes shot open.

"You missed me, huh?" Murphy's voice was husky.

Ben nodded, his stomach fluttering.

"I know why you really came to find me," Murphy said with a cheeky smirk.

"Shut up."

"You can't sleep without it, can you?"

"Shut up." Ben pushed him playfully, but Murphy grabbed him tight, pulled him in close, and planted ten little kisses all over his face, ending with one on his nose.

"There." Murphy tucked a strand of hair behind Ben's ear. "Now we can both sleep."

About the Author

Blue Jones is a British author who writes sweet and sexy romance, full of offbeat characters and happy endings.

Her books have been published by Dreamspinner Press, NineStar Press, and various UK & US literary journals. When she's not writing or painting, she loves *Twin Peaks*, Daniel Clowes comics, and watching *Call Me By Your Name* on repeat.

Twitter: @bluejonesauthor

Website: www.bluejonesbooks.wixsite.com/home

Also Available from NineStar Press

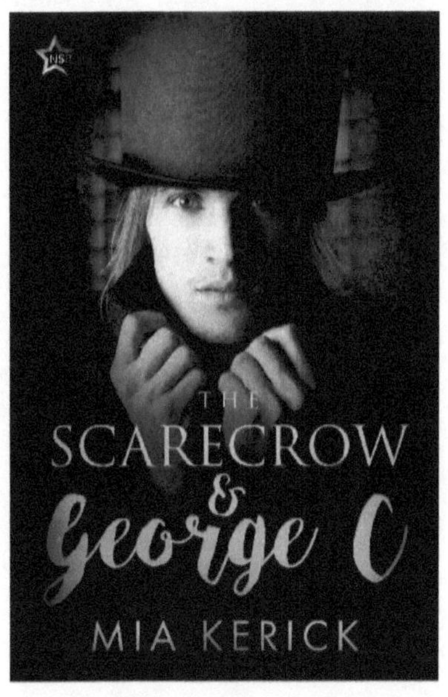

Connect with NineStar Press

www.ninestarpress.com

www.facebook.com/ninestarpress

www.facebook.com/groups/NineStarNiche

www.twitter.com/ninestarpress

www.tumblr.com/blog/ninestarpress